WITHDRAWN FROM STOCK

The Liar's Room

SIMON LELIC

PENGUIN BOOKS

PENGUIN BOOKS

UK | USA | Canada | Ireland | Australia
India | New Zealand | South Africa

Penguin Books is part of the Penguin Random House group of companies
whose addresses can be found at global.penguinrandomhouse.com.

First published 2018

001

Copyright © Simon Lelic, 2018

The moral right of the author has been asserted

Set in 12.5/14.75 pt Garamond MT Std
Typeset by Jouve (UK), Milton Keynes
Printed and bound in Great Britain by Clays Ltd, Elcograf S.p.A.

A CIP catalogue record for this book is available from the British Library

PAPERBACK ISBN: 978–0–241–29656–1

www.greenpenguin.co.uk

Penguin Random House is committed to a
sustainable future for our business, our readers
and our planet. This book is made from Forest
Stewardship Council® certified paper.

For Sarah, always

Who am I?

She wakes to find herself broken, and it is the first question that enters her head. The next: *where am I?*

She feels drugged, sluggish. Her head is heavy, her senses dulled, as though she were underwater. And there is a fire in her throat. The sensation when she swallows is of trying to ingest crushed glass.

She blinks. Her vision clears but it is the smell of this place she's in that is revealed. The room stinks of damp, booze, days-old urine. It hits her and makes her gag. The only thing that stops her vomiting is that her stomach is so utterly empty. When did she last eat? How long has it been since she even allowed herself to think about food?

She rolls from her makeshift bed – a too thin blanket, already as soiled as its surroundings – and on to all fours, and her right arm immediately gives way beneath her. She screams out in pain and hits the floor hard, shoulder first, which makes her yell out again. She waits, sobbing, for the pain to clear, then examines her unclothed arm. There's no wound but there is a bruise like a rotten sunset running from her elbow to her wrist, and she has no idea how it got there . . . until she remembers.

Him.
He hurt her arm. He put her *here.*
And the cold reality sinks in.
Where she is. Why.

3 p.m. – 4 p.m.

I

Right away when she sees the boy she has a feeling she knows him. Or, somehow, that he knows her. The woman she's hiding, as much as this person she's become.

He's dressed as though for a special occasion. Most people probably wouldn't notice but Susanna is familiar with teenage boys and although this boy is slightly older – nineteen, perhaps? Twenty? – it's clear he's selected what he's wearing with a sense of purpose. His jeans are dark, clean, unripped. His shirt is untucked but neatly buttoned and there's a designer logo above the left breast. The shoes he has on are dress shoes really, not meant to be worn with jeans, but like the rest of the boy's outfit they've been chosen, Susanna suspects, because they're the best he has. It is the same attire he would pick for a first date. Which is sort of sweet, actually. Touching, that he should have made such an effort just for her.

The sense she knows him fades like déjà vu. What she puts it down to after the initial jolt is the boy's – the young *man's* – unquestionable good looks. His is a face borrowed from a magazine, the kind Susanna can no longer bring herself to read but has fanned on the coffee table in the waiting room outside. Less a waiting room, more a co-opted landing, one she shares with a dentist, Ruth, who practises in the room at the other end of the converted mews house. Between them, in an opened-out bedroom at the top of the stairs, is the desk used mainly by Alina – the Ukrainian woman who doubles as Ruth's dental assistant and their receptionist – and downstairs, with a separate entrance, is an antiques shop. It's fully stocked but never open and neither Susanna nor Ruth has ever met the owner. They joke that the antiques business is just a front. For money launderers, the Devon mafia, ISIS. The truth, Susanna thinks, is that the owner runs his business mainly online and only ever meets clients by appointment. The truth is boring and Susanna prefers it. But Ruth has a predilection for the dramatic. Sometimes Susanna wonders how Ruth would react if she were to discover the truth about *her*.

The young man, though. His face. He could be a model. He has the bone structure and the blemish-free skin, as well as the eyes – brown and brooding – if not the haircut or the swagger. When he enters the room he does so as though untrusting of the floorboards. His fringe falls across one eye and he gives the impression of peeking out from behind a curtain.

Across his torso is a messenger bag. He unwinds it from his shoulder as he steps a little further into the room.

'Er . . . hi,' he says, a greeting that sounds as much a question.

'Adam?' Susanna is standing and she offers out a hand. The young man meets it with his own, which Susanna takes as confirmation he's the person she's been expecting. Adam Geraghty. The first of two new clients scheduled for that afternoon. Unusual to have two in one day, though given her finances of late not entirely unwelcome. 'I'm Susanna. Come in, please.'

'Susanna?'

'Or Susie, if you prefer. Anything but Mrs Fenton or I'll constantly be checking behind me for my mother.' It's a joke and a lie rolled into one, which in Susanna's mind makes it mostly OK.

Adam smiles. 'Susanna,' he repeats.

'Have a seat.' Susanna gestures and Adam follows the path laid out by her outstretched arm. There are two upholstered chairs – upright but comfortable – angled across from each other in front of the disused fireplace, a small table bearing glasses and a jug of water positioned between them. The chairs are purposefully identical and Adam selects the one furthest from the door. Which makes Susanna wonder whether Adam hasn't received therapy of some kind before, because in her experience first-timers tend to try to preserve an easy escape route.

He sets his bag down on the floor close beside him and perches on the edge of the chair. He takes a moment to survey his new surroundings. The room is small but relatively bare. There's Susanna's desk, haloed by the Georgian windows and as tidy as she can ever seem to get it. There's the coat stand in the corner by the door, which but for the hat Susanna bought specifically to adorn it would look as spindly and forlorn as a winter tree. There are the bookshelves, loaded and dishevelled, and her framed certificates beside a Matisse print on the party wall (Susanna wouldn't have bothered with the certificates if Ruth hadn't insisted they would lend her gravitas) but nothing otherwise except the plants and the crisp white paintwork.

'Susanna,' the young man says again. 'It sounds wrong.' A pause. 'What I mean is, shouldn't I call you, like, Doctor or something?'

'Sure, if you want to,' Susanna says, 'although I'm not one.' She flags the joke this time with a smile. 'I'm a counsellor,' she clarifies. The joke has fallen flat and she attempts to re-establish a tone of professionalism. 'A counsellor isn't the same as a clinical psychologist and it's a completely different field to psychiatry. Which isn't to say I'm not qualified.' She shifts. 'All I'm really trying to explain is that you don't need a doctorate to practise in my field. In fact in some circles it's actively discouraged.'

She tends to do this: use humour as a defence mechanism, then lurch too far the other way. Whether she recognizes the young man or not, there's definitely something about him that has set her on edge. Those good looks again, probably. Good God, Susanna. Are you *flirting*? Shame on you! You must be thirty years older than him at least.

Susanna feels herself glowing and drops her gaze towards her lap. She picks some fluff from the black of her trousers.

'So,' she announces and re-hoists her smile. 'Why don't you start by telling me a little bit about why you're here?'

The boy seems startled. 'You mean just launch into it?'

'Let's start with the basics. Shall we? Your name, age, a bit about your background. That sort of thing. And after that we can move on to what specifically you're hoping to get out of this conversation.'

Adam adjusts the way he's sitting. 'OK,' he says. 'Sure. My name's Adam. Adam Geraghty. I was born here. In England, I mean. In London, actually, not *here* here. And I suppose . . .' He stops, shuffles again, winces. 'Look, do you mind if I just come out with it? The way you said. Can I just tell you why I'm here and then you can tell me whether you think you can help or not?'

'Well . . .'

'I don't want to sound rude or anything. It's just, I don't want to waste your time and if I'm honest I don't really have that much money. And actually, I'm also feeling slightly nervous. More than slightly.' He grins bashfully. It's a schoolboy grin and Susanna feels a tiny fracturing in her heart.

'Sorry,' Adam is saying. 'Sorry. That's not how this is done, is it? Sorry,' he says again, running his hands through his hair. 'You'd never guess this was my first time, would you?' He reddens, then adds somewhat hastily, 'Talking to someone like you, I mean.'

Susanna warms as well at the unintended innuendo. 'It's fine, Adam. Really. You're in charge here, not me. We can start however you want to start and we don't have to talk about anything you don't want to unless you're ready to do so.'

Watching Adam's reaction, Susanna realizes why she

thought she knew him. It's not his looks. It's his smile. The way the left side of his mouth pulls higher than the right; the little glimpse he allows the world of his milky teeth. It's a goofy smile. Innocent. *Familiar.*

'I guess what I'm wondering about is how long this usually takes,' Adam says. 'You know. To fix things.'

Susanna blinks and locks her eyes on Adam.

'There's a common misconception when it comes to counselling,' she explains, 'that what we're working towards is the resolution of a particular problem.' She pauses, watches Adam's eyebrows arrow slightly in the silence. 'That's not what counselling is really about. I'm here to help you, yes, but what I'm most interested in is helping you to find a way to help yourself. In all circumstances. Holistically.' She believes this, passionately, but she's worried Adam will be put off by the terminology.

'All I'm trying to say,' she goes on, 'is that it's a process. An open-ended one. Your question was how long this usually takes but I'm afraid I can't give you an answer. It could be we see progress after six sessions. It might equally turn out that you and I aren't suited to each other at all. Sorry to sound so woolly but there are just so many variables.'

'Like what's bothering me.'

'I'm sorry?'

'Like what's bothering me. You said there are lots of variables, and one of them, I guess, is what it is that's actually bothering me. Right?'

'Well, yes. Although . . .' Keep it simple, Susanna. 'Yes, that's one of the variables, absolutely.'

'So about that . . .' Adam says. 'I mean, is it OK if we talk about that now?'

Susanna can see he's desperate to get it off his chest. This thing. The perceived problem that brought him to Susanna's office in the first place, which Susanna can pretty much guarantee isn't what's really bothering him at all. That's the way it usually works. A client comes in focused on one thing – some experience they're convinced is at the centre of their unhappiness – and it turns out to be something else completely.

'Of course,' she says. 'If you think it would help, by all means let's address it.'

Adam doesn't shuffle the way she's expecting him to. From the way he's so far referred to his 'problem', his obvious embarrassment about whatever it is that's troubling him, she expects him to shift, to clear his throat, to take a moment to summon up the courage and at the last to mumble it towards the floor.

But he doesn't do that. He sits perfectly still and when he speaks he looks Susanna squarely in the eye.

'There's something I want to do,' he says.

'Something you want to do?'

'Something . . . bad. And the thing is . . .' He hasn't moved. Hasn't once dropped his gaze from hers, but there's a tiny smile now playing on his lips. And it's not a goofy smile this time. It's not a goofy smile at all. 'The thing is, Susanna,' Adam goes on, all innocence now drained from his expression, 'I don't know if I can stop myself.'

2

'You haven't responded,' Adam says. He runs his hands through his hair again. He is tearing at it almost, the way her ex-husband used to do whenever he and Susanna argued – which, by the end, had been virtually every time they were together.

'I shouldn't have said anything,' Adam goes on. 'You don't even know me and I . . . I mean, I haven't even asked you about confidentiality. About whether, you know. You would have to say anything. If I . . . were I to . . .'

'Adam.' She uses his name to focus him. To focus herself. 'Adam, listen. It's fine. I promise. You should feel free to say anything you want to. Anything you need to. That's what these discussions between us are all about. Openness. Honesty.'

Adam is looking at her dubiously, the way a school kid might look at a teacher who's caught him doing something he shouldn't but has assured him it's OK to go on. Like it's a trap, in other words. Like she's trying to trick him.

'As for confidentiality,' Susanna says, 'what transpires in this room is entirely privileged. That means you can trust me as much as you would trust your doctor, say, or your solicitor. The only exception is if I were to deem you to be a threat. To yourself, I mean. Or to others.'

It is so subtle that Susanna almost doesn't notice it: Adam shows a shadow of a flinch.

'Adam? I promise you I would never breach our bond unless we'd absolutely come to a dead end. I'm here to help you. That's my priority. And I know I can't possibly hope to do that unless you feel able to trust me. To confide in me.'

'So that's a rule,' Adam answers. 'Like a law? You're not allowed to say anything unless I agree you can? To . . . I don't know. To the authorities, I guess. Like' – Adam's eyes peek out at her from beneath his fringe – 'to the police.'

Susanna does her best not to react.

'That's right,' she responds. 'I can't tell anyone anything about you, not unless I believe you're about to hurt someone – yourself included – and there's nothing more I feel I can do to keep you safe.'

Adam is considering. Deciding, Susanna assumes.

Finally he puffs out a breath. 'Can I start at the beginning?'

'Please do,' Susanna says.

'So there's this girl . . .'

If Susanna had been put on the spot, she probably would have guessed Adam's story would begin like this. Girl/boy – one or the other. Adam doesn't come across as being homosexual but Susanna has been surprised before by her clients' sexual proclivities. Not that she's judgemental. For all her faults that's one thing she's never been. Not like Neil, her ex-husband, who'd once confessed to her that his biggest fear was that their son, Jacob, Jake to his parents and his mates, would turn out 'queer'. Which Susanna was shocked by at the time but now finds almost laughable: Neil's prejudice, yes, but also that there was a time when her husband's biggest fear centred on the manner in which their only son would fall in love.

'She's younger than me. This girl. Not a lot. Just, like, three years younger.'

Susanna realizes she still doesn't know Adam's exact age. If he is indeed nineteen or twenty, that would make this girlfriend of his sixteen or seventeen. Two or three years older than Emily, then: Susanna's daughter, her only child other than Jake.

'She's pretty, I guess. Not just pretty. She's beautiful actually. She's slim, kind of short I suppose, and she's got this amazing hair, like, I don't know. Like polished wood. It's sort of brown but also red in places, gold even, and it shines like she's advertising shampoo. And she's got this laugh. I don't really know how to describe it. It's kind of a dirty laugh, you could say, but at the same time it's exactly the opposite. It's just pure. With no malice in it. It's like she laughs and you want to laugh too. You know?'

Susanna nods and Adam, instead of continuing, all at once clamps his lips tight, as though he's embarrassed. And perhaps he's worried that he's coming across as soppy, daft even, which maybe in his terms he is but to Susanna's ear all he sounds like is a young man who is very much in love.

'She's obviously a very attractive young woman.'

Adam appears worried at first that Susanna is mocking him but then he allows her a glimpse of that schoolboy grin.

'She is,' he says. 'Absolutely, she is. And that's why I'm so worried, I suppose. About . . .' The grin freezes, fades.

'About what, Adam? What is it you're worried about?'

'I'm worried about . . .'

Susanna waits.

'I'm worried about hurting her,' Adam states, and there's a silence as understanding blooms between them that he's not talking about hurting her *feelings*.

Susanna is careful to remain quite still.

'What is it that makes you think you might hurt her?'

And the way Adam looks at her now . . . it's like before, when he first alluded directly to his 'problem' (*There's something I want to do*) and all innocence drained from his expression. It occurred to Susanna then that Adam was more troubled than she'd initially assumed and that maybe she was right to be wary of him.

But the instinct is fleeting and quickly the notion re-establishes itself that, whatever it is about Adam that has been niggling at her, it's linked to Susanna's past, not his. It's her problem, in other words; her baggage.

'Adam? What is it that makes you think you might hurt her?' Susanna repeats.

'It's just . . .' Adam takes a breath and expels the air

slowly. 'It just feels *right* somehow,' he says at last. 'That's the only way I can think to describe it. Like . . .' He is on the brink of speaking again, then shakes his head.

'Keep going, Adam,' Susanna says. 'Remember, I'm not here to judge you. If the words don't sound right the first time, no one's going to stop you taking them back. We have all the time we need to get this right.'

She waits.

'Adam? Why is it you think you might –'

'Because she *deserves* it,' Adam suddenly gushes. And this time there is genuine anger in his expression. He is leaning forward, elbows on knees, and there is a passion – a fervour – in his eyes. 'Except, maybe I don't even mean her,' Adam continues. 'Maybe who I really mean is . . .'

Susanna watches him, still startled by the intensity of Adam's outburst. Is . . . who? Ordinarily Susanna's instinct would be to say Adam was alluding to himself; that *he* is the person he feels should suffer, perhaps because subconsciously he doesn't believe he deserves to be in the relationship in the first place. But it's odd. For some reason she can't escape the feeling that in fact he has in mind someone else entirely.

'Oh, I don't know,' Adam announces, reclining and folding his arms.

Susanna allows an extended pause.

'Let's go back a bit,' she says at last. 'Shall we?'

Adam looks at her questioningly.

'Can you tell me a little bit about your parents?' Susanna says. 'About what things were like when you were young?'

There is another flash in Adam's eyes that Susanna doesn't fully understand. Irritation, perhaps? Anger again? *Triumph*, even? It could be any of those things. All of them. None.

'You said you grew up in London, for example,' Susanna persists. 'Is that right?'

'Yes. No. I mean, I was born in London,' Adam tells her, 'but I didn't grow up there. I grew up sort of all over the place really.'

'Your parents travelled?'

'My old man did. Although I'm not sure *travelling* is quite the right word. Running, more like.'

'Meaning?'

'Meaning he was a waste of space.' A flash of anger again, barely contained. And beneath it, Susanna judges, something more, something she can't quite put her finger on.

For the moment she decides to let it slide. 'What about your mother, Adam?' she asks instead.

Adam's lips crease at one corner. He ignores the question Susanna asked him. 'I know what you're thinking,' he states instead.

And Susanna is convinced for an instant that he does.

'You're thinking about my background,' Adam goes on. 'You're wondering whether that's part of this. Part of the way I've been feeling.'

Susanna smiles, as much for her sake as for Adam's.

'I am, as it happens.'

'You're probably right,' Adam says. 'In fact, I'm sure you are.'

Susanna feels her eyes go narrow. 'What makes you say that?'

'That's the way it is for everyone. Where we come from, our secret pasts: we can't escape them. They define us. Control us. Trap us even, sometimes.' Adam looks at her intently. 'Don't you think?'

Susanna, paralysed, stares back. And a grip of ice closes around each of her shoulders.

She stands. Conscious that Adam is watching her, she moves across the floor until she is hovering at the visitor's side of her desk.

'Is everything OK?' There is the sound of Adam leaning forward in his chair. 'Did I say something wrong?'

Susanna forces herself to smile. She tries to show it to Adam without fully turning round. She needs a moment. Just a moment.

'No, of course not, I . . . I was looking for a pen, that's all. And my notepad.' She makes a show of searching her desktop.

'You're going to take notes? I thought you weren't supposed to take notes? The last therapist I saw, he said something about it interfering in the process.'

And there it is: the first time Susanna understands categorically that Adam hasn't been entirely honest with her. He claimed that he'd never had counselling before, and yet with one simple observation he's given himself away.

'Like, I say something,' Adam is explaining, 'you write it down, then I change what I say next based on what you've chosen to record. Right?'

Something bad.

Because she deserves *it.*

So he lied. It's no big deal. Clients cover up all the time. And truth, Susanna knows, is subjective. Isn't that what her training taught her? What *feels* true to the client is what counts, not what's fact and what's fiction.

Our secret pasts . . .

There is a pen beneath Susanna's hovering fingers and she forces herself to pick it up. 'Right,' she says. 'That's exactly right. The pen, the notepad – they're for after.'

She re-establishes her smile. She turns . . .

. . . and is rocked by what she sees in Adam's eyes: sheer, unadulterated hate.

It is as though he has been unmasked. He looks . . . older? Younger? *Crueller*, certainly, and with that somehow also more familiar: the way he seemed to Susanna when he first walked in. As for that innocence she detected earlier in his demeanour, it's like a sheen that has cracked and peeled away.

Trust herself. How many times has she been over this? She knew something was off, so why didn't she *trust herself*?

'Are you OK, Susanna?'

'I beg your pardon?'

'You look afraid, all of a sudden. I'm not scaring you, am I?'

He sounds pleased.

'Scaring me?' Susanna laughs. 'No, of course not, why should you . . .'

But he is. Absolutely he is. There's no denying it any more: something about him frightened her from the beginning. She can rationalize all she wants but now she's acknowledged it, it's as obvious as the fear itself.

'You've been lying to me,' she finds herself saying. 'Haven't you?' This is something in ordinary circumstances Susanna would never do. Force a client to confront their inconsistencies. Accuse them, basically. But she has no doubt that Adam is pushing her – testing her? – and instinctively she feels an urge to push back.

There is a moment when Adam remains perfectly still.

Then, 'You've got me,' he says. And it is not only Adam's appearance now that seems altered. It is his posture, his voice, everything. He unbuttons the collar of his shirt, slumps slightly in his chair. Susanna thinks of actors, slackening as they slip off stage. Of news anchors, ridiculously – of how their personas must alter the instant the camera light blinks off.

'It was the notepad, wasn't it?' Adam is saying. 'Me saying you weren't supposed to take notes?' He shakes his head, laughs at himself. 'I was trying to impress you, I guess. I've done a lot of research, you see. I know my stuff.'

Research? Susanna is about to echo, when Adam hits his forehead with the heel of his palm. Hard.

And then he laughs again.

'But that was all,' he says. 'I've seen other counsellors, I admit it. But my problem. My dilemma, I suppose you could call it. That was genuine.'

Susanna's throat is clogged with questions. With shock, with confusion, with fear.

'Here,' Adam says. 'Maybe this will help you understand.' He leans sideways, and slips his hand into his rear jeans pocket. From it he produces a piece of paper.

At first Susanna doesn't move.

'Here,' Adam repeats and this time when he waves the piece of paper Susanna finds herself reaching for it. She takes it, turns it over.

And sees her daughter looking back at her in a photograph.

3

The memories fizz in free association, bubbling and then bursting at the surface.

The pregnancy, which was horrendous. Not like before. Not like the first time. Somehow with Emily *everything* was different. Unless, equally possible, it wasn't and Emily, her little girl, was just a fluke. A pearl chafed into perfection.

But the sickness. Certainly the sickness was new, something she'd not experienced with Jake. It hit her early and instead of passing only gathered intensity. She was hospitalized. Twice. The second time for almost a fortnight. It became so bad that Neil suggested termination. No, that's not right. He didn't *suggest* anything. He alluded, insinuated. Tried to coax her so that the decision – the responsibility – would become Susanna's. And looking back, as Susanna has relentlessly, that was the moment, she would say, that their relationship finally broke apart. It had been crumbling anyway. By the time Emily was conceived it was as much a memory of something tangible as a thing itself: an edifice ready to fall at the slightest tremor.

Termination, though; the mere suggestion of it . . . for Susanna that was the beginning of the end. It was like the time Neil had confessed his fears about Jake's sexuality, except worse, more fundamental, because prejudice was something Susanna could at least account for. What Neil said was he was only thinking of her well-being. That it was nothing to do with the fact that he hadn't wanted a second child in the first place; had argued for months that it was precisely the wrong thing to do. Which maybe it was but that didn't alter how desperate Susanna was for her baby to be born. Her little girl, as things turned out. A baby *girl*.

Susanna wasn't some radical. She was as pro-choice, she felt, as it was possible for a mother to be. But after everything they'd been through Susanna couldn't believe the thought would even enter Neil's mind. Kill it, was what he meant. Murder her baby.

She overrode Neil in the end, of course she did, and the joy of Emily's birth for the most part rinsed away the pain. Of the pregnancy, that is. Of labour. But afterwards, and until Neil and Susanna went their separate ways (separate? Try opposite. Diametrical) Susanna had night upon night of sleepless fear. It had finally dawned on her that she was living with a stranger. Husband, father: *impostor*.

Bottom shuffling. Ha! They both did it. Meaning maybe there were some commonalities after all. Except Jake's method of movement was like a lurching, sitting-down limp, whereas Emily was always more elegant. It was almost graceful, the way she sculled across the floor, if you could describe dragging your bum across the linoleum as a thing of grace. That was the thing, though. She almost floated. Zen-like. A pink-skinned, talcum-powdered Buddha.

Emily with a photograph of Jake. Older now. Six? Seven? And the Jake in the picture, coincidentally, not that dissimilar in age.

'Who's this, Mummy?'

Susanna turning to look. Realization dawning as she sees.

'Where did you get that?'

'Hey. Give it back.'

'I said, where did you get it? You shouldn't be going through my drawers, Emily. I've told you before about going through my things.'

'I wasn't. I just found it!'

Even if Susanna hadn't been able to read Emily so easily, she would have known her daughter was lying to her. There were no photographs of Jake anywhere in their house that weren't at least two sealed layers from being 'found'. This one, Susanna knew – the way a librarian knows the location of the books she minds, a curator the story of each exhibit – was in an envelope in a shoebox in her junk drawer. Junk being a euphemism for hallowed treasures, a label she'd only chosen in the first place in a bid to deter Emily.

'Mummy? It's mine, I found it, let me see.'

'It's not yours, young lady.' Susanna felt anger in spite of herself. Fury without warning or good reason.

She tried again.

'It's not *yours*, Emily. It's Mummy's. It's . . . precious,' she settled on, for want of a better word.

'But I want to see. Show me, Mummy, please.'

She hesitated at first but then gave in. What harm, she remembers thinking, could it do?

For a long time Emily just stared, trying to decipher what had made her mother so cross.

'But who is it?' she asked.

Susanna looked from Emily to the photograph. She allowed her thumbtip to graze her son's cheek. 'Just a boy,' Susanna responded. 'No one you know.'

And she distracted her daughter with a plate of biscuits.

Their perfect day. The absolute happiest Susanna has been in what she has learned to think of as her life, part two.

It was just her and Emily. No one else. No bystanders even who betrayed in glances that they knew exactly who Susanna and Emily were. No imagined scrutiny either, which for a long time had been almost as much of a problem. More even, her counsellor would have said. Her counsellor being Patti Moorcock. Introduced to Susanna by her bereavement counsellor and the person who in turn introduced Susanna to her new career. For two, three years Patti had been Susanna's mentor, confidante, friend. Perhaps the only true friend Susanna has ever really had. There's Ruth too, of course, but as much as Susanna adores Ruth there's still that secret that will always exist between them, which by omission has ripened into a lie – and has, in Susanna's mind, downgraded their relationship to an illusion. A light show. Something beautiful yet insubstantial. Something she knows will eventually come to an end.

But that day. Her and Emily's perfect day. A walk on the beach, sugared doughnuts while sitting on the pier. Talking. Just talking. Emily was ten at the time and soon enough, Susanna knew (was acutely, painfully aware), conversation with her mother would be something she would shy away from. Yet that day she was garrulous, cheerful, open. She answered when Susanna asked, laughing and smiling as she did so.

And it wasn't one-way traffic. Emily asked questions of Susanna as well, seemed genuinely interested in what Susanna had to say. It was silly really, Susanna taking such pleasure in a conversation. Except it didn't feel silly. To Susanna it felt like the opposite: the pinnacle of what a parent is able to do. Talking to your kids. *Listening* to them. Loving them by blessing them with your full attention.

'You know God?' Emily came out with, veering from a conversation about rollercoasters – the type of tangent only a ten-year-old will attempt.

Susanna was taking a sip of her daughter's Coke at the time, which they'd bought to wash down the doughnuts. At her daughter's question (statement?) she found herself struggling to contain her mouthful.

'I do,' she replied at last, swallowing and running a finger across her chin. 'Although not personally.'

It was a feeble joke – a Mum joke – but Emily, bless her, gave a giggle. 'Mu-um,' she chastised.

'What about God?' Susanna asked her, frowning slightly to suppress a glimmer, which she feared Emily would misinterpret.

'Do you reckon She's really real?'

Again Susanna had to suppress her smile. 'She?'

'Sure. Or He, I guess.'

'Well . . .' No, was the true response. She wanted to believe, and after Emily was born had considered allowing herself to, but ultimately couldn't permit herself the self-deception. 'I suppose it's possible. Plenty of people would say they didn't have the slightest doubt.'

'But you don't agree. You don't believe She does exist.'

Susanna's policy of always trying to be honest left her no wriggle room and anyway Emily had discerned the answer already.

'No, I don't. Although if God's real I'd bet money He's a man.'

Emily, as they ambled, looked at her sideways. 'What does that mean?'

Susanna shook her head. 'Nothing, darling. Just a joke, that's all. Not a very good one.'

Ordinarily Emily would have insisted her mother explain it, deconstruct it so she could examine its precise make-up. Emily's mind, though, was evidently on higher matters.

'But what if She *is* real?'

There was something in Emily's voice that caused Susanna to frown genuinely. Fear? Not quite. But anxiety of some sort certainly. 'What do you mean?' Susanna asked.

For a moment Emily didn't respond.

'Emily? Is something worrying you?'

Her daughter shook her head. 'Not worrying me, exactly.'

'What then?'

'I'd be sorry, that's all. If God exists and no one believes in Her. I mean, not no one. But lots of people. You know?'

Susanna stopped walking and turned to face her daughter. A breeze slid gently across the pier and she had to tuck her hair back to stop it blowing in her eyes.

'You feel sorry,' she said. 'For God.'

Emily stopped walking too. She half frowned, half squinted against the sunlight. 'Well, yeah. And sad, I suppose. Because it would be lonely. Wouldn't it? If you were God and no one believed in you?'

God, Susanna loved her. Ha. How about that for a prayer, a statement of what Susanna believed in. I love you, Emily. I believe in *you*.

'I don't think you need to feel sorry for God, darling,' Susanna said. 'I think, if God exists, I would imagine She's feeling pretty pleased with Herself.'

'Because of the world.'

'Pardon me?'

'God's pleased with Herself because of the world. Because of all the cool stuff that's in it. Is that what you mean?'

'Well . . .' Again, it wasn't. But if it should have been, would Susanna agreeing count as lying? 'What I meant was,' she clarified, sidestepping, 'it must be pretty cool being God and that's why She's probably quite happy. You know, being able to summon lightning bolts at will. Having people worship you every Sunday. Living, basically, on a cloud.' She looked down as Emily gave another giggle.

'But yes,' Susanna went on, 'I think you're right. I think if there really is a God then overall She deserves to feel proud. There's a lot of unpleasantness in the world but there's a whole lot of brilliant stuff too.' Susanna took her daughter's hand, felt Emily's fingers coil around hers. 'Often . . . Well. I suppose it's just easy to forget that.'

For six, seven paces they walked on without saying a word. Then Susanna caught her daughter smiling.

'You said She,' Emily declared, triumphant in a bashful sort of way.

'Ha.' Susanna looked into the wind, used a palm to wipe away a tear. 'So I did,' she said, turning back. And she held her daughter's hand tighter.

The opposite. The nadir. The worst day, at least since Susanna, part one.

Although really it boiled down to a single incident. They were, what? Out shopping, she supposed. The precise details of their outing have receded in her memory into irrelevance. Again, though, it was just her and Emily, and Emily at the time had been in the pushchair. She was three months, two weeks and four days old. Susanna worked it out after. Would she remember? That was what Susanna fixated on. Which on the one hand seemed ridiculous given that her own earliest memory (sitting on a pedalo with her father, ice cream dripping on to her knees) came from a time when she was four years old. But they say children are shaped by events that occur even when they are in the womb. They say a child's entire personality is moulded by what they experience in their first few months. Meaning Emily would surely remember something, even if only in the deepest part of her.

She was so unprepared, that was part of it. It was over, she thought. The worst had happened but they were getting past it, and she simply assumed the rest of the world was moving on too. *Assume makes an ass of you and me.* That was one of Neil's favourite sayings. Also, *at the end of the day* and, worst of all, *it is what it is*, which in five words was about as close as you could get to distilling his philosophy on life. A verbal shrug is what it amounted to, and it made Susanna want to hurl something every time.

Boys will be boys, that was another one. Another shrug. Another abdication of responsibility.

'I know you.'

It was that pronouncement that caused Susanna to turn.

'Excuse me?' she said to the woman who'd approached them. This was on the street. The pavement somewhere. Outside Tesco?

'I said, I know you. I recognize you from the television.'

Tesco, that's right, and they had been shopping because Susanna recalls how at that stage she was wrestling with the carrier bags. There were tins, packets, bags of loose vegetables that were coming untied, and Susanna was struggling to hook the carriers on the handles of the buggy. Things kept spilling out, though. She remembers a can of peaches rolling towards the stranger's foot, the woman spotting it and trapping it beneath her toes. And then, a second later, knocking it with the side of her boot towards the gutter.

'Hey,' Susanna protested – but feebly. Scared now. Not just of this woman, who was shorter than Susanna, and slighter. Younger too. She must have been twenty-seven, twenty-eight, definitely no older than thirty. And she had a child herself. That was the worst part. There was a little boy holding her hand. Watching. Learning.

'You're scum. That's what you are. *Scum.*'

OK, so maybe she was scared of the woman but she was scared of the situation more. It was like one of those dreams, where you find yourself in public naked. That's how she felt: utterly, unbearably exposed.

'You may have fooled them but you didn't fool me. I know. I *know.*'

Susanna glanced about her, afraid of how many of the shoppers bustling around them would be listening. 'I think you've got me confused with someone else.'

She tried to move off then, leaving her shopping where it lay. And maybe it was that – the willing abandonment of what was rightfully hers – that the woman took as an admission of guilt. She became emboldened, dragging her son so that together they blocked Susanna's path.

31

Red hair, green eyes, a chin that jutted like an accusing finger.

'She yours?' the woman said. That chin of hers flicking towards Emily. Emily staring up at them from the pushchair.

For an instant Susanna considered claiming Emily was her niece, her goddaughter, anything. Yet even by that stage she'd instilled in herself that devotion to honesty. Telling the truth seemed such a clear principle by which to live her life: sacred, almost, in its purity. If she was truthful, upfront, always, how could anyone ever hold her to blame?

So *yes*, she intended to say. *She's mine.*

As it was she didn't get that far.

The woman spat. Not at Susanna. She raked the mucus to the back of her throat and then heaved it full force into Emily's buggy.

Susanna shrieked. Her first and only honest-to-goodness *shriek*. She'd had occasion to make the sound before but it was only on seeing her daughter sprayed by a stranger's vitriol that her anguish found voice. She was aware the little boy had started to cry, sensed a passer-by veer away from her in alarm. She remembers the woman – the spitter – barging past her, hindering her for a moment from succouring her child. And Emily's face when Susanna bent to her: shocked, yes, but too innocent to be properly afraid.

And then, after that, the memory blurs, the way her vision did from the onrush of tears. She doesn't recall getting home, has no idea what happened to the shopping. She remembers *being* at home, and crying obviously, endlessly, and immediately dunking Emily in the bath. She remembers scrubbing at her daughter's face, how red Emily was from the flannel. And she remembers her daughter screaming – from the pain of it: her soap-scraped skin.

And Neil yelling. 'Stop! For Christ's sake just stop it, won't you?'

Susanna thinking he was yelling at Emily.

It finally dawning on her that he was talking to her.

Running, in the middle of the night. To her brother's at first, where she knew if she remained she would be found, but it was only for one or two days, assuming Peter would let them stay even that long. He would rather not have helped them at all, that much was obvious, but when a family member turns up on your doorstep at three o'clock in the morning, an infant wrapped shivering in their arms, what choice really does that leave you?

Emily frightened, upset. Susanna doing her best to comfort her. To comfort herself as well. To reassure herself that she was doing the right thing. One more lie, was what she told herself. A big one, a whopper, but without it she didn't know how they could go on. She'd managed to convince herself, before, that the truth would set her free. She finally realized, paradoxically, that only a lie would. And it was Neil in the end who'd forced her hand. Neil's fault this time, absolutely and categorically. At least Susanna had the balm of knowing that.

Again though, would Emily remember? At five months old now, what impressions would she retain of the life they were leaving behind? And how much would Susanna eventually choose to tell her? That was the real question, and another challenge to Susanna's vow of honesty.

Everything, therefore, was the answer. Eventually Susanna would tell Emily everything. Who her father was. Why they'd left. Her real surname, her mother's real first name. Just not yet, obviously. When she was . . . how old? Six? Nine? Twelve?

Not yet.

It became a refrain. A get-out clause. She *was* being honest because the lie was only temporary. Not even a lie. An omission. Like her omission with Ruth, which Susanna permitted because it was tied to the lie she'd allowed herself. That one, final lie that she and Emily so desperately needed.

And besides, she would tell Emily one day.

Some day.

Just not yet.

Teenager-dom. The early years. And how Emily had flourished. Who says a daughter needs a father? Who says working single mothers can't cope? And OK, so maybe Susanna never quite fulfilled her promise to herself, allowed Emily to continue living in ignorance instead, but that was another aphorism, wasn't it? *Ignorance is bliss.* Aphorism or truism – Susanna isn't sure there's a difference. All that matters in Emily's case is that the lie proved good for her. The lie helped her daughter thrive.

And Susanna too. She completed her training, even set up her own practice. Admittedly there were things that . . . haunted her. But compared to her former life – compared to strangers spitting at her daughter, for heaven's sake – the challenges of her current circumstances are ones Susanna feels able to cope with. Like Emily herself. Her daughter is a teenage girl, Susanna an older mother, so inevitably they've had their share of difficulties. Yet difficult, in Susanna's mind, is relative.

Yesterday morning. The last time Susanna saw her before Emily went off to school, and then slept over at her friend's house. The breakfast rush, the bathroom crush. Once Susanna stood taller than her daughter, so that as they shared the mirror in front of the sink Susanna could position herself to the rear and still see over the top of Emily's head. These days they have no choice but to squash in side by side, swapping places when they need to. It's become a dance, a morning ritual that Susanna has learned to treasure.

Her favourite part is when Emily squeezes the toothpaste. It's a small thing, silly really, but every morning, almost without fail, Emily will hold the toothpaste tube and deploy a dollop on to Susanna's brush. Sometimes Susanna will be standing there with her toothbrush in her hand. Other times she'll be fiddling with her hair and Emily will simply get her toothbrush ready for her.

Susanna tried explaining to Ruth once why that

small act makes her so happy. There are a thousand reasons, is the problem, most of which she found impossible to voice. The biggest, though, the one she did express, was that it makes Susanna feel like she is loved. More than flowers on her birthday, more even than her daughter declaring that she loves her out loud. Toothpaste on her toothbrush. Nearly two decades living with Neil and Susanna would never have guessed it could be that simple.

But yesterday. The morning had started as normal. *Emily* seemed normal. Didn't she? She was cheerful. If anything more cheerful than usual, and –

Oh God.

Was that part of this?

Was that part of *why*?

Sex. Yet again it came down to sex. Not *sex* sex necessarily but girls, boys; boys, girls . . .

Emily. Oh Emily. Susanna's precious little girl. Susanna considers Ruth her only friend now but Emily is her friend and so much more. If something's happened to her. If anything threatened to . . .

Susanna has died for her daughter once already. If she were to lose her – if somehow they were to lose each other – Susanna would die all over again.

4

'Who are you?'

The photograph is still in Susanna's hand. The picture of Emily.

She looks at Adam and says it again. 'Who are you? *Really?*'

'I told you,' Adam replies. 'My name's Adam. Just as your name's Susanna. Right?'

Susanna swallows.

'Are you a reporter? From the press? Or a private detective or . . .' But she knows that Adam is none of these things. Whatever he is, it's something far worse.

'Sit down, Susanna. Please. Why can't we just continue our little chat?'

Susanna shakes her head. 'Get out,' she says. 'Whoever you are, just get out. Get out or I'll call the police.'

Which rings so hollow Adam doesn't bother to react.

From being afraid Susanna is suddenly furious. At herself for having been duped. At him – 'Adam' – for having duped her. And for not just letting her be. She's been doing what she can. Living as honourably as she can. She's been trying to *help* people, doing the only thing she is left with that might enable her to make some amends.

But it's not enough. She was a fool ever to have believed anything she could do would be enough.

'You're some kind of . . . of *tourist*,' she says. 'Is that it?'

She's come across them before. Not since she left. Not since she ran. But in letters, on the telephone, sometimes even at her door. *Fans*, they called themselves. Which made Susanna feel physically sick. One time she was sick, after reading a letter she would have been better off burning. This was back near the beginning (the end? She still doesn't know what she's supposed to call it), when she still bothered to open the letters she received at all. One or two, admittedly, had helped, which is perhaps why she persisted with her mail as long as she did. But it was like trying to taste sweetness in sewage. In the end the effluence had drowned her.

Susanna barely waits for Adam to respond. All at once she is marching towards the door. 'Alina!' she yells, calling for their receptionist. She reaches for the door handle. 'Alin—'

'I wouldn't do that if I were you.'

The look Susanna gives him is needle-sharp.

'Why? Because of a photograph?' She looks at it again and realizes from the cut of Emily's hair that it is a day or two old at most. And the background: Susanna doesn't recognize it. It looks industrial: breezeblock wall, concrete floor: nowhere her daughter would ordinarily be. But, 'You could have got that anywhere,' she insists, desperately. 'For all I know you found it on the Internet.'

The Internet in Susanna's mind is somewhere foul. A swamp, somewhere sullied – a source of squalor and a reservoir for it, both. She lets Emily use it but only because she accepts she has no choice. If she could she would cut their cable connection, coat the walls of their house in lead. As for Twitter, Facebook, all the rest, Susanna can only imagine what would have been waiting for her in those places had they existed eighteen years ago. She would stop her daughter using those as well, would have denied her a mobile phone if that, in this day and age, were remotely feasible. Susanna would go as far as to say that it was because of the Web, because of (anti) social media, that she has so far shied from telling Emily all the facts. Maybe that's true, maybe not, but in her mind it's as good an excuse as any.

'Because of the photograph,' Adam agrees. 'Also, because of this.'

Susanna is focused once more on summoning Alina, her intent to open her office door. But when she looks Adam's way she freezes. Her hand floats uselessly in front of her.

He has a knife. It's a hand span in length, gun-metal grey, and dull everywhere but on its edges. There it gleams, like a smile waiting in the dark.

The knife is laid openly on Adam's lap, as though it had been resting there all along.

'Oh my God. Oh ... God ... I ...' Susanna covers her mouth with both hands. She is aware that her head, her whole body, has begun to shake. 'Please ... whatever you want ... whoever you are, I ...'

'Calm down, Susanna.' Adam lets his fingertips touch the handle of the knife. 'You really don't want to make me use this. If that happens, you'll never know what I've done to your daughter.'

What I've done to your daughter. The words cut more deeply than the knife would but before Susanna can react the door to her office swings open.

Instinctively she blocks it with her foot.

From the landing there is an *oof* sound. Alina's lungs venting her surprise.

'Susanna?' she demands.

'It's fine, Alina,' Susanna responds, her voice artificially high. Her eyes all the while are on the knife. 'Everything's fine!'

The door moves against Susanna's foot. Alina is trying to force her way in. The door hinges towards the seating area, so that Adam remains hidden from view.

'I was just wondering whether my next client was here yet,' Susanna blurts. 'That's all.'

'You shouted. For this?' The affront in Alina's voice is plain to hear and Susanna realizes that this is probably why she has responded so quickly. Normally when Susanna calls Alina never comes, irrespective of whether she's involved with helping Ruth. She's here now, not to check whether Susanna needs help, rather to take issue with her means of summons.

Susanna catches Adam's eye. He's settled into the role of spectator, more fascinated now than threatening.

Susanna shifts her foot to allow the door to open a fraction further. The gap is just wide enough to allow her to show Alina her smile.

'It's fine, Alina, really,' Susanna repeats. 'And I'm sorry I shouted. I wasn't thinking. Sorry,' she says again.

Alina's face is one she's seen on Emily. But as a three-year-old, a toddler, after some perceived injustice that's left her contemplating how far she's been wronged.

Alina exhales. 'You have intercom,' she states. 'Please: use this.'

'I know. I will. I can never get it to work, that's all.' This much, at least, is true. Susanna isn't good with modern technology, perhaps because she spends so much of her time refusing to acknowledge it exists. 'You should tweet, Mum,' Emily has told her. 'Or get on WhatsApp at least. Everyone's on WhatsApp these days.' Which is precisely what Susanna is afraid of.

'They are not here.'

'Pardon me?'

'Your next *client*,' Alina clarifies, placing an emphasis on the final word that is almost scornful. 'They are not here.'

'Right. OK. Well, let me know when they do arrive.' Susanna realizes a second later what she has said. 'No! Wait! I'll come out. In . . .' She makes like she's checking her watch. Really she's checking behind her. 'In a while,' she settles on, reasserting her smile. 'OK?'

Alina presses her over-glossed lips into a pout, then sighs and retreats along the landing. For a moment Susanna stares out after her, contemplating the route to the staircase. She could just run. Adam wouldn't be able to stop her. But who knows what he would do in Susanna's wake, what retribution he might exact against Ruth and

Alina. And Emily. It is just a photograph. So far Adam hasn't demonstrated he has any greater hold on Susanna's daughter than his possession of that single image. But there's no way Susanna is willing to take the risk.

Gently she closes the office door. She leans against it, breathing, then forces herself to face into the room.

'You're better at this than I am,' Adam says. His tone is self-effacing, almost humble, but Susanna doesn't trust it. She's learned already not to trust anything about him.

'Better at what?' she finds herself asking, the response more instinct than genuine enquiry.

'At lying.'

Susanna looks up then.

'To be honest, I'm surprised I managed to keep going as long as I did,' Adam says. 'I was so worried I'd give myself away. I've had some practice lately but on the whole I'm really not a very good actor. That's why I stuck mainly to the truth.'

The falseness in his modesty this time is plain to hear. In fact he sounds so pleased with himself for having taken Susanna in that, as before, it fires up Susanna's anger. You didn't fool me, she's thinking. You *didn't*. I fooled myself, is what happened. I didn't listen to *myself*.

Susanna finds herself marching towards her desk. She doesn't care about the knife all of a sudden, nor what Adam might do to her. All she cares about is Emily.

She picks up her mobile phone. She is aware Adam is watching her and is only moderately unsettled by the fact he makes no move to stop her. She scrolls to find her daughter in her contacts. She taps the number to initiate the call and, turning from Adam, holds the phone up to her ear. It's two weeks into September and after a long summer holiday her daughter is back at school, so she expects the call to go straight to voicemail. Instead it rings, and for an instant Susanna succumbs to a surge of hope – until, as well as the ringing in her ear, she hears a ringtone going off right behind her.

She turns, the hand holding her own phone falling from her ear as she does so. Adam is fishing once again into his back pocket. He pulls out an iPhone – two models old, in a case bearing images of pressed flowers – and frowns at the screen as though puzzled at who might be calling. He acts like he's screening: turns up his nose and slips the phone back where it came from.

The dialling stops, the ringtone too, and from close beside her Susanna hears her daughter's voice.

'Hi, this is Emily. I'm either, a, at school, b, asleep, or, c, all of the above. Leave a message and if you're lucky I'll get back to you.'

Susanna looks at the phone in her palm. Ridiculously, she has to resist the urge to speak to Emily's voicemail, to beg her daughter to call her right away. *This very second, young lady. I'm not kidding.*

'You could, I don't know. Try one of her friends?' Adam suggests mock-helpfully.

He has her phone. More than the knife, more than the picture, it is the fact that he has her daughter's iPhone that convinces Susanna this is really happening. Emily would no sooner be parted from her mobile than she would be from her right arm.

Nonetheless Susanna does exactly as Adam suggests. She calls Frankie, Emily's best friend, who Emily was supposed to be staying over with last night. Susanna realizes she has no way of knowing whether her daughter even made it to school that morning.

Frankie answers on the second ring.

'Hey, Mrs F.'

'Frankie. Listen. Is Emily with you?'

'Em? Nope. I haven't seen her since Wednesday.'

'Are you sure? Are you certain?'

'Sure I'm sure. She texted me yesterday morning saying she wasn't feeling well so wouldn't be coming round later. Which was a real bummer because we've got this project at school. And Emily said she'd –'

Susanna hangs up. She can feel the shallowness of her breaths, the panic welling from her stomach. 'Where is she?' she says, rounding on Adam.

Adam frowns like he's unsure who it is Susanna's talking about. 'Emily?'

Yes, Emily! Yes, my daughter! 'I'll call the police,' Susanna says. 'I'll scream and Alina will call them for me.'

Adam doesn't answer. He knows there is no need.

'What have you done to her?' Susanna presses. 'You said before you'd *done* something to her. If she's hurt . . . if you've touched her . . .' All at once Susanna's legs feel like they've been punctured and her fury is swept away by a rush of fear. 'Please,' she says, gripping the desk. 'Please, just tell me . . . Emily . . . is she . . .'

She is crying, she realizes. Adam is looking back at her through a blur.

44

'We'll get to Emily, I promise,' he tells her, the playfulness – the mischievousness – gone from his tone. 'In point of fact, it's mainly because of Emily that I'm here.'

'What do you mean? Look, Adam . . . whoever you are . . . if there's something you want . . . money, or . . . or whatever, I . . . I'll give it to you. OK? Everything I have.'

'Susanna . . .'

'My purse,' Susanna goes on. 'Look, here's my purse. I've got . . .' She searches for cash, finds a five-pound note and some change. 'My bank cards. Take my bank cards. I won't cancel them, I promise, I'll just let you draw out whatever you –'

'*Susanna!*'

Susanna stops talking. She feels the edge of her desk press into the back of her thighs.

'Just *stop*,' Adam says. 'OK? Stop *whining*,' he tells her. 'Stop *begging*.' As they were earlier his hands are tearing at his hair but if it was an act before, there's no sign he's pretending any more. And that anger Susanna has so far only seen in flashes: it's come undone.

'We'll get to Emily,' Adam hisses. 'I told you already that we would.' His hand has closed around the knife handle. It looks instinctive, as though he isn't fully aware of everything he's doing. 'But let's start with the reason you ran, Susanna. Before your daughter, before we discuss how you might save her, let's talk about what you did to your son.'

Emily

8 August 2017

So it's been a while. I remember when I got this diary in my stocking last Christmas, wondering what I was ever going to write in it. Which I don't mean to sound ungrateful. It was good of Mum to buy it for me, it really was. But at the same time, there's also a certain amount of irony. You know, that my mum buys me a diary to keep a record of all the stuff I'm doing, when Mum is also the person who basically stops me from doing *anything*. You know? I mean, I re-read those entries I wrote after Christmas, to try to get myself into the swing of it, and it's basically this massive *bleeeeuuuurgghhh*. Just, so I did this and then this happened and this was nice and isn't everything wonderful. Not exactly Anne Frank, right? Who, by the way, is my absolute hero.

But yeah. Since Christmas I've had nothing to say. Since I was born, in fact, it sometimes feels like. Which, again, makes me sound like a spoilt little brat, probably – like, 'Poor me, my life's so easy and uneventful.' I wonder what Anne Frank would have made of that! All I'm trying to say I guess is that my life so far – it hasn't exactly been some great adventure. Me and Mum, we live in this *nice* little house, with these two *nice* cats, and we do

49

nice things together. Going shopping, going to coffee shops, going for walks. But literally that's *it*. We don't even go on holiday, because there's no way Mum would ever leave her precious clients. Which I guess I admire, and I love my mum, I really do, more than I can imagine loving anyone. But sometimes it feels like *aaaaaarrrrgghhhh!!!!* You know? Like, I'm fourteen, Mum! I shouldn't *always* have to be back before it gets dark. And I should at least get to choose my own friends! Which obviously I do, in the first instance, but then Mum always insists on me inviting them over. *Always.* And I know exactly what it is she's doing, even though she tries to pretend she isn't. She's vetting them, checking them out. Making sure they're appropriate, basically. I mean, seriously – she won't even let me watch a fifteen-rated movie!

But I'm getting sidetracked. What I wanted to say – the reason I'm writing in this diary after all, after thinking I never would again – is that at last in my life something has happened.

So I met a boy.

Which, haha, is like the definition of *bleeeeuuuurgghhh*, right?

But the thing is it's nothing like that. He's older, for starters. Which I can imagine what Frankie would say if I told her but that's because she'd assume it was about sex. And it's not. It's definitely not. OK? (Mum? OK?? If for some reason you're reading this – which I hope – I know – you would never do – but if you are I want to make that clear. I am not having sex with a seventeen-year-old. In fact, for the record, I'm not having sex with anyone. God. I can just imagine what you'd say if you thought I was.)

But that's another reason I'm writing this, because I know if I even told Frankie (who's been my best friend since for ever) there's a chance even she wouldn't understand. So that's why I'm keeping this private. Not counting Adam, of course. Obviously Adam knows too, otherwise there wouldn't be anything to write *about*.

That's his name. Adam.

He's tall. He's got this hair that falls across his eyes, which I like because it makes him look shy. You can always see them, though, just peeking out. They're brown, kind of like mine. They look better on him, though. Way better, actually, because to be honest I hate my eyes. I mean, brown's boring, right? Except not on Adam. On Adam they look kind of intense. Which probably makes him sound like some sort of psychopath or something but all I mean is he's deep. A grown-up. And what's nice is that he treats me like a grown-up too. And if you think about it, the age thing, don't they say girls mature faster than boys? So really, mentally, me and Adam are about the same age. Right?

That's the way I'm looking at it, anyway.

But how I met him. What I can't believe was that it was only eight and a half hours ago. Because it feels like a lifetime.

We were in Starbucks. The one in the shopping centre. It's where everyone's been hanging out in the summer holidays. The people who aren't in Spain or visiting relatives or whatever. Which obviously me and Mum never do because, a, the whole client thing, and b, we haven't got any relatives, none that I've ever met anyway.

But that's the routine. Breakfast with Mum, mooch until about midday, then head down to the shopping centre. Sit in Starbucks for maybe an hour or two, then kill time looking at clothes and whatever in the shops. Which is what I mean about my life being uneventful. And it's not just Mum, to be fair. It's also the fact that, where we live, there isn't much else to do *anyway*, not for kids my age. Although, thinking about it, it's that whole chicken and egg thing, isn't it? Like, maybe that's *why* we're living here: precisely because there's nothing for me to do. No way for me to get myself in trouble.

Anyway. The summer holidays have been pretty tedious, is my point, and today was shaping out to be even more boring than normal. Until:

'Is this seat taken?'

Frankie, she'd texted me at the last minute to say her mum was making her go with her to visit her Aunt Laura. And when I say last minute, I mean the exact second we were supposed to meet. It's like, she must have known before then. If she was going to meet me at one, then she would have had to leave her house by twelve-thirty at the latest, and if she'd texted me then, maybe I would have had a chance to turn round, to save on the bus fare at least. Because I'm not going to sit in Starbucks on my own, am I, not when I know no one's coming. It would be social suicide, what with Amy Jones there with all the others.

Is this seat taken?

I'm looking at my phone when he says it, trying to decide how to reply to Frankie (I'm torn between *bummer* with a little sad face – you know, to try to make her feel bad – or like, *wtf?!?*, which is basically more how I feel) and also trying to figure out if Jess or Rosie or any of the others would be free to meet up if I called, and it's only when I glance up that I see him standing over me.

And to begin with I don't notice how hot he is, this boy who's asking me if this seat's taken. But I see Amy and the others all staring and at first what I figure is they're staring at me. You know, poor old Emily-no-mates. But they're not just staring, I realize, they're *ogling*. And when I look at him I realize why.

'Er, sure. I mean, no. You can take it. If you want. It's, um. All yours.'

UGH! You'd think I'd never been asked a question before. Yes or no, Emily! He wanted a seat, not your life story.

But he sits down opposite me anyway, like diagonally opposite, which he probably figures is far enough away that he can make a run for it if I start foaming at the mouth.

'Sorry . . .' It's him again, talking to me when I'm sitting there praying he won't. I'm staring at my phone and basically glowing like a beetroot. 'I don't suppose you happen to know the Wi-Fi password, do you?' He waggles his iPhone.

I tell him what it is and he types it in.

'Thanks,' he says, smiling, and my head, it's like a beetroot now that's been set on fire. I have to hold my iced coffee up to my cheeks to try to cool myself down.

It's at that point I become aware of the tittering. Amy and the others, they've seen me and Adam talking, and obviously this becomes hilariously amusing to them. I mean, they're jealous, basically, so what else can they do except take the piss? Seriously, grow up. It's people like Amy Jones that make me think maybe Mum's right to be worried about who I choose to hang around with. Not that I would *ever* want to hang around with her.

'Friends of yours?' Adam (I don't know his name's Adam yet, but that's what I'll call him), he's playing it cool. Looking at his phone, sipping his smoothie. Amy and that are behind him, so when he moves his eyes to gesture towards them, he does it so as only I can see.

I act like I'm looking at my phone too. In reality I've texted Frankie ages ago and there's no real reason for me to still be sitting there. Or, there wasn't.

'Not exactly,' I say. 'More like the opposite.'

Adam makes this face, then. He freezes and his eyes go wide. 'So like, *enemies*?' he whispers, aghast.

Laughing is the last thing I'm expecting to do, so when I do I give this little snort. A snort! *Smooth*, Emily. *Real* smooth.

'Deadly enemies,' I reply, recovering myself. 'The deadliest.'

Adam checks across his shoulder. 'They look pretty deadly,' he says. 'I mean, I'm practically choking on all the perfume from here.'

I laugh, and this time manage not to sound like Frankie snoring.

'It gets worse,' I say, leaning in. 'The one in the middle? With all the hair? She'll freeze your blood with just a smile. And if you say something bad about her behind her back? She'll look at you and turn you to stone.'

Adam tries not to smile. 'Like Medusa,' he says. He looks behind him. 'Maybe that's what all the hair's for,' he adds, turning back. 'To cover up all the snakes.'

I'm sipping my drink and when I laugh this time some goes up my nose. It hurts, the way it does if you do a somersault underwater, but at the same time it only makes me laugh more.

We carry on like that for a while. I mean, just for a few minutes it seems like but long enough that Amy's stopped sniggering and instead starts giving me evils. Which obviously plays right into our hands and soon it's not even a challenge. You know, coming up with stuff that makes her seem ridiculous. Which I guess is cruel but it's her own fault because it's exactly what she does to everyone else. And besides, there's five of them and two of us so it's not as though we're ganging up.

But then Adam gets up to leave. It seems like he's only just sat down but when I check my phone after I realize he's been there twenty minutes.

'Watch your back, soldier,' he tells me as he gathers his things. 'And don't forget to eat plenty of garlic.' He winks then, which could be like *eeeww*, but somehow he makes it look sweet. Like a secret, basically. Just for me.

And then he's gone.

So that's that, right? That's what I'm thinking. Even Amy's smiling now she can see I'm sitting on my own again. But I don't engage. I make like I'm sending another text and finish my drink and then casually get up to leave. Playing it cool, you know? Like I won already, so why would I bother playing her stupid games? And it feels good. And it keeps feeling good, so I hit a few shops, buy a magazine, a new case for my phone, pick up some smellies for Mum. Just some Body Shop stuff I know she likes. So that kills about an hour, after which I reckon it's time to leave. Amy and the others will be around somewhere and I figure get out while I'm ahead. So I do, I head to the bus stop. And guess who's there, *waiting for the very same bus!*

I mean, what are the chances? Right??

So that's when we get talking properly. On the bus ride. We're upstairs. He's got one front seat and I've got the other but then it gets busy and he asks if it's OK if he moves across. He acts all shy about it, as though he's worried it'll make me uncomfortable, but just as this guy is about to sit down next to me, Adam gets up and gestures to the place next to mine. 'Is this seat taken?' he says.

And I grin. I couldn't have stopped myself grinning if I'd wanted to.

And we just chat. We ride the bus for three round trips. And Adam's asking about Amy and about school and about everything, basically. He's so interested in my life and it's refreshing, you know? Me and Frankie talk all the time but we've known each other so long, sometimes it feels like we've said all there is to say. Also, with Frankie, it's often like she's just waiting for her turn to talk. She *acts* like she's listening but she's not really hearing what I'm saying. I mean, don't get me wrong, I love Frankie to bits (except when she stands me up, of course) and she is absolutely, positively my best friend. But with Adam it's different. He's a boy, obviously, so that's part of it. But also, it's like he knows me. Like, *really* knows me. And when I talk to him, when I tell him stuff . . . the thing with Adam is, he really listens.

4 p.m. – 5 p.m.

5

'You know him.'

Susanna looks up, half expecting to see someone else in the room. Alina or Ruth or . . . or Emily. But there is just her and Adam in opposite chairs, the ticking clock on the wall between them.

'What?' Susanna says.

Adam looks at her questioningly.

The voice comes again: *you know him*, and it takes another moment for Susanna to realize it is in her head. She has heard it before. The voice, not the words themselves. She has even seen things. Faces, figures – forms she would rather have forgotten. The voices, the visions, they came fairly frequently at first and for a while Susanna was convinced she was losing her mind. Steadily though, and in particular as she started her training, she came to realize that what she was experiencing was a psychological manifestation of her guilt. Which, at the time, didn't make it any easier to bear.

'I said I want to talk about Jake, Susanna.'

Susanna feels a pang that forces her to focus.

Adam tips his head. 'Did you ever care? About Jake, I mean. Was there ever a point you loved him?'

The room, the voice, the memories that have come

raging back, everything slips into a void. There is just Adam and the charge he has laid before her.

'What are you talking about? How can you even . . .' Adam doesn't interrupt her but Susanna stops talking as though he does. She is speechless. The opposite. There is so much she wants to say – *needs* to say – that she doesn't know where to start. 'Of course I loved him. I never stopped loving him. *Never.*'

Adam seems pleased. That he has riled her again? That she is responding to his accusation so vociferously? Or that Susanna has chosen to engage at all?

She shakes her head. She will not do this. She *won't*.

'Where's Emily? Tell me what's happened to Emily or so help me God I'll . . .'

Adam gives her time to finish. 'You'll what?'

'I'll . . .' Scream? Shout? Kick? Cry? Take your pick, Susanna. Each would be about as effective as any other.

'I'll take that knife and I'll cut your throat from ear to ear.'

Susanna hears the words as she utters them and is shocked by them. By the violence, not only in the words themselves, but in her tone. Yet that's not all. She is pleased too, she realizes. Reassured that she is still capable of standing up for her children. Of protecting them, at whatever cost.

Until Adam starts laughing.

It is not an act. His amusement is real. The implied dismissal, terrifying.

'Go ahead.'

Susanna just stares.

'Here,' Adam prompts, suddenly serious. 'Take it.' He offers her the knife hilt first.

He is baiting her, yet Susanna can't help but consider the odds. She is standing perhaps six feet away from the chair in which Adam sits, meaning the knife is now two feet closer. And it is pointing towards him. He will be primed for her to make the leap but that doesn't mean he'll be ready. If she moves quickly, there's a chance she could seize the handle, or Adam's arm at least, and then it would come down to whoever was fiercer. Her chances aren't even, Susanna figures, but they're not far off.

Minutely Susanna turns her head.

'I didn't think so.'

Susanna doesn't look up but she senses Adam place the knife on the arm of his chair.

'Still, at least that's settled. Now, hopefully, we can get on with things.'

'Please.' So much for being capable. So much for being fierce. 'Please,' Susanna repeats. 'Just tell me she's OK. Tell me she's safe, that you haven't . . .'

'Haven't what?'

Susanna flinches from Adam's gaze. 'Haven't . . . touched her, or . . .'

Adam's lips twist sideways. 'No, I haven't *touched* her. As for whether she's safe or not, that's entirely up to you.'

'But –'

'Look. It's quite simple. The sooner you talk, the sooner this is over. OK? I mean, is that so difficult to understand?'

Susanna recoils. She finds herself nodding.

'So let's begin. Shall we? In fact, let's start with that.'

'With what?'

'With whether or not you ever loved your son.'

It's not as straightforward as she made out. She told Adam she never stopped loving Jake and she did love him, of course she did. Susanna is as sure of that as she is of her love for Emily. Which is overpowering sometimes. So intense that it stops her sleeping, so smothering that every so often she finds she can't even draw breath. But with Jake . . . although Susanna *knows* she loved him, it is a love she struggles to remember. It's like trying to bring to mind a sunset, when all you can recall clearly is the night.

Susanna has spent a long time over the years exploring how other parents like her have dealt with the emotions she's experienced: reading memoirs, listening to transcripts, searching archives for interviews. Parents of fundamentalists, for example; of terrorists; of kids who shot up a school. And while Susanna has been able to draw certain parallels, she has also remained acutely aware that her experience was completely apart, not least in how it all ended. That's confounded Susanna more than anything. How could it not?

'You haven't answered me.'

'I'm trying to,' Susanna responds. 'And anyway I already have. I said to you!'

'Said what?'

'That I loved him. Always. Through it all!'

She needs to calm down. She needs to be able to think clearly, to allow herself to concentrate on Adam. Her best hope is to work out what he wants – and, more specifically, how she can give it to him. He knows who she is, obviously. He knows – or at least suspects – what really happened. And it's obvious he feels some empathy for Jake, which means he could indeed be a 'fan'. In which case it's possible that Adam has no direct connection to Susanna or her daughter whatsoever, and that Susanna's best strategy would be to focus on addressing Adam's sense of self-worth. Of disabusing him, basically, of whatever misconceptions he's allowed to take root.

Except, *you know him*. The voice, this time, is like a breathless whisper in her ear.

Adam notices her jump. 'Are you OK, Susanna?'

She clasps the desk to steady herself.

'Why don't you sit back down?'

'No, I –'

'Sit.'

It is not a suggestion. Susanna allows her feet to carry her to her chair, where normally she feels so comfortable. It is usually a safe place for her, in spite of how exposed the act of counselling sometimes makes her feel. But it is exposed in a good way, and – crucially – to other people's demons instead of her own.

As she takes her seat, however, she can't help noticing how claustrophobic this room of hers is making her feel. The rug beneath her feet, the comfy upholstered chairs, the normally calming presence of her plants and books – even the sunlight reaching through the slatted blinds: none of it distracts from how close Adam is. Their knees must be two rulers' lengths apart. Two daggers' lengths, in fact. Adam's knife rests on the arm of his chair, in front of his elbow. Susanna cannot help but stare. And, looking at the edges of the blade, all she can think about is Emily.

'You were saying?' Adam prompts.

Susanna feels the strength drain out of her as she exhales. Her head is all at once in her hands.

'Look, you know what happened. Clearly. You think you do, anyway, otherwise why are you here? So if you *know*, you know as well that what you're asking me about isn't that simple. *Love* is never that simple.'

Adam doesn't hesitate in his response. 'It should be. For the mother of a child, a father of one, it should be.'

Susanna looks up. Is this another clue? Another hint about why Adam is here?

'You say that,' Susanna ventures, 'but what does that even mean? "It should be",' she quotes. 'Are you saying I had no right to be upset? To be conflicted?'

'Conflicted,' Adam scoffs. 'Yes, Susanna. That's precisely what I'm saying. No parent has the right to be conflicted when it comes to loving their child.'

'Why not?'

'Because that's not what they're there for! They're there to protect them. To *love* them. Unconditionally!'

From nowhere Susanna recalls the song she used to sing to Jake when he was small. The tune was something she'd appropriated from a nursery rhyme, the lyrics made-up nonsense, but almost without fail it would make Jake laugh. She even sang it to him when he got older – ten years old, eleven – and though he would squirm in embarrassment, not once did he ever ask her to stop.

'And is that what your parents offered you?' Susanna asks Adam.

'Ha.' Adam has been leaning forward. He slumps back, disgusted, and with the knife starts picking at the upholstery on the arm of his chair. 'I told you before, my parents were a waste of space. They were even worse at it than you are.'

The barb cuts, even though Susanna is half expecting it. 'You said your father was a waste of space,' she counters. 'You didn't tell me anything about your mother.'

'There's nothing to tell. My mother died when I was five. The week before my sixth birthday.'

In spite of everything, Susanna feels a pang of sympathy. They say that when a parent loses a child it's the worst pain of all and for a long time Susanna believed that to be true. But objectively, and having seen first-hand with her clients the damage it can do, she knows that for a child who's lost a parent the anguish is often on another scale entirely.

'I'm sorry, Adam. That must have been very hard for you.'

Adam is prodding at the chair, using the tip of the blade to worry at a thinning patch of thread. He stops and looks up. 'I barely knew her. And anyway it was worth it, just to see the pain on my father's face.'

Susanna is well practised at keeping her reactions neutral but she is powerless to disguise her shock. 'What did he do to you to make you hate him so?'

The question, Susanna knows, represents another slip. There is no way, in a normal session, she would ever be so direct.

Even so, for a moment it seems as though Adam might answer. Clearly he is thinking of nothing but his father as the blade pierces and then slices into the fabric of the chair. 'Just . . . everything. He . . .'

And then Adam looks up. His expression – astonishingly – is close to one of elation. 'You are!' he declares. 'You're good at this!' He laughs, shakes his head, places the knife lengthwise along the chair arm. 'You nearly had me,' he says. 'You genuinely almost got me speaking. Not that I'm hiding anything,' he adds, spreading his hands. 'Ordinarily I'd be happy to tell you anything you want to know about my background. But I'm conscious we don't have much time and really I'm here to talk about you. About *your* failures as a parent.'

Another barb. Another opening of old wounds.

'Trust me,' Adam says, 'I know exactly how *my* parents fucked *me* up. I . . .' He stops himself. 'I can say that, right? That word, I mean? Because of the poem. All you counsellor-types love that, I know. "They fuck you up, your mum and dad, blah-di-blah-di-blah."' He checks Susanna's reaction, presumably to see if she's impressed. 'I told you, I've done my research.'

Larkin. The poem he means is by Philip Larkin. And Susanna doesn't like it, as it happens. Not because

68

she doesn't like swearing (which she doesn't) but because Larkin's words cut so close to the bone.

'You can say what you like,' Susanna responds, 'use whatever language you like.' In a session – a *real* session – she would say the same thing; encourage the client to use whatever vocabulary most helps them to get across their feelings. She only says it now, however, because she knows she's in no position to object.

'Wait.'

Something has occurred to her.

'What did you mean?' Susanna says. 'What you said just now, about us not having much time?' There is something hateful filling her insides: a bulging, sick-inducing warmth.

From Adam's reaction, Susanna can't escape the impression that somehow, for some reason, he is pleased with her.

'Just what I said,' he answers. 'I'm guessing you and I could stay here all night if we had to. It's your office, after all. But Emily . . .' He lets the sentence dangle, like bait.

Despite the photo, despite the phone, Susanna has until this point been clinging to the hope that Adam is bluffing. It is not a bluff she has been willing to call but she has at least been able to reassure herself that even if Emily *is* in danger, she is safe while Adam remains with Susanna in this room. Abruptly, however, even that slight comfort has been ripped away from her, and with it the delusion that the worst is not really happening.

'Susanna. Hey, Susanna!'

It must look to Adam as though Susanna is about to fall apart because the sharpness of his words is like a slap. He claps: once, twice, each time closer to Susanna's face.

'Don't go to pieces on me, Susanna.'

All Susanna can do is shake her head, and she feels the tears jostle free as she does so. If she weren't so wary of Adam's anger she is sure she would already have collapsed in on herself. Physically, mentally: all she feels capable of doing is curling up into a ball.

'Focus, Susanna. Focus on Jake. On what I asked you.'

'But I've answered already!' Susanna blurts, repeating herself for what feels like the umpteenth time. 'I *did* love him! I did!'

'I don't believe you.'

'But that's . . .' *Not fair*, she wants to yell. Like a child would. *That's so unfair!* She breathes, sobs, breathes again. 'You asked me a question and I answered it,' she says. 'I can't help it if you don't like what I say!'

Adam considers. 'Prove it then.'

'I beg your pardon?' The challenge sobers her.

'Prove it. You say you loved Jake. *Prove* you did.'

'*How?*'

'Tell me something about him that you loved.'

'Just . . . everything! I loved *everything* about him. He was my son!'

Adam's face shows clearly that he is growing tired of this. 'Answer me this then,' he says. 'And remember, Susanna.' He holds up a finger. 'Don't lie to me. I promise you I know when you're lying.' He pauses, then asks his question. 'Do you deny you're responsible for what Jake did? For how it all ended?'

Susanna shakes her head. She does curl up then, briefly, until a surge of anger makes her rigid. 'I lost my son,' she hisses. 'Do you understand that? Whatever happened, whatever you *think* happened, why ever the hell you *care* – I've already been punished! It's not possible I could have been punished any worse!'

'Ah.' It is an argument Adam has clearly been expecting. 'But you've been reborn, *Susanna*,' he says, emphasizing her name. 'Is that fair, would you say?'

'Reborn? No, I . . . My life isn't about me any more. Don't you see? I've made it so it's not about me!'

Adam sneers. 'Do you really believe that? You with your cats and your three-bed semi and your neat, cosy little office. Do you really, genuinely believe that?'

She can't win. Clearly. Whatever game Adam has her playing, it's obvious it's been rigged from the start. 'I'm not going to sit here and defend myself,' Susanna says, before adding in barely a whisper, 'Not again.'

And Adam's smile, this time, is triumphant.

'Oh, but you are,' he says. 'In fact, that's exactly what you're going to do. And I'm going to judge you, Susanna. That's why I'm here. I'm going to judge you – and I'm going to watch as you judge yourself.'

6

Jake hadn't always been a boy of extremes.

As a toddler, a young boy, he'd been sociable, cheerful, and so easy-going that right from the first few months he'd reminded Susanna of Neil. That laid-back nature was the very thing that had attracted Susanna to Jake's father in the first place, when – at the age of nineteen – she'd first got talking to him in the pub. He was the one who'd come up to her, which in itself for Susanna was something new. And after the upbringing she'd had – the upbringing they'd both had, it turned out: so constricted, so controlled – Neil had seemed to Susanna like a remedy for all her ills. He'd cured himself of the discipline his parents had imposed on him – and though Susanna had gone in the other direction, winding herself tighter and tighter the older she got, she hoped Neil would be able to cure her as well. He made her laugh, made her *giggle*, in fact, and in that respect and others he made her feel like the teenager she'd never been allowed to be.

So seeing that same carefree attitude in Jake had delighted her. And Jake was self-contained as well, happy just doing his thing. He would sit with his books, his colouring, his Lego, and rarely cry for Susanna to intervene. If anything the opposite was the case. If a problem presented itself, he would prove determined to solve it himself. To think, Susanna and Neil had been so proud of that once: Jake's reluctance to ever ask for help.

It was only as Jake grew older that this side of his personality seemed to evolve. He began to take the setbacks he encountered more personally. From Jake's perspective, anything less than total success corresponded with abject failure. He wouldn't rage about it, though. He would simply move on to other things.

So football, for example, lasted half a season. At one point Jake was training four nights a week, playing both mornings on the weekend – before deciding, after a game he'd spent sitting on the substitutes' bench, that it wasn't for him after all. And music. Every fortnight there was a new CD on repeat on his stereo, a new idol scowling down at him from his bedroom wall. When he did something he would do it wholeheartedly, commit to it with his body and soul – but when he decided he'd failed at it, or whatever it was had failed *him*, he would discard it with barely a shrug.

'It's healthy,' Neil had declared. 'It means he's not got the same hang-ups we had, that bullshit need to always *see it through*.' That had been Neil's parents' thing: an almost self-flagellating insistence that if you started something, you finished it, no matter the personal cost. And Neil was right, Susanna decided. Far better that Jake be exposed to a variety of experiences than be railroaded into persisting with something that made him unhappy. (Susanna had another theory too: that

Jake was searching; looking for meaning – a purpose – he would never find. But she never said as much to Neil. She barely said it to herself.)

It was the same with friends.

With Scott Saunders.

With Peter Murray.

With Charles Bell.

Scott, Pete and Charlie. Strangers, one day. Blood brothers, the next.

And girls. Girls! Though Susanna didn't know about that until it was too late. She didn't know about a lot of things, as it turned out, until it was too late.

But on or off. All or nothing. The older he got, the more that was Jake in everything he did. Everything – right up until the day Susanna came home from one of her walks and found his body swinging from the banister.

So in answer to Adam's question, of course Susanna feels responsible for what Jake did. If she could have she would have held up her hand, bowed her head, and cried for everything she should have done. The same way any parent would have. The thing is, though, Adam must know she could never have admitted the way she felt publicly, not given the way things turned out. And these things he's been saying, his accusation that she never loved her son. It makes Susanna wonder: did Adam mean the question the way she assumed he did? Or was he alluding to something more, something there's no earthly way he could know? A secret Susanna has kept for so long, she would deny it even to herself.

*

'Scott Saunders. Peter Murray. Charles Bell.'

He lists their names the way, a few moments ago, Susanna recalled them herself. He wants to start at the beginning, he says. Which is in itself a curious statement because, for Susanna, by assuming it all started with them, Adam is bypassing almost fifteen years of Susanna's failings.

But Scott, Pete, Charlie: they were the catalyst, in one sense at least. Everything that followed sparked and ignited because of them.

'They were friends of his, right? Because that's one of the things I don't get.'

'What do you mean?'

'They denied it, for a start. Claimed they barely even knew Jake.'

The taste this brings to Susanna's mouth is wearyingly familiar. 'Of course they'd say that. What would you expect them to have said?'

'No, I know. But it wasn't just them. From what I've read it was only Jake who seemed to think they were ever mates. The other kids, the witnesses or whatever, they all said –'

'There *weren't* any witnesses,' Susanna interrupts. 'Not a single one.'

'You know what I mean. And anyway, that's not strictly true.'

'It is true! It's a fact! I thought you said you'd done your research.' It's a reckless provocation but Susanna can't help herself. She's had enough of rumours, of hearsay. It's like with the magazines out in the waiting area that these days she can't bring herself to look at. Isn't the truth sensational enough? How does distorting it help anyone? That's what frustrated her with what happened more than anything: the way people grew tired of the facts so quickly that they resorted to twisting them, manipulating them, until by the end everything was back to front, upside down, inside out. The story moved on, is what they said, whereas Susanna simply *couldn't*.

'It's not true, Susanna. There were witnesses. Scott, Pete, Charlie: they were there.'

'You can't be a witness if you were one of the guilty. It doesn't work like that. It *shouldn't*.'

Adam could press the point, Susanna knows, but instead of doing so he lets it slide.

'So are you saying they *were* friends of Jake's? Right from the start?'

'No. Not from the start. In fact they were never friends. Not real friends. They tricked him. Trapped him.'

Although even as Susanna says these words, she knows the real trick was one she played on herself. Jake wasn't tricked by his friends. Susanna, rather, tricked herself into believing he remained the same happy, healthy boy he'd always been. Or, perhaps, had never been. She fooled herself into ignoring the anguish that was consuming him, rendering him hollow.

'Careful, Susanna. It's beginning to sound like you're trying to shirk responsibility. Like they're the ones you think are most to blame.'

'Of course they're to blame! I bla[ ]
I blame lots of other people too.'
she's narrowed it down to five.

Jake, naturally.

Neil.

Scott, Pete, Charlie.

Six people, actually, although she tri[ ]
about the sixth.

Adam reclines in his chair, folds his hands in his lap. 'I'm sure you do,' he says. 'And we'll get to that. But for the moment let's start with those three. Shall we?'

It happened one day after school had finished. The beginnings of their . . . association. Susanna wasn't there herself, obviously, but she was by Jake's side as he went over and over the entire story with the police. Indeed, she has read the transcript so many times and pictured the scene playing out so often, it is like a movie she has come to know frame by frame.

Jake, not for the first time, had stayed behind after school. Whenever Susanna asked him, which she rarely did because she was so often late home herself, he would claim he had stayed behind to do his homework, to help a teacher, to finish off a kick-about he was involved in with his friends. Lies, it turned out: every one. Jake did his homework but rarely until the last minute, and only because if he didn't he knew his parents, his teachers would start asking questions. But *helping* a teacher? Playing with *friends*? Susanna had no idea how much of a loner Jake had become. From being

formed friendships easily, he'd become some-
no struggled to maintain them. It wasn't that he
out with people. It was more that he simply lost
interest, the same way he lost interest with everything
else. And Susanna would have seen it, if she'd looked.
But it was far easier to take what he told her at face
value, to believe Jake was the same sociable, self-
contained kid he'd always been. And as for that day
itself, Susanna doesn't actually remember it. If the
occasion hadn't later assumed the importance it did,
she wouldn't have been able to pick it out from any
other.

So Jake was on school grounds, alone, after hours –
doing, it turned out, what he often did. He was *watching*:
on this occasion a group of boys in the year above him.
Scott Saunders, Peter Murray and Charles Bell quite
often hung around on school grounds as well, mainly
because they knew they weren't supposed to. Rules, to
them, were like dares, and Jake had become fascinated
by the sort of things they got up to.

Today Jake saw them gathered near a bin, which at
first he didn't connect with the smell of smoke he'd
noticed hanging in the air. He assumed the caretaker
was burning leaves nearby. There were enough of them
about at that time of year. The front section of the
school grounds was thick with trees. When you entered
through the main gates, they formed an honour guard
along the length of the drive, and for several weeks
during the autumn the driveway itself was a dense red
carpet.

78

But the smoke didn't smell like leaves. And as Jake spied on Scott and the others from the shadows of the treeline, he came to see what it was that was actually burning. He saw the flames, anyway, tonguing at the air from within the litter bin. And as the fire began to lick higher, Scott, Pete and Charlie drew closer, cackling like witches around a cauldron.

Jake had no intention of getting involved, he later told the police. Not because the older boys were trouble-makers and it was clear they were up to no good, which is what would have deterred most kids. Rather, Jake didn't know how to engineer an approach. Not only were Scott and the others a year older, they had a reputation for bullying. If they decided to pick on Jake, he wouldn't have stood a chance. Scott, the ringleader, was a good head taller than him, and Pete two T-shirt sizes broader. Charlie was short but he was all tendons and bones, making him almost the toughest-looking of the lot.

So Jake just stood there, hypnotized, and might have remained in the shadows until the fire went out had events not followed the course they did.

'Hey! What's going on here?'

Jake couldn't say where the young teacher appeared from. There was a doorway from the main building close to the bike sheds, so it was possible Ms Birch had just exited through that. She was new, barely qualified, and weighed about as much as the stack of sandwiches Pete alone would eat for lunch. But for a small woman – a girl, practically – her voice was remarkably forceful.

Even Scott and the others jumped when they heard it, their shoulders only settling when they realized its source.

'Nothing, Miss,' someone said. Scott, Jake thought, because he was the one to step in front of the bin to deliberately try to block the teacher's view.

'Are you boys *burning* something?'

'No, Miss. Why would we do that, Miss? I dropped my cigarette, that's all,' Scott answered.

'His lighter, he means, Miss,' put in Charlie, as he tucked into formation beside Scott. 'We're all too young to actually smoke, you see, and we'd never *dream* of lighting up on school grounds.' Charlie may have been small but he was sharp. In looks, too: from his gel-jagged hair to the jut of his chin.

Pete, behind them, had made a start on trying to extinguish the fire but the flames lashed out at him each time he attempted to draw near. From where he was standing, Jake could see it all clearly. Pete looked like a lion-tamer trying to hold back a vicious animal. In fact, Jake said, the fire looked exactly like that: like something alive. It was mesmerizing. Almost beautiful, he said. Those were the exact words Jake used.

'You don't smoke but you carry a lighter. And some-how you dropped your lighter into the bin and then the bin, miraculously, caught fire. Is that what you're telling me?'

Ms Birch edged past Scott and Charlie to try to deal with the blaze herself. The flames were flicking so high that when she tried to move the rubbish in the bin to

80

try to smother them, she was driven back in the same way Pete had been.

'Ow! Shit!' A tongue of fire had lashed out and licked her.

Scott, Charlie and Pete, watching on, just laughed.

'You shouldn't swear, Miss,' Charlie said. 'If you swear we'll have to tell a teacher.'

Ms Birch was too concerned with the fire to worry about the sniggering, though it was clear by this point she was unlikely to succeed in quelling either.

'Here.'

As Jake crossed the driveway, he stooped to gather up an armful of leaves.

'Here,' he repeated, as he carried the mound of leaves towards the bin.

'No, wait, don't –'

Ms Birch was caught unawares by Jake's appearance. Belatedly she tried to pull him back but before she could he had deposited the entire armful of leaves on to the fire.

'What are you –' she protested, thinking at first that Jake's actions would only make matters worse. But the leaves were damp, and the effect was as if the fire had been stifled by a sodden blanket. There was smoke, lots of it, but soon even the smoke faded into nothing.

'Well.' For a moment that was all Ms Birch could summon herself to say. But then she appeared to remember her duties, her anger, and she whipped round to address Scott. 'You realize how stupid that was, don't you? You could have burned down the entire school!'

Rather than being cowed, Scott immediately bridled. The problem was, Scott Saunders *was* stupid. Susanna saw evidence of that countless times over the coming months. He was stupid and he was cruel and he was vindictive. But he had been called stupid so many times – by other kids, by his older brother, by his father – that the word itself had become a trigger. He'd once swung a chair at a staff member who'd dared to suggest he was 'slow', and had only avoided expulsion because the chair in question had missed. The incident was common knowledge among the faculty and only a teacher as raw as Ms Birch would have been so careless as to use the s-word in Scott's presence.

He stepped forward, forcing Ms Birch to back up against the bin, which no doubt would have been warm from the fire. And if Scott looked down on Jake, he positively towered over the young teacher.

'You shouldn't say things like that,' Scott said. 'You shouldn't call us *stupid*.'

'No, I . . .' Ms Birch was afraid, Jake could see it. But she attempted to exert her authority, standing as tall as she could in the space Scott allowed her. 'You boys need to come with me. We're going to see the headmaster.'

Scott sniffed and edged closer, so that Ms Birch was literally bent backwards over the bin. 'The bald old coot's gone home for the day,' he said. '*Everyone*'s gone home. Look.' He tipped his head towards the teachers' parking area and there were indeed only two or three cars left, one of them being Ms Birch's own battered Beetle.

Scott smiled then. *See?* that smile said. *You're on your own.*

'You started a fire,' Ms Birch persisted. 'On school property. That's not something I can allow to go unpunished.'

Jake exchanged glances with Pete and Charlie. He couldn't tell what Charlie was thinking but Pete's thoughts couldn't have been clearer had they been written in a bubble over his head. *Shut up. Just shut up, you silly cow.*

'We told you what happened, Miss. We didn't deliberately start anything.' This from Charlie, who somehow always managed to look like he was sneering.

'Do you really expect me to believe –' Ms Birch started to say, and that's when Jake saw his opportunity.

'It's true,' he said, and all heads turned towards him. 'I saw it happen.'

Ms Birch looked at him for a moment, then back at Scott. Some light seemed to come on behind Scott's eyes and he ceded the young teacher half a step of ground.

'They were just walking by,' Jake went on. 'Scott here threw something in the bin and then there was a bang. When I saw them they were trying to put the fire out. They didn't deliberately start anything.'

Ms Birch considered for a moment. 'Do you know these boys?' she asked Jake narrowly.

'Not really.'

'What's your name?'

'Jake.'

'Well, Jake . . .' She looked at Scott, Pete and Charlie in turn, then back at Susanna's son. 'I suppose that clarifies things. Thank you. Perhaps we should draw a line under the matter there.' She was trying to sound assertive but when she caught Jake's eye, the relief – the gratitude – was written in her smile.

And not just hers. Pete let out the breath that he'd clearly been holding for longer than he realized. Charlie, his sneer deepening, nodded. And Scott, as he brushed past the diminutive teacher and led his cohort off towards the gates, tipped Jake a conspiratorial wink.

'See you around,' he said.

Adam has been listening intently. Not once has he moved to interrupt.

'So he covered for them. That's how it started. That's what led them to becoming friends.'

'I told you –'

'Right, right, they were never "friends".' Adam draws the quote marks in the air. 'But let's keep things simple, shall we?'

Susanna opens her mouth to argue. It's *not* simple, she wants to say. That's the whole entire point. Instead, 'Fine,' she answers.

'And after that? What happened after that?'

'They started hanging around. And Scott and the others, they were into things that Jake had never come across before. Had never really *considered* before, for all I know.'

'What kind of stuff?'

Susanna looks at Adam blankly.

'What kind of stuff were Scott and the others into? You said before that . . .'

Susanna doesn't need him to finish the sentence. Her nod turns into a head shake and then back again. 'Violence, basically. Rap music, horror films, computer games, the bloodier, the more graphic, the better. And fire, obviously. They liked to set things on fire. They set a park bench alight once. Also . . . other things. *Living* things.'

Adam smiles at this. Susanna, disgusted, turns away. 'What else?'

Susanna contemplates refusing to answer. But they have been down this route already and she knows where it will end.

'Pornography. Scott had mountains of pornography.'

'What kind of pornography?'

'What do you mean, *what kind*?'

'There're all types of pornography, Susanna. Soft core, hard core, ethnic, fetish. There's anal porn and oral porn and kiddie –'

'Just pornography! OK? I don't know exactly what *kind*.'

Although she can still picture some of the images in the magazines she later found hidden beneath Jake's bed. That was something else she ignored, in the sense that she left it for Neil to deal with. Neil said later that he had, though he wasn't explicit about how. A quiet word, probably, softened by a nudge and a wink. All Susanna cared about at the time was that the magazines were gone from her house. And she managed to convince herself they didn't belong to Jake, that he must have been holding on to them for a friend.

Adam holds up his hands. 'I was only asking. Like I say, I'm just trying to get a few things straight. The reports, the news stories: they're pretty messy. Most of the stuff they couldn't even report on. You know, because of Jake's age.'

Susanna, in reply, says nothing.

'So Jake was into all of that?' Adam goes on. 'The violence, the horror films. He got a kick out of that stuff too?'

Susanna is categorical. 'Not the boy I knew.' Which she realizes is as damning as it is defensive. 'He was curious. That's all. It made an impression on him. Clearly it did.'

'Meaning, what? That you blame the rap music for what happened? The computer games? Scott's *porn* collection?'

It was tempting to, at first. Susanna can't deny it. But as she wanted to tell Adam before, it wasn't that simple. What happened, what Jake did, was the result of a confluence of factors. It's not as straightforward as blaming *Grand Theft Auto*. 'It didn't help,' she says. 'Scott and the others were older. They were showing Jake things he had no business seeing, not at his age. Not at any age. And he'd never been in a *gang* before. He'd had mates but . . .' Susanna trails off. She remembers Jake's friends when he was younger. Timothy Thompson. Josh Green. Harry Kirkwood. Nice boys. Sweet boys. About whom, when Jake was playing with them, Susanna's only worry was whether or not they were sharing their toys.

Adam waits until he's sure she's finished talking. 'So basically, what you're saying is, they weren't friends at first but then they were. Right? And Scott and the other two, they were lying when they claimed they barely even knew Jake.'

'Of course they were lying. I already said that. Scott Saunders, Peter Murray, Charles Bell: they drew Jake in. And Jake, he was . . . not innocent. But unprepared. In the end he was like . . . like . . .'

Susanna doesn't finish the sentence. Her thoughts are drawn to that burning bin, to the image she has of Jake standing there, watching it from across the driveway. There's a phrase that's come to mind but she doesn't say it. In the end Adam utters the words for her.

'Like a moth to a flame.'

7

Outside, a cloud occludes the sun and a shadow sweeps across the room. Susanna didn't think that it was possible for the world to feel any darker.

'They drew Jake in, you say. But you did nothing. You didn't even bother to find out what Jake was getting up to, who your son was hanging around with all of a sudden.'

Susanna looks up. 'He was fifteen. And he never told me.'

'Don't you think it was your responsibility to find out?'

Susanna does. In retrospect, she does. But it's easy to say that now, far harder, as a parent, to balance the need to know your son is safe with respect for a teenager's right to privacy. And she trusted Jake. Wasn't that what she told herself? Or did she confuse trust with something else – an excuse to justify her failure to scrutinize his friendships more closely? But he'd never had any trouble with any of the mates he'd chosen before. There was one incident at school that same year, when Jake had been hauled before the headmaster for allegedly headbutting another child, but it was so out of character (Susanna thought) that she believed Jake's excuse that it had been a scuffle blown up out of all proportion, and that he'd only got involved in the first place to protect a friend – a friend he'd jettisoned soon after. And that was further proof, as far as Susanna was concerned, that she and Neil had raised a young man who was well on the way to becoming fully independent. Jake didn't *need* Susanna looking over his shoulder. He would watch out for himself – exactly as he always had.

'Is that how this works?' Susanna asks. 'I tell you what happened, what I did, what I failed to do, and you decide whether or not I'm genuinely sorry? That's how you choose whether or not to let Emily go?'

Adam waggles his head from side to side. 'Something like that.'

Meaning Emily's being held somewhere? Imprisoned somehow? If there's a chance Susanna could find out where, might there be a possibility as well that she could get a message to someone, to the police or Alina or Ruth or *anyone* really, without Adam knowing? A telephone call is out of the question, obviously, but a text maybe or an email or . . . WhatsApp? Should she have signed up to WhatsApp after all? Would WhatsApp have helped her?

Susanna knows she isn't thinking straight. It makes no difference what medium she employs. The difficulty will be sending a message without Adam seeing her. And, more importantly, working out what that message should contain. Because she could scream for help right now, dial 999 before Adam could stop her. But until she knows for certain that her daughter would be found, wouldn't spend the hours, days, weeks that followed starving or suffocating or bleeding to death in some makeshift prison – a basement somewhere? A warehouse? The back of some van? – Susanna can't risk doing *anything*. Her only choice is to play Adam's game. More: she has to win.

'So what if I said it to you now? If I admitted it, that it was my fault entirely. No one else's. Not Scott's, not Pete's, not Charlie's. Not anyone's. Just mine.'

The face Adam pulls makes him look like an official sitting behind some desk somewhere. He wants to help her, his expression says, but his hands are tied.

'The thing is, Susanna, you've had eighteen years to accept responsibility. Why should I believe anything you say now?'

'But that was different. You know that! Just because I couldn't say anything publicly doesn't mean I didn't think it was all my fault. With the people who were there, the people it affected, I've *always* maintained I was responsible. Always. I meant it then and I mean it now.'

'Do you?' Adam answers, his head tipping sideways. His fringe falls across one of those chocolate-coloured eyes of his and he uses his fingers to draw it aside. 'OK, Susanna, let's try this. Here's your chance. Your opportunity to save your daughter. Tell me. Explain to me exactly what you accept responsibility for and I promise I'll take it at face value. I won't doubt you. Whatever you say, I'll believe.'

Adam sits waiting.

'Just . . . everything,' Susanna says. 'OK? I should have been a better mother. I should have known my son better: what Jake was doing, who his friends were, what they were teaching him. I should have found out about his obsessions, about his worries, his heartbreak. I should have read the signs better, been around more, spent less time at work, not been so proud that he never asked me for help. I should have intervened, and ... and ... I should have stopped him.' Susanna looks at Adam, her face open, her hands open. 'OK? I should have stopped him. It was my *responsibility* to stop him. No one else's. I was his mother. So that's ... that's ...' She flounders. She's not sure what else she can say. 'There,' she finishes, her hands dropping into her lap. 'There.'

The silence is torturous.

'That's it?' Adam says. 'That's all?'

'Isn't that enough?' Susanna blurts. 'What else *is* there?'

All at once the knife is in Adam's hand. He's on his feet, the knife raised level with his ear, before in one sharp motion he stabs it down, towards Susanna. She yelps, flinches, scrabbles away, and when she looks the blade is buried to the hilt in the cushion of her chair, just behind her left shoulder.

Adam, leaning over her, seizes hold of the knife. He pulls, until the blade slides free and he is able to point it at Susanna's throat.

She swallows and feels her neck bulge against cold metal.

'One last chance, Susanna,' Adam hisses. 'I'm going to give you one last chance.'

Susanna shuts her eyes. She can feel the warmth of Adam's breath as he exhales, hears it waver as it carries

91

with it his anger. This could all end, right now. The game goes on or everybody loses.

There is a knock.

Susanna opens her eyes. Adam's flick up and glare across Susanna's shoulder.

It comes again, a gentle knuckle-tap against Susanna's door.

Adam moves fractionally away and withdraws the knife from its position at Susanna's throat.

'Alina,' Susanna croaks. 'I told her I'd come out. My next client . . . they'll be waiting.' According to the clock on the wall, it's already almost half past the hour.

'You don't have a next client.'

'I do, I –'

'You don't have a next client,' Adam repeats, more emphatically, and Susanna grasps what he is telling her. The second slot, the second new client Susanna was expecting, even though she knew how unusual two new clients in one afternoon would be: there's no one coming. Adam has arranged it that way: used a bogus name (another one), booked a bogus appointment (another one), to ensure he and Susanna wouldn't be interrupted.

The knock comes again, louder this time.

'Send her away,' Adam instructs. He takes his seat and tucks the knife out of sight beside his thigh. 'Now.'

Susanna gets up. She is unsteady on her feet but uses the furniture to support herself as she crosses the room.

'Alina, I . . .' she is saying as she opens the door but it is not Alina who stands waiting on the other side. It is Ruth.

'Hey, honey,' Ruth says. Her voice is low, apologetic. 'Listen, I'm sorry to interrupt but I wanted to make sure you were OK?' Her eyes flick to scan Susanna's office but her view is restricted by the half-open door.

'OK?' Susanna echoes. 'What do you . . .'

She hears Adam behind her, clearing his throat.

'Listen, Ruth – I'm kind of in the middle of a session at the moment.'

'No, I know, but Alina said . . .' Ruth lowers her voice further. 'Alina said you'd been in with the same guy for an hour and a half.' She tests a smile. 'Who have you got in there, Leonardo DiCaprio?'

Susanna, much as it pains her, smiles back.

'Seriously, though, is everything OK? You don't need an emergency dentist?'

It's an old joke this time. When Susanna and Ruth had first agreed to set up shop together, it was one of the benefits that appealed to Susanna the most. She wanted her own private practice but at the same time she was afraid of the isolation, of being in an office on her own with a parade of strangers. Disturbed strangers, some of them. And Ruth, when Susanna admitted this, assured her that if they were going to rent together, that was one thing Susanna wouldn't need to worry about. If anyone caused her any trouble, Ruth would come at them with her dentist's drill and – even more terrifying, she maintained – a sharply honed lecture on flossing.

'No, it's fine. Really. I had a free hour, that's all, and Adam, he . . .' Susanna hesitates, worrying for an instant that Adam will be angry that she's used his name – though of course it's *not* his name, and anyway he already gave it to Alina when he booked the appointment. 'We're doubling up, that's all,' Susanna recovers. 'Adam is away next week and we were making progress so we thought – that is, *I* did – that, rather than stopping we'd . . .' Adam coughs again. Susanna tenses. '. . . we'd double up,' she concludes.

Ruth is trying to peer through the gap between the door and its frame. She looks at Susanna, who does her best to convey the impression that everything is normal. She has told Ruth before about the importance of keeping time in counselling, of starting and finishing precisely on the hour, but she hopes and expects her friend was paying about as much attention as Susanna typically does when Ruth talks to her about teeth.

'Well, OK,' Ruth says. 'But remember it's Friday.' She smiles and taps her watch face. On Friday afternoons, by long-standing if unstated agreement, Ruth, Susanna and sometimes Alina head down to the Nanny State, the pub on the corner of the mews. It's the one time of the week Susanna permits herself to behave the way she always used to: with her workmates in her old company, with Neil before they'd begun to lead separate lives, with her friends from university – from the first year at least, before she'd dropped out after falling pregnant. Ordinarily she and Ruth will have at least a couple of drinks each before heading home to their respective families. In Susanna's case this means Emily and their two cats. In Ruth's, a three-legged lurcher named Betty and two slightly mangy parakeets. The usual time for them to leave for the day is five o'clock, which is when Ruth officially shuts up shop. Sometimes, though, if she's already finished with her patients and Susanna has wrapped up her paperwork, they'll sneak out half an hour early and use the time to guzzle an extra drink.

Either way, after five o'clock the rest of the building will be empty, and it strikes Susanna that Adam must have known this as well. *I've done my research*, she can almost hear him gloat.

'Are you heading off now? To the pub, I mean.'

'Well, we were going to,' Ruth replies, before adding quietly, 'But we'll wait if you want. I've got some invoices I need to go through and I'm sure Alina's got something she can be getting on with, so if you'd rather we stick around it's really no –'

'Don't be silly.' *Please don't go.* 'You go ahead. I'm feeling a bit under the weather anyway, so a night off the booze will do me good.'

'You're not going to meet us down there later?'

'I . . . probably not. Not this time. But next week, I promise.'

Please don't go! There is an instant when Susanna almost screams it because she knows that this is her final chance; that once the others leave she will be well and truly on her own. She could attempt to communicate her panic with a look, one she would be able to keep hidden from Adam's view, and Ruth, she is certain, would understand. Once again, though, it comes down to what would happen next. Adam has shown he is capable of violence, that he is barely holding himself back. At least if Ruth and Alina leave they will be safe. Once Susanna is able to discover what has happened to Emily, she will be free to take whatever risk she feels necessary. If she took a chance while the others were still in harm's way, and somehow one of them got hurt, Susanna knows that there is no way she would be able to live with herself. And not just in figurative terms.

'Well, if you're sure,' Ruth says. '*Are* you sure, Susanna?'

Susanna, this time, doesn't hesitate. 'Perfectly,' she says. 'You two go and enjoy yourselves. It's been a long week.'

Ruth rolls her eyes and gives a snort of agreement.

'I'll see you Monday,' Susanna says. And with a smile and a little wave, she shuts the door. Her forehead comes to rest on the painted wood and she listens to her friend heading back along the landing – until from outside, from behind her, there is silence.

8

A building burns. It starts with a single flame, like a burst of red in a scan of an otherwise healthy body, before steadily the cancer metastasizes and the deadly glow begins to spread. On the first floor, through the floorboards, there are candle-trails of smoke. The wisps billow into plumes, and soon the smoke is being chased upwards by the whip of the crackling flames. The desks burn, the books, the schoolwork fixed so lovingly to the walls. The fire crawls upwards from storey to storey, until it eats into the timbers of the roof. In a matter of minutes the blaze is more deafening than the fire alarm, more insistent than the approaching sirens. The walls char and blacken, the windows bubble and burst. Even the air warps in the impossible heat. It is unreal, horrific, glorious: a shimmering pyre that leaps towards the stars. It is an appalling image, unspeakable . . . and one that Susanna cannot help but savour.

'Whose idea was it, do you think?'

Susanna is back in her chair. The rug beneath her feet is wrinkled, and all it would take to nudge it straight is a simple movement of her foot. She keeps both soles flat on the floor.

Adam has recovered himself. He hasn't said as much but Susanna suspects he has been placated by having witnessed her lie. He seems to regard Susanna doing so as justification somehow for what he's doing. Proof, almost. Vindication.

He is pacing beside the fireplace, tapping the knife against his jeans as he talks. Susanna frowns in response to his question.

'Their plan,' Adam clarifies. 'The fire. Whose idea was it?'

'Scott's. Obviously.'

'Do you believe that?'

'What do you mean?'

'Just what I said.'

'He admitted it. He never even tried to deny it. He said it was a joke of course, that he never meant for it to happen, but he never disputed that the idea was his.'

'Yes but knowing what you know. Do you still believe that?'

'I don't understand what you mean.'

'You don't think it could have been Jake's idea?'

'Jake's? No. I mean . . . no.'

Adam purses his lips, bobs his head. 'No,' he says. 'Me neither.' He seems reassured in some way, which puzzles Susanna all the more.

'What difference does it make?' she asks. 'Given what happened. Why does it even matter whose *idea* it was?'

Adam stops moving and looks at her. For a moment he seems to be genuinely considering the answer. In the end, however, he shrugs. 'None, I guess,' he says. 'Not to you.' And with that he resumes pacing.

Susanna is getting tired just watching him. As the

minutes have passed – the hours, almost: according to the clock it is coming up for two – Susanna has felt the energy drain out of her. It's not that she doesn't have the will to fight. It's more frustration that she doesn't know how. She's a hamster spinning on a wheel, a mouse running mindlessly through a maze. She knows she should be looking for a way out but the longer the pursuit goes on, the harder she's finding it to believe that she hasn't already been cornered.

'That's another thing they couldn't talk about much,' Adam is saying. 'The newspapers, I mean. That's why I asked.'

Susanna can't help but scoff.

Adam stops pacing and turns towards her. 'What?'

'Nothing.'

'No, really. Tell me.'

Susanna scowls up at him. 'The newspapers. That's where you did the "research" you're so proud of? In the *newspapers*.'

Adam is genuinely intrigued. 'Sure. Some of it. Why? Is that so awful?'

'Not awful. Idiotic.' The word is in her mouth before she can suppress it. It tastes good, though. Bracingly bitter.

Adam just laughs. 'You see? That's what I'm talking about. I'd have thought you would have approved. They were on Jake's side, after all. Eventually.'

Susanna laughs right back at him. 'The papers weren't on anybody's side. They never are.'

'Well, not yours, I suppose,' Adam concedes with a

smirk. 'They really didn't like you much, did they? How did that make you feel, I wonder?'

'I don't care what they said about me. I don't care what the newspapers said full stop. Neither should anyone. Neither should *you*.' Something strikes her, distracting her for a moment from her anger. 'But then, you don't actually believe what they said either. Do you? It doesn't make sense that you do.'

Because Adam was right. The newspapers eventually took Jake's side. From everything Adam's said so far, however, it's obvious he's as certain that Jake was guilty as Susanna is. And, more than that, he admires him for it, believes he should have been exalted rather than suffer the end he did. Isn't that what Susanna has decided, the reason she's identified for Adam being here?

Except, if that's the case, why does he also seem so determined to punish Susanna for what Jake did? *Do you deny you're responsible?* That's what he asked her, a question that was as much an accusation.

'I used the newspaper stories as a framework, that's all. Just, you know. To establish the facts.'

Susanna barks out another laugh. 'Facts! Ha. That's a good one.'

'Tell me, then,' Adam responds. 'Because I don't know everything, you're right. That's part of the reason I'm here.'

He tilts his head, as though seeing Susanna for the first time.

'You know,' he says, 'I actually have to admit you

look way better than I thought you would. I figured you'd look older, obviously. But the longer hair, that colour on you. It's a bit darker than I would have chosen – I prefer your more natural blonde – but it suits you. It does.'

Susanna doesn't like the way Adam is looking at her. She pulls her cardigan tighter across her bust. 'Tell you what?'

'Huh?'

'You said, *tell me*. Tell you what?'

Adam grins. He knows she's riled and he doesn't resist the temptation to gloat. He would sit and mock her all day, Susanna reckons, if time – in his words – weren't so pressing.

'The plan,' Adam says, returning to business. 'Tell me what you know about the plan.'

It sounds so official. But there *was* no plan, not at first. Scott, Pete, Charlie, even Jake – they all admitted it. They were just messing about, they said. Like, *if* you were going to kill someone, how would you do it? *If* you were going to break into some rich twat's home, what would be the first thing you stole? A game essentially. One, it turned out, they played all the time. It was a bit of fun, was the phrase Charlie used in his statement. Just, you know. A laugh.

Jake by now was well and truly one of the gang. And the stuff they talked about, the things they got up to, right down to these hypothetical 'games' they played . . . it excited Jake. In Susanna's mind, ridiculous as she knows it would seem to anyone else, she compares it with the first time she remembers opening a book. Not the actual first time but the first time she realized that these words on the page, these lines and lines of what had once seemed impenetrable text, were gateways to whole entire worlds, all of them waiting to be explored. For Jake she imagines it felt similar. His own world thus far had been painted in foggy greys and cloying whites. Scott, Pete and Charlie: they showed him how full of colour life could be. Dashing colours, daring ones. They could smoke cigarettes, weed, if they wanted to, pore over all the filth and violent movies they could get their hands on, do whatever they could get away with, basically. They weren't *kids* any more. Right, Jake? You're fifteen for fuck's sake and you've never even seen a girl's snatch.

That's how it worked, from what Susanna gathered. The four of them, they egged each other on. At first Jake was more of a spectator, soaking everything up: a new-found audience to which Scott and the others could demonstrate their daring. So Charlie would brag about something he'd done at school, for example, some prank he'd pulled on one of the supply teachers, and then Scott would try to go one better. Yeah, well, that's nothing. You should have heard what I said to the headmaster when he had a go at me for the state of my uniform. Told him it was a political statement, *sir.* That I didn't want to get mistaken for a member of Hitler's Youth, *sir.* Reckon I'll get detention for a week, *minimum.*

And so on and so on, each of them trying to outdo the rest, until Jake joined in the fun too. It emerged later that he'd bullied some of the younger kids, smoked marijuana, tried ecstasy, even stolen from several shops on the local high street. Other things as well that Susanna would never have believed he was capable of. He knew right from wrong. He *knew* it. But knowing what he was doing was wrong was part of the thrill. More importantly, and the way it looked to Jake, the worse you got up to, the better the others liked you. The more they approved.

Plus, doing what was right had never made him happy. That was what Susanna learned, when it was too late for her to try to help Jake work out the reason why not. Doing wrong may not have made him feel happy exactly either but it made him feel *something*. It filled the hole he carried around inside of him, made him forget his frustrations and growing anger at the world.

Again, Susanna only found out afterwards that this was the way Jake was feeling. Part of the reason she didn't spot the change in him was that he didn't outwardly appear any different. He wore the same clothes, followed the same routines. At least as far as Susanna knew because she was working as head of HR for an accountancy firm at this stage – a job she'd initially taken on part-time but one that had steadily demanded more and more of her week, until she found herself staying late most days – and would only usually get home in time for dinner. He was moodier, she supposes, ruder, but he was also awash with hormones, so even that she put down as something that was to be expected. He was a teenage boy, for heaven's sake. And Jake's teachers didn't notice any change in him either. He was smarter than the others, was the thing. He kept his transgressions covert, below the radar, so only Scott, Pete and Charlie would see. Smarter? Or more cowardly? Given what it all eventually led to, you could just as easily make a case for both.

The fire.

The plan.

They were playing that same old game. What if, just imagine, wouldn't it be cool. Except this time their flight of fancy morphed into something real.

They'd been building a bonfire, their accounts later revealed, scavenging anything that would burn from the local dumping ground and transporting it to the barren patch at the eastern end of the nearby common that tended to default as their base. It was just Charlie, Pete and Jake at first. Scott hadn't shown up when he was supposed to, so sod him, they'd said, he knows where we'll be, and they'd gone ahead and started the fire without him.

Again, Charlie claimed later they were just having a laugh, mucking about, but Susanna quickly became convinced that fire, for each of them, had some deeper attraction. Heavens, she's known grown men who've turned positively primeval at the mere suggestion of setting something alight, so yes, perhaps partly it was simply that: a caveman-like obsession that was all the less inhibited because of their age. But she also remembers how Jake described the fire he saw Scott and the others set in the litter bin that day at school, the adjectives he used to describe the flames. And Pete. Fire definitely held some unhealthy fascination for Pete. He was the quietest of the bunch, the least prone to bragging, and at first, after the whole story had come out, he'd been the one who'd frightened Susanna the most — at least before that mantle passed to Scott, and after Scott to her very own son.

So playing with fire: it was more than a game to them. And on this occasion it lent their version of *let's pretend* a distinct and exhilarating edge.

'What would you burn? Free choice. It could be a building, an object, a *person*. Anything.'

Charlie later admitted he raised the subject, and he confessed to using pretty much those exact words.

'Why, what would you?' Jake was still at the solicitous stage at this point, worried about saying the wrong thing. And he could tell Charlie *wanted* to be asked. That's why he'd voiced the question.

'My neighbours' house. With everyone in it. No question. Fucking pikeys. My dad's been round there like a million times telling them to shut the fuck up, said next time he'd go back there with a cricket bat. Figure I could save him the trouble.'

Susanna imagines Charlie throwing something on the fire then, the splash of sparks mirrored in his soot-black eyes.

'If you burned down your neighbours' house,

wouldn't your own house burn down too?' Jake had been thinking the same thing but it was Pete who pointed out the obvious.

'So what? It's a shithole anyway. We could build a new one with the insurance. Put in a pool.'

A cackle of laughter then, mimicking the flames.

'Your turn, Jakey-boy. What would you burn?'

'My dad's computer.'

Pete and Charlie laughed.

'His *computer*?'

Jake admitted later he thought he'd said the wrong thing. That his suggestion, compared to Charlie's, was pretty lame. But he stuck to his guns.

'Yeah. And I'd make him watch too. He's on that thing all the sodding time, like from the minute he gets home from work. Actually, he probably wouldn't even notice if it was on fire. He'd still be trying to play his stupid games.'

'What kind of games?'

'I dunno. Like *Tomb Raider*, sometimes. Poker and stuff after me and Mum have gone to bed, even though he denies it to Mum.'

'Your old man plays *Tomb Raider*?' Charlie asked. 'Sweet!'

'It's not sweet. It's pathetic.'

'Yeah, well,' Charlie said. 'A computer probably wouldn't even burn, not unless you doused it in petrol.'

'Yeah it would.' This from Pete, who'd been following the exchange mutely. 'Everything burns if the fire's hot enough.'

'Ha! Says the fucking pyro over there. What would you burn, Petey? No, wait, let me guess . . .'

Everything, Jake had expected him to say. *Anything*. Because even among his friends Pete's fascination with fire was considered abnormal. Not bad necessarily, just peculiarly intense. Before Charlie had a chance to finish his sentence, however, Scott appeared from the line of trees that served as a fence around their private patch of common.

'What are you three homos gassing about?'

He looked angry, the others said later. His cheeks were all fiery and his heavy eyebrows were set in a frown. He was carrying a bag, like a holdall, and he tossed it down as he drew near. The odd thing was that the bag, when it landed, seemed to *squirm*.

'Where have *you* been?' Charlie said.

'Where do you think? Fucking detention, that's where. The first of five she's got me in this week.'

'Who?'

'That slag. The new one, with the tits. She's had it in for me since she spotted us trying to melt that bin.'

'Ms Birch?' Jake said.

'Miss Bitch more like,' said Charlie, who always knew how to draw Scott from one of his funks.

'Ha, yeah, Miss *Bitch*. Her.'

'What did you do?' Jake asked.

'Nothing! That's what I'm saying! Forty-five minutes she had me cleaning paintbrushes. I tell you where I'd like to stick those paintbrushes. Right up that skinny cow's gash.'

Apparently, Scott had tried to reach up the skirt of one of the girls in his class. By the time the girl in question had squealed and Ms Birch had turned from the whiteboard to look, though, Scott had his hands in the air, a parody of *who me?* innocence. When he said 'nothing', what he meant was, nothing anyone could have proved. So Ms Birch had given him a week's detention on the only charge that would stick: the language he'd used when the girl had accused him, which everyone else in the class had heard all too clearly.

Pete, chortling, changed the subject.

'What we'd burn. That's what we were talking about. Person, place or thing. Free choice.'

'That's what you're *always* talking about,' Scott replied, looking at Pete. He turned to the bonfire. 'And anyway that's easy. The school. And I'd start it from that skinny slag's desk, so that the cops or whatever would pin it on her.'

The school. It was so obvious an answer it was almost cheating but Scott's slight twist on the suggestion meant it just about counted. Besides, Scott's suggestions *always* counted. He'd thump anyone who suggested different.

'You should do it. *We* should,' said Charlie, who was still trying to improve Scott's mood.

'I would if I didn't think you lot were too pussy,' Scott replied, warming his hands against the fire.

'Who's pussy?' countered Charlie. 'Jakey-boy's the only pussy here. How many girls have you fucked, Jakey?'

Jake glared. 'Shut up,' he snapped.

'Come on,' Charlie persisted. 'How many girls have you *snogged*?'

This was something that would come to define Jake's position within the group. For each of them, other than Scott of course, a deficiency had been identified that the others would return to again and again. So, when Pete was mocked, it was about his appetite. The joke was, if Pete wasn't burning something, he was eating it. Charlie was ragged about his size. He wasn't *that* short but he was shorter than the others and for Scott and Pete that was enough. Jake's perceived inadequacy was his sexual inexperience, which Charlie in particular enjoyed highlighting at every opportunity. As for whether Jake really was as inexperienced as Charlie liked to make out, Susanna, at the time, could not have said.

'What's in the bag?' Jake said, eager to change the subject. But he admitted later that he was also genuinely curious. As before, when he'd looked at it, he was convinced he'd seen the holdall move.

'See for yourself.' Scott was grinning. 'Go ahead. Pick it up.'

Charlie and Pete were looking on. Jake was reluctant but in the end he reached for the bag. What was the worst that could happen? He'd seen Scott carrying it himself, so it wasn't like it was going to *bite* or anything.

'Shit! Fuck!'

Jake leaped back from the holdall an instant after he'd grasped the handle. Not only had it moved, definitively this time; whatever was in it, he would have sworn, had also *screamed*.

Scott cracked up. The others, even though they were as baffled as Jake was, laughed with him.

Jake glowered, furious at the feeling he'd been tricked. 'What the hell? What have you got in there?' His first thought, he later confessed, was that inside the bag was a *baby*. Only because of the size, the sound it made. Which just went to show: what happened next: it could have been worse.

'Your face!' Scott was practically crying. 'Honestly, Jake. You should have seen your face!'

The others, still laughing along, edged closer.

'Seriously. What's in there?' Charlie prodded the bag with his toe. Another 'scream', although this time the sound was distinctly *feline*.

Jake bent closer to the bag. He reached for the zip. 'Is that a cat in there?'

'Don't open it!' Scott leaped forward and hauled Jake back. 'Do you know how long it took me to catch that thing?' He gave the holdall a short, sharp kick, hard enough to elicit another wail.

'A cat? Ha! You caught a cat? What the fuck, Scott!' Charlie's grin sparkled with expectancy. This, right here, this was exactly why Scott was *numero uno*. He did stuff, thought of stuff, that no one, not even Charlie, would ever dream of. Crazy stuff, *hilarious* stuff.

'It's my next-door neighbour's. Was, rather. It's called Snuggles or Sniggles or something like that. No, wait. *Squiggles*. Fucking thing keeps me up all night.' He kicked the cat once more.

'Why'd you bring it?' This from Pete – who, quicker

than any of them, had already figured out precisely why.

'We're having a bonfire, right?' Scott replied. 'And if you have a bonfire you've gotta have something to toast.'

There was a pause as the others caught up. Then: 'Fucking brilliant! Fucking genius!' Charlie was practically dancing with excitement.

'Well,' said Scott. 'Who's gonna do it?'

Charlie stopped jiggling. He looked at Pete.

'Go on, Petey,' he said. 'Toss it on.'

'You toss it on,' said Pete back. 'Or let Scott. It was his idea.'

'I fucking caught it. I've done all the hard work. Come on, you faggots. Man up.'

Neither Charlie nor Pete showed any sign of relenting. They told the police they didn't want to do it because they knew it was cruel but it was obvious even to Susanna that basically they didn't have the guts.

'I'll do it.'

The others turned to face Jake.

'For real?' said Scott.

Jake's eyes swept the faces around him. 'Give it here,' he said.

'No way,' said Charlie. 'No way he's really going to do it.' But like Pete he was wide-eyed with anticipation. They edged closer, and Scott, grinning, handed Jake the wriggling bag.

They crowded around as Jake carried it towards the fire. It was as though they realized the same thing

Susanna did, the first time she heard Jake recount this story. After she'd come to terms with her initial horror, she was able to see as well that this moment was a tipping point. For Scott and the others, what Jake did next would decide whether or not he was truly one of their group: a lifetime member or a temporary guest. More than that, it would show them how strong they were. How far, if they acted together, they could go.

Jake paused when he reached the edge of the bonfire . . . but not for very long. He couldn't exactly back out now. And actually, when he picked up the bag, when he pitched it into the middle of the fire, he didn't even feel that bad. He felt sorry for the cat, a little bit. But it was only a cat. And it would die eventually, just as everything does. If anything he was putting it out of its misery. And, on the flipside, he felt *good* about how the others were looking at him. The admiration they showed: it was real, like he'd exceeded their wildest expectations.

So he focused on that: his friends' approval. He didn't look at the holdall as it burned, not after he'd made sure he hadn't thrown it too far. He could hear it, though. The cat, that is. And, even more than before, the way it screamed made it sound almost human.

It is not what he asked her. Adam wanted to know about the plan but what Susanna has ended up telling him is the part that was important to *her*. The bonfire, the cat, Jake's fingers around the handles of the bag – it's a scene she revisits often. It's so vivid in her memory, it's as though she was actually there. Some days – some nights, in particular – she would swear that she genuinely was. The only difference in her nightmares is that it's not the cat she sees burning. In her dreams, rather, it is Jake.

'I know that's not . . . that you wanted to know about the plan. But that's how it started. That's how they came up with the idea.'

'To burn down the school.'

Susanna nods and finds she can't stop. For a moment it feels like she is rocking. 'And after that . . . I don't really know what happened after that. It became like a project for them. A secret scheme. Whenever they got together it's what they talked about. Working out the details: when to do it, how, in a way they wouldn't get caught. They realized the building would have to be empty, for their sake as much as anyone else's. But it . . .' Susanna trails off. There doesn't seem to be anything more she can say.

'A secret scheme,' Adam repeats. 'Meaning you had no idea. Is that right? *Nobody* had any idea.'

He isn't expecting an answer and Susanna doesn't offer one. Of course no one knew. How could they have? And what would they have thought even if they had discovered some detail of what Jake and the others were spending their time talking about? It was just adolescent nonsense, they would have said. Just boys being boys, mouthing off to try and make themselves feel big. Susanna can almost hear herself saying it. Dismissing it, the way she had when Jake was hauled in for fighting. At the very most she would have tried to talk to Jake about it but he would have fobbed her off with the same explanation. *It was just a game, Mum. We weren't being serious. I mean, is that what you think of me? Do you really think I'd be that stupid?*

'Tell me something, Susanna.' Adam perches on the arm of his chair. He leans in. 'Do you wish it had all worked out the way they'd meant it to? The plan, the fire, all that. Do you wish it had happened as they'd intended?'

Susanna thinks again of the burning building, of people running from the roaring flames. She thinks of their soot-blackened faces, of the lines drawn by their tears.

She blinks, looks up. And even though she's always known the answer, she's surprised when she hears herself say it.

'More than anything.'

9

Ruth is doing something she would never, ever normally do. Not if someone paid her. It's Friday afternoon, all her patients have been scraped, drilled and polished, so there's simply no good reason for her to be sitting in her gloomy little back room doing paperwork. This – checking invoices, writing cheques – it's a Monday job. Fridays are for going out with the girls. A Singapore Sling, a few shots of tequila, and then off to the local meat market for a grind on the dance floor and a snog on the sofas.

Ha.

She wishes.

In her younger days that was most Friday nights. Most Thursdays and Saturdays too, if she's honest. Nowadays it's a civilized G&T with Susanna and Alina, then a slightly tipsy drive home. Sometimes she can get the others to stay for three, on rare occasions even for four, but then Susanna starts to worry about Ruth getting behind the wheel, which kind of puts a dampener on the fun. Although, to be fair, the thing Ruth most feels like doing anyway right now is heading straight home, running a bath and pouring a large glass of Chablis, and dissolving in water that is almost scalding while Alfie Boe serenades her from the stereo.

Rock and roll.

Christ, Ruth. When was it exactly that you turned into your mother? (About twenty years ago is the depressing – and distressingly accurate – answer, because the fact is Ruth is older now than her mother was when she died. Bloody hell, Ruth. Talk about putting a dampener on the fun. *You've lost that Friday feeling . . .*)

And anyway, she will have to go to the pub first because she has already said she would to Alina. Which she only did when she thought Susanna was coming as well.

Alina. God.

Alina's . . . fine. She's good at her job and she can be quite dry, which Ruth likes, but on the flipside she's not exactly a barrel of laughs. And she's got a pout on her that makes her look like a cat's bum.

The problem is that Alina's lonely. She's got no family here and the friends she talks about don't, to Ruth, sound like anything more than passing acquaintances. It's almost as though Alina isn't able to tell the difference. Ruth is her friend, though Alina treats her more, ironically, as her counsellor. Susanna *should* be Alina's friend but rather than looking to cultivate that friendship, Alina rubs against her like sandpaper, then complains to Ruth that Susanna 'does not like her'. 'Well, it's hardly surprising,' Ruth has said to her. 'Try, I don't know, just being nice to her for a change. You're allowed to be friends with some-one even if you take exception to what they do, you know.'

Because that's another problem. Alina, part of whose job it is to act as the receptionist and administrator for a BACP-registered counsellor, doesn't, it turns out, believe in counselling. 'You listen,' Ruth remembers her repeating after Susanna had tried explaining to her once what being a counsellor entailed. 'These people. They talk. And you just. What? Are silent?' With Ruth Alina converses in full sentences. Susanna is lucky to get more than two syllables between silences that punctuate her disapproval.

'Well,' was Susanna's answer. 'Basically. Although of course there's more to it than that.'

She'd lost Alina at 'basically', Ruth could tell. And ever since then Alina has seemed determined to clash with Susanna on points of principle ('they are the ones to talk and yet you are the one who gets paid!'), when a woman of her age (what is she? Twenty-eight? Twenty-nine? More than old enough to act the grown-up) should understand that isn't what friends do. Hell, Ruth has plenty of friends who take exception to what *she* does. That's what it feels like when she catches sight of the condition of their teeth. And though Ruth would *love* to lecture them about their dental hygiene, somehow she manages to hold herself back. And if she can do it, *anyone* can. She's said to Alina, if you really feel a need to vent, you should sign up to Twitter.

Which was a joke, of course.

Which naturally Alina didn't get.

So, no. The prospect of an evening with just her and Alina doesn't exactly fill Ruth with joy. So why not get it over with? Set aside the paperwork, pop along for one, then head home and draw that bath. She could be naked and in the company of Alfie Boe by . . .

Ruth checks her watch.

. . . half past six. A quarter past if she's lucky with the traffic. After the day she's had, the week, it's no less than she deserves.

Susanna, though. Susanna is the reason Ruth's delaying, much as she would welcome that G&T.

She *seemed* fine. When Ruth listened at the door – just for a moment or two, just to make sure it wasn't a bad time to interrupt – she didn't hear anything she considered out of the ordinary, not that she could hear very much. And then, when Susanna opened the door and the two of them spoke, Susanna acted perfectly normal as well. A little on edge but wasn't that to be expected? Ruth has never interrupted her before when she's been in session, mainly because she knows it isn't something she's supposed to do. So naturally Susanna would be flustered. Ruth knows how *she* would react were someone to interrupt her when she was with a patient, and she can guarantee she wouldn't be as measured as Susanna was. Objects would fly, put it that way. And some of the objects within a dentist's reach tend to be sharp.

But she worries. That's the thing. Partly, again, because that's what friends do. Mainly because of Susanna's past.

Ruth has always known there was *something*. It was obvious from the day they met, when Susanna first came to view the office. She was evasive, edgy, constantly checking in corners. Ruth's instinct was to stay well clear, to sublet the room to someone else, but what it came down to in the end was that Ruth *liked* her. Susanna was clearly a decent woman: kind, funny, *honest*. To a fault, sometimes, it later turned out. And she was obviously desperate to make this counselling thing work. The space was *perfect*, she declared, and what she most appreciated was the prospect of not being stuck in an empty building all on her own. Which was another clue, one Ruth cottoned on to even at the time.

At first Ruth assumed Susanna was running from an abusive ex-husband. Husband, boyfriend, one or the other. Ruth has had her share of degenerate ex-partners herself. No one who hit her but abuse isn't always physical. Ruth's first husband, one of three before she finally realized she was better off on her own – just her and Betty and the twins, as she likes to refer to her parakeets, and which she thinks of as her dog's younger siblings – used to restrict her access to the money she earned. *Her* money, for pity's sake! He used to insist it was paid into a 'shared' account, for which he held the only chequebook and debit card. He used to give her an allowance, like pocket money: a more effective method of controlling her than physically walking her around on a leash. The craziest thing is not that Ruth allowed herself to be manipulated like that, but that it was a mistake she later repeated. With John, husband number two, and Cliff, her third and final. She's free now, which on the whole she considers a blessing, but the point is, if Susanna was going through something similar, Ruth would have done everything in her power to help her. What woman wouldn't?

It was only by accident that Ruth found out the truth. This was ... three years ago? God, no, more. Five. Obviously it was well established by then that Susanna didn't talk about her background, so Ruth was aware she considered her secrets shameful. No news there, Ruth thought. What woman doesn't blame herself when she's been abused? But then one day in the waiting area, when Susanna was at the desk talking to Alina and Ruth had come out to call the name of her next patient, Susanna had reacted as though Ruth had called to *her*.

She laughed it off afterwards, claimed she'd misheard, and though Ruth realized right away that Susanna was dissembling, she didn't consider it a particularly big deal. So 'Susanna' wasn't her real name. So what? It made sense that she would change it if she was in hiding. Except soon after that, when Ruth had been scanning the Saturday supplements, she found herself reading an article about the way women are portrayed in the press, about how they're so often *demonized*, basically – and there she was. Her Susanna. The photograph they ran looked nothing like her, not at first glance. But the details of the story, that first name, *something* anyway caused Ruth to lean a little closer ...

And then it clicked.

She was shocked at first, of course she was. Hurt, a bit. Angry as well that her best friend – which is what Susanna by that point had become – had chosen to conceal from her such a fundamental aspect of who she was. It explained everything. *Everything.* Susanna's bearing, her beliefs, her behaviour in just about every incident in their shared history that Ruth could bring to mind. She'd always known Susanna had her secrets. She'd just never imagined that the door she'd hidden them behind would open to reveal such darkness. Such *depth* too. It wasn't some cubbyhole Ruth found herself peering into. It was a dungeon.

She said nothing. She made her peace with the fact Susanna hadn't confided in her (her life, her choice, Ruth reasoned. It wasn't as though Ruth had confessed every shameful secret from *her* past) and resolved to carry on just as though she'd never found out. Although, oddly, knowing what she did somehow made Ruth love Susanna all the more. She didn't know the ins and outs of what had happened; she wasn't sure which version of events she should believe. All she could go on was her instinct and the relationship she and Susanna had already forged, and in *that* context Susanna appeared both stronger and braver than Ruth ever imagined. She felt sorry for her friend, yes, but she had also never felt so proud. Look at what she was doing. Look at who she'd become!

And Ruth thought she was doing well substituting a pair of parakeets for a husband.

One thing that did change was how responsible for her friend Ruth began to feel. She'd always looked out for Susanna, had always been careful not to leave her in the building alone, not without warning, and had always cast a discriminating eye over any thuggish-looking middle-aged men she passed while on her lunch break, say, or on the walk to and from her car. But having found out the truth – having realized what it was Susanna was running from – Ruth took her role of guardianship to another level. More than anything, Ruth has come to realize how afraid Susanna must feel. How afraid, and how alone. What she would most like to do is enfold Susanna in her arms and assure her that she loves her in spite of everything. And yet to do so, she feels, would be a betrayal, strange as that might seem. So doing this, looking out for her: it is to Ruth's mind the next best thing.

Sitting here in her office now, she isn't sure what has made her so uneasy. Partly it's that: the prospect of leaving Susanna with a stranger. A young man too, someone so close to the age Susanna's son was when he died. Susanna *told* Ruth she would be fine but she would say that, wouldn't she, especially when the client was there listening in. And what she said about . . . how had she put it? *Doubling up.* Ruth is sure that isn't something Susanna would normally do. In fact she's told Ruth before, something about timekeeping, about how important it is in counselling to stick to the schedule, unless Ruth is getting mixed up? She does listen when Susanna tells her things but she would imagine it's the same for her as it is for Susanna when Ruth talks to her about teeth. Sometimes she can *see* Susanna tuning out. Ruth doesn't hold it against her. Other people's passions: frankly they're not always that interesting.

Maybe she's just tired. She's had a long week and

now she's just . . . what's that word Susanna uses? *Projecting*. She's feeling blue, basically, and she's allowing that to influence her perceptions of what's happening around her. Maybe when Susanna said she was fine she really meant it. She's had long enough to judge whether she's in any danger, and if she was feeling in any way threatened she would have signalled for Ruth's help when she had the chance. And the fact is, she didn't. If anything she seemed impatient to be left alone. So maybe Ruth should mind her own business; stop treating Susanna as though she were a child, when in reality she is a tough, middle-aged woman who's been through more in her life than most people could begin to –

'Ruth?'

She looks up. She checks the time again and curses. She's been sitting here for the best part of twenty minutes when she told Alina she would be ready to go in five.

'Coming!' she calls back. 'I'm just this minute putting on my coat!'

Alina grumbles something from the hallway about meeting her downstairs, which is Alina-speak for *get a bloody move on*. Which is fair enough, actually. Alina was wrapped up and ready to go when Ruth had turned from Susanna's door, and is no doubt gasping for that G&T as much as Ruth is. *Was*. All of a sudden she doesn't much fancy it, nor even the bath with Alfie Boe. Not the one on the stereo, anyway.

She hauls on her coat even so. She shoves aside the paperwork she's been pretending to tackle and switches off the overhead light. A minute later she is through her surgery and casting one last glance at Susanna's office door. She hesitates, just for a moment, and then she is downstairs, hoisting a smile for Alina and pulling the door into the building closed behind her.

Emily

19 August 2017

It feels like me and Adam have had our first argument. Which we haven't, at least I don't think we have, but today . . . let's just say it didn't go the way I hoped it would.

We've seen each other a few times since the bus ride but only ever for a couple of hours. Mainly we've been chatting by text. So today was supposed to be our first proper day out. Not even anything that exciting really, just a picnic on the common. But anything is better than sitting in Starbucks, right? Plus it was a chance to spend the entire day with Adam. An evening would have been even better – a meal or a movie or something – but there's no way Mum would have allowed *that*. Not without getting Adam's life story first, and at the very least running some kind of background check. As it was I had to tell her I was planning to spend the day with Frankie. I didn't like lying to her, and she's made me swear more times than I can remember that it's some-thing I will never, ever do, but if I hadn't, today might not have happened. Although, looking back, maybe that wouldn't have been such a bad thing after all.

So, me and Adam, we're walking along, looking for a spot to lay the blanket, and we're heading towards this little private patch of trees. Even from a distance I can see there's no one else sitting there, meaning me and Adam would have it all to ourselves. And we haven't kissed yet, we haven't done anything more than hold hands, so what I'm thinking about is maybe today will be the day – you know, when we finally get to have our first kiss. But then Adam stops walking.

'How about right here?' he says.

And we're basically in the middle of the field, right on the edge of the kids' play area.

'Here?' I say.

Adam is already spreading out the blanket.

'Sure. Why not.'

'You don't think it's a bit . . .' *Public*, I want to say, still thinking about that kiss. 'Noisy,' I end up saying.

'Noisy?' Adam looks up at me, then around. His eyes fix on the play area. Today was like twenty-five degrees, not a cloud in the sky, so it's heaving. 'I guess,' Adam says, 'but it's a nice noise, don't you think?' Which, when he says it, this little kid lets out this humongous *screeeeeeeaaam*. Adam, he kind of half winces, half smiles, like, *Thanks, kid*. You know?

'OK, so maybe it's a *tad* noisy,' Adam concedes. 'Here, let's go a bit further back.'

Which we do, a bit, and it's better, a bit, but it's not like it's the noise I'm really worrying about.

'You really like that sound?' I ask him as we settle. I gesture with my head towards the playground. 'The kids playing?'

Adam gives this embarrassed little shrug. 'Not the

screaming, obviously. And the crying I can live without. But the laughing, the running around . . .' He shrugs again. 'Kind of, I guess.'

I must have looked at him funny because rather than letting it go he tells me to lean back and shut my eyes. And this time I *definitely* look at him funny but he's like, go on, it's not a trick, *trust me*.

So I lie back.

'Shut your eyes,' he tells me again.

'Why, though?' I say but by the time I've finished asking my eyes are shut anyway because when I lean back the sun is directly overhead.

'Are you comfortable?'

I wriggle until I am. 'Physically,' I tell him, which he laughs at.

'Right. Now listen.'

There's movement on the blanket beside me and when I peek I see Adam is lying down next to me. On his back, the way I am. Eyes closed, the way mine are. *Were*, anyway. I shut them again.

And at first I'm just waiting for something to happen. For Adam to start tickling me or something, or maybe, right out in the open, for him to lean over and deliver that kiss. But after a moment I've forgotten all about that and instead I'm doing what Adam told me to do. I'm *listening*. And you know what? He's right. The sound of those kids playing . . . This is going to sound stupid, I know, but all of a sudden it isn't like noise any more. What it sounds like, as I'm lying there with the sun on my face, is the happiest, most cheerful kind of music.

When I open my eyes Adam is propped up on one elbow. He's looking at me, smiling. 'See?' he says.

And I do. I get it. It's like listening to waves on the shore, or rain when you're lying in bed. And to show him I get it, what I do is, I reach up and I kiss *him*.

Now, ordinarily this would be fucking momentous. Right? If it wasn't for what happened after, it would be the whole point of me writing what I'm writing. Except now, looking back, what I'm wondering about is whether it happened because of that. Because of that kiss. I mean, it only lasted for a couple of seconds, probably not even that, but right away Adam starts acting all weird.

He sits up. He's surprised, I guess, probably almost as much as I am. 'Emily,' he says. I like that, by the way. That he calls me Emily. My mates, even Mum sometimes, they tend to call me Em. It's a silly thing probably, not even that big a deal, but Emily just sounds way more grown up, and I get treated like a kid enough.

'Emily,' he says, 'you haven't told anyone about us. Have you?'

'What do you mean?' I say. Because what I'm expecting is for him to say something about the kiss. Or not to say anything but to smile or laugh or *something*.

'Frankie, for example. And your mum especially. You haven't told her that we've been seeing each other, have you?'

'No. Of course not. You asked me not to, remember?' Because he did, right after that time on the bus. I mean, setting aside the fact that I would never have told anyone about him anyway, Adam had this bee in his bonnet about the age thing, about what my mum and other people might think. So what I figure is, that's what's bothering him now.

'Relax,' I tell him. 'No one *saw*. And anyway . . .' I touch his arm. 'So what if they did?'

Adam's looking towards the playground, at the parents chatting around the sandpit. He half smiles back at me, and for a second I think everything's all right. But then he's looking back where he was looking before and that smile of his dips into a frown. He gets up then, and starts walking towards the play area. Towards the little fence, which comes up sort of level with his belt.

'Adam?' I say, calling out. When he doesn't answer I get up and follow him. 'Adam!' He stops at the fence and I realize he's spotted this little kid. So I stop too and from then on I'm just watching, from a few yards away, back up the hill. The whole time, from then on out, all I was doing was standing there *watching*.

'Hey,' Adam says, and he bends down, so that he's talking to the kid through the railings. 'Hey, buddy. Are you OK?'

Because the kid, the little boy, who must be five or six or so, he's crying.

'Did you hurt yourself?' Adam asks him. 'Did you trip or something?'

The kid just wails. His crying doesn't change. It's like he doesn't even realize Adam's there. And his face is this mess of snot and tears. There's dirt too, and sand all glued to his cheeks where the snot has smeared.

'Hey. Hey, buddy.' All Adam's doing is trying to comfort him. He slips a hand through the railings and gives the boy a little shake on his shoulder. Just, you know. Nicely. He's not being weird or anything, I swear.

Then: 'Get your hands off him!'

This woman comes up to Adam and she says it again. 'Get away from him! Get your hands off him!' And at this point Adam isn't even touching him!

Adam says, 'Are you his mother?'

'*Todd*,' the woman barks, blanking Adam completely. And she's furious, even though her little boy is sitting there crying. '*Todd*,' she goes, 'come here! *Now!*'

Todd, the boy, he carries on wailing.

'Are you Todd's mother?' Adam says again.

'Yes, I'm his bloody mother,' the woman snaps. 'Not that it's any business of yours. *Todd!*'

She goes to grab Todd by his arm but Todd gets up and legs it past her. And I can hear him crying as he goes, I can virtually hear him crying now, but the thing is – the thing I've just realized – is that him running off was the last we saw of him. I don't even know if he's OK, or what the matter was in the first place. Which on the one hand makes me feel bad, because I'd like to know, you know? But on the other hand, I guess Todd isn't really my point. My point is Adam.

He's glaring at the woman. 'You do realize he was crying, don't you? You realize your son was upset?'

'Todd!' The woman is yelling after her son but then,

when Adam speaks, she whips her head back round. '*Yes*, I realize he was crying. He cries all the bloody time!'

'I wonder why that is.'

'I beg your pardon?' the woman says, smiling this *ugly*-looking smile. 'Who the bloody hell do you think you are?'

Up until this point no one else was really watching. They stopped when Adam went to talk to Todd (like, thank God *someone*'s dealing with it . . .) But the woman raises her voice this time, and it's obvious she's not just shouting at her kid, so people are starting to take notice.

'I'm wondering who you think *you* are,' Adam replies. 'Your little boy's sitting there, bawling his eyes out. But rather than going to him, rather than acting like a mother should, you just, what? *Ignore* him. Hope some stranger will deal with it instead?'

'I told you, he cries all the time! And I didn't *ask* you to –'

'Do you even know why he was upset? Did you even bother to check whether he was OK?'

The woman, she's having one of those moments where she'll probably come up with a million clever things to say afterwards. I can almost hear her telling her mates later, about how this nutter accosted her on the common and she was like, boom, back in your place, when really, in reality, all she was doing was standing there like a fish.

Then she does think of something. What she thinks of is, 'Piss off!'

Which is the point I should probably have stepped in.

'How fucking dare you!' the woman goes. 'What are you, some kind of kiddie fiddler? Hanging around kids' playgrounds, looking for little boys to go and *rub*.' She mimes rubbing a kid's shoulder, the way Adam did when he was comforting Todd.

'A kiddie fiddler,' Adam repeats. And his smile . . . I mean, I hate to say it, but it's not exactly all that pleasant then either. 'You know what,' he says, 'I'm surprised you even noticed me. What were you doing while your son was crying?' He gestures to the phone in the woman's hand. 'Checking Facebook? Looking at Twitter? If I *was* a kiddie fiddler, I could have snatched Todd away before you even realized he was missing.'

'What's going on here?'

This from some dad-type. And I don't know if he knows the mother but all of a sudden he's there at her side. 'Is there a problem?'

'Yes, there's a fucking problem!' the woman yells. 'This *pervert* is threatening to kidnap my son!'

Which is NOT what Adam said!! Not even close! Again, though, I don't say it. I just think it. Loudly – but I realize that still doesn't count.

'You what?'

The dad, he's all outraged. It's kind of pathetic, actually. He's like one of those big fat hippos on *Planet Earth* that tries to stop other hippos muscling in on its territory.

'Back off, pal,' he goes. 'Go on, piss off out of it. If you haven't got kids you've got no business being here.'

'I'll call the cops, that's what I'll do,' the woman chips in, all loud and whiney. I didn't notice it till then: how shrill she was. Her voice is like Alvin and the chipmunks.

'Go ahead,' Adam tells the woman, and I can tell he's losing it too. 'Call the police. In fact, here, I'll do it for you. Let them know what a great mother you are, see how many laws you've broken by being such a waste of space.' And then, what he does is, he reaches for the woman's phone. There's the fence between them obviously but they're standing so close it hardly even matters. And the point is, Adam reaching out like that, trying to grab the woman's phone: it's a mistake.

The woman squeals. The dad steps forward and gives Adam a shove. Adam stumbles, almost falls, but then he's up and leaning over the fence. Then *he* shoves the dad, who gets hit at the same time by the woman, who's flailing at Adam, and I guess the dad, he must have thought it was *Adam* who hit him, because it's all this big thrashing mess, and what he does is, the dad, he punches Adam. Hard. Right in the face.

And then I *do* move.

I yell, 'Stop! Don't! Leave him alone!'

Adam's bent over. He's virtually kneeling on the grass. I can't see his face because it's covered by his hands but I can see there's blood so I'm panicking, you know? 'He didn't do anything!' I shout at the dad. 'He didn't even do anything!'

And the dad, you can tell he's worried about what he's done because he's looking at Adam and he's looking at his hand, at the blood on his hand, going 'He hit me first! He hit me first!' to himself and to me and to all the other people who have started gathering round.

I try to help Adam. I'm the only one who can because everyone else is on the other side of the fence. They're all peering at us, like we're some exhibit or something, like in a zoo, but no one's saying anything helpful. Just 'What's going on?' and 'Is he OK?' and 'What happened, did anyone see?' And the dad is still all, 'He hit me first! He hit me first!', sounding like some stuck CD.

Adam gets back on his feet. He's holding his nose so I can't see how badly it's damaged but there's red all between his fingers, all down his T-shirt, and I'm asking him, 'Are you OK? Adam? Let me see. Are you OK?'

But Adam shrugs me off. He starts walking. Staggering. He heads up the hill, away from the playground, from all the mums and dads, who are standing there staring as he goes. I go after him. I'm touching his arm, asking if he's OK, telling him to show me, to let me help, just *please Adam, please,* when all of a sudden he whips round to face me. And the blood, it's all in his teeth. In the gaps, I mean. And I can see it's there because he *snarls.*

'Go the fuck away from me!' he spits. So violently I feel myself flinch.

And then I don't know what to do. I just stand there, basically, watching Adam walk away. I want to apologize but I don't know what for. I want to go after him but I don't want him yelling at me again. And I start crying as he storms up the hill. It's pathetic, I know, but

```
----------------------------------------
Loans
----------------------------------------

Mr James McCallion
22 Apr 2023

Measure of darkness
Kellerman, Jonathan
Item barcode: C902878020
Due date: 13 May 2023


Liar's room
Lelic, Simon
Item barcode: C902905420
Due date: 13 May 2023

----------------------------------------
```

I couldn't help it. Adam doesn't look back, doesn't even pause to pick up his stuff. And all I can think is, what did I do? I don't even know what I did! Even now I don't understand it. That snarl, the blood in his teeth . . . it's like, the little boy crying, the woman shouting, the dad punching Adam in the face: it's like it was *my* fault.

Like more than anyone Adam blamed me.

5 p.m. – 6 p.m.

10

The room shudders slightly, then stills. It is barely noticeable, nothing more than a ripple in the air, but both Susanna and Adam fall momentarily silent, each of them conscious what it means. Ruth has gone. Alina has gone. The rest of the building is finally empty.

Susanna knew this point was coming and she thought she was braced for it. She was but that doesn't mean she was prepared. It feels like she's taken a leap into the ocean, and the water is colder than she could possibly have anticipated. The loneliness – the *aloneness* – hits her hard, all at once, in every part of her. She finds herself gasping, struggling to fend off the encroaching panic.

'Susanna? You look very pale, Susanna. Are you OK?'

Susanna looks towards the window. She could run to it, now. She could hammer on the glass, use her chair to smash the pane, and scream into the street below for Ruth to rescue her. Adam couldn't stop her. He *wouldn't*. All Susanna has to do is *move*.

'Susanna? Where are you going, Susanna?'

She gets as far as her desk. She stops when she sees the framed picture on the surface of Emily. Her little girl, grinning out at the world as though nothing that was looking on could possibly harm her. As though monsters weren't lurking just out of shot.

Susanna turns it to her chest.

'Please,' she says. 'Wouldn't it be easier if you just told me who you are? What it is you want from me? I don't understand why you're hiding it. Why you're so intent on playing these *games*.'

Adam affects surprise. 'Games? Nobody's playing any games, Susanna. Just ask Emily if you don't believe me.'

Susanna squirms at that, hugs the photograph tighter.

'And I told you before,' Adam continues. 'I'm not hiding anything. Didn't I say that? Right at the beginning? It's a question of time, that's all. *Your* time, remember. Emily's time.'

Susanna hasn't forgotten. Ruth and Alina's leaving has only reinforced in her mind the sense that time is slipping away. But she still doesn't understand what that *means* exactly: how much time they had to start with, or how much (if any) there is left. And though there is nothing Susanna wants to do more than concentrate wholly on her daughter, she knows that if she is going to find a way out of this, Adam is the riddle she needs to solve.

And that's the other thing that's made her focus again on Adam. Susanna has the beginnings of a theory. Half a theory would perhaps be more accurate, although possibly not even that. She almost doesn't want to look at it too closely because she knows if she does it will fall apart. Or, just possibly, it will come together, and Susanna isn't sure what would be worse.

'You really don't have any idea? Do you? About me, I mean,' Adam says.

Susanna doesn't like that. Adam's knowingness, above all, but also the fact he seems so able to scrutinize her thoughts.

'How could I?' Susanna answers. 'You haven't told me anything about you. You claim you're not playing games but as far as I'm concerned that's *all* you've been doing. The game for you seems to be the point.'

Adam makes a face, like he is the innocent party here and Susanna is the one who's not being fair.

'Your name, for example,' Susanna presses. 'I don't even know your real name.'

'But you do,' Adam insists. 'Adam Geraghty. Adam *Donald* Geraghty if you want my full name, though you'll understand why I kept the Donald part quiet. These days it's not exactly a badge of honour.'

Susanna is about interrupt but Adam raises a hand.

'I know, I know,' he says. 'I probably gave you the impression it was a pseudonym but it's not, I swear.' He clocks Susanna's doubtful look and moves to pull out his wallet. 'Here. Look.'

The wallet is thick, jammed with loyalty cards and receipts from the look of it. Not like Susanna's, which contains her bank cards, her driving licence and little else. Old Susanna used to carry around her entire life history. New Susanna's existence is pared virtually to the bone.

'Here,' says Adam again, and he offers Susanna a collection of cards. There is a debit card with Mr A Geraghty embossed on the lower-left corner; a library card after that showing the same; then Adam's own driving licence, a provisional one, clearly showing the name he claims is his, as well as his address and date of birth.

'I haven't had a chance to take my test yet,' Adam explains. 'I've been a bit busy lately. You know. What with one thing and another.'

Susanna focuses on the driving licence. The address it shows is Flat 2, 9 Clapham New Road, SW4 0HL. Adam claimed before that he was born in London, and the driving licence seems to bear this out. Or at least that he lived there, once, before he trailed Susanna *here*. As for Adam's date of birth, it is recorded on the licence as 30.11.1999, making him just under eighteen years old. Which means he is younger than Susanna thought he was initially but, actually, and now Susanna has time to consider it, precisely the age he claimed he was. He never revealed his age specifically but he did tell Susanna that his 'girlfriend' was three years younger than him, and Emily is indeed fourteen.

More importantly, however, and the thing that strikes Susanna hardest, is that Adam's date of birth doesn't fit with Susanna's theory. At the very least it *distorts* it, and the relief, briefly, is breathtaking.

But then Susanna realizes what that means. She is back where she started, for one thing, working on the assumption that Adam is a fan, a fanatic, a

(oh God)

a *copycat*, and if that's the case Susanna is no better off, *Emily* is no better off. If anything they have more to fear, assuming that for Emily it isn't already too late.

Oh Emily. What has he done to you? It is her daughter Susanna is most afraid for but she cannot help a corollary of that fear following in its wake. What about *you*, Susanna? What does Adam plan to do to *you*?

Something else strikes her. Adam has shown her his ID. Susanna knows his name, his registered address, everything. Either Adam doesn't expect to get out of this himself or, worse, he doesn't *care* whether or not he gets away. Which surely means neither Susanna nor Emily is getting out of this either.

'Susanna?'

Adam is frowning, leaning forward in his chair. He gets up and crosses to where Susanna is standing.

'Breathe, Susanna. You're not breathing.'

Adam seizes the photograph of Emily and for an instant Susanna tries to resist. Adam is stronger though and Susanna hears it clatter as he slides it on to the surface of the desk.

'Look, just . . . just sit down or something.'

Adam attempts to guide Susanna into the chair behind her desk but Susanna bats him away. If his hands were to touch her skin she is sure she would gag but she is shielded by the fabric of her cardigan and anyway there is no space in her throat. The panic that has been threatening has overwhelmed her. It is a full-on, full-frontal attack. The first time Susanna succumbed like this was the first anniversary of Jake's death. She was seated at her dressing table, doing her hair ostensibly but really just staring in the mirror, when her son all at once appeared behind her. And not just in the mirror's reflection. When

Susanna spun round, Jake was standing there as clear as the air between them. Except he *wasn't* standing. Susanna saw the gap below his feet, the dressing-gown cord looped around Jake's neck, and she realized that, somehow, he was hanging.

And then he was gone. There were repeated appearances, repeated panic attacks, but few so severe as this one.

Adam is glaring at her, convinced she is trying to provoke him. 'What's the matter with you? It's not asthma. I know you don't have asthma. If you're faking, I swear to God I'll . . .' Adam finishes the thought with a head shake. There is confusion in his voice but for the most part it has manifested as anger. 'For Christ's sake, Susanna, *sit down*.' This time he practically forces her into the chair. 'And get a grip on yourself. Put your . . . I don't know. Your head between your knees or something.'

Adam starts rifling through Susanna's drawers, searching presumably for the asthma inhaler he was so certain before that Susanna does not need. She wants to stop him (they're *my* drawers, my *things*) but even though she is struggling to breathe there is a part of her that is relishing his alarm. Susanna reacting like this: for once it isn't part of his plan.

'For fuck's sake.' Adam slams the final drawer shut, his hands coming out empty. He whips round to face Susanna. 'I said get a grip on yourself! Stop *wheezing* like that. I know you're faking. Do you hear me, Susanna? I said I know you're faking!'

Breathe, Susanna. Forget about Adam for a moment and just *breathe*. Because enjoying his agitation is one thing. But if you don't do what he says and snap out of it, there's no telling what he will do.

She clings to the arms of her chair, feels her knuckles whiten as she grips.

Adam has collected the knife. He's holding it in front of him, waving it, the way a wizard would brandish a wand.

'I'm going to count to ten,' Adam says. 'Do you hear me, Susanna? If you don't pull yourself together by the time I get there, I swear to God your daughter dies.' He waits for her to speak. 'Susanna? I'm not kidding around, Susanna!'

And he isn't, Susanna can tell. Knowing this – understanding it – only makes the panic attack worse.

'One . . .'

Susanna leans forward in precisely the way Adam suggested, her head down between her knees.

'Two . . . three . . .'

She spots her handbag in the footwell of her desk. The bottle of water she bought at lunchtime is poking out. Fumbling, focusing at the same time on breathing, she attempts to unscrew the lid.

'Four . . . five. You're going to kill her, Susanna. You're going to kill the both of you. Six.'

Susanna sits straight – as straight as the tautness across her chest will allow. Her airways feel clearer but there is something constricting her ribcage. If she didn't know better she would swear she was having a heart attack. But she has been here before, coped with this before, which means if she focuses she can cope with it now.

'Seven.'

She raises the bottle and feeds herself a succession of sips. She tries to ignore the plasticky taste, the echo in the water of tuna sandwich.

'Eight. Nine.'

'Donald.'

It comes out as a croak and Adam, reacting, moves closer, bringing the knife with him. 'What was that? I'm on nine, Susanna. Nine and a half.'

'*Donald.*' She forces it out, almost like a cough. And somehow this helps. Her lungs draw nourishment from her breath. Her pulse is still racing but it is slowing, slower, slow enough that she can count the beats. And, again, this soothes her: the moderating rhythm of her heart. 'How did. How did you end up. With the name. Donald.'

For a beat Adam is silent, and Susanna is convinced in that instant that he will snap. That he'll construe the question as another challenge. A final, intolerable show of dissent.

Instead, abruptly, Adam laughs. It is the first time he's done so and it sounds completely spontaneous. He has a nice laugh, Susanna realizes through her fug. Deep and genuine and warm. It doesn't endear him to her. On the contrary, she finds herself hating him all the more. And she does hate him, it strikes her. Susanna, who these days never allows herself to hate anyone, would cheerfully shove Adam through the window. Never mind that the fall wouldn't kill him. He'd break his legs and then suffer all the more. *Good.* Because that laugh of his proves this isn't him. That he's *choosing* to do what he's doing rather than being subject to some inner compulsion. More than that, he used that laugh to trap Susanna's daughter. He gazed at her with those beautiful brown eyes of his and hypnotized her into thinking he was her friend. He must have done. How else would he have been able to get close?

Again Adam laughs, and this time it is his false laugh. His persona laugh. The laugh he thinks makes him sound all big and clever.

'You really want to know?' he says. 'You almost choked to death, and you're sitting there asking me how I got my middle name?'

Susanna shivers, pulls her cardigan more tightly around her. She always feels like this after suffering an episode. Weak, cold, faintly sick. She aches too. There is an arc of pain running from her fingers to her neck. Oddly (or perhaps not) it is the type of ache she remembers from when Jake was a baby. Emily never had trouble sleeping but Jake . . . sometimes Susanna would be up with him all night. Singing, pacing the nursery, patting him gently on the curve of his little hunched back. That tension across her neck the next morning, as though she had spent the night shrugging suitcases: it was exactly the same as she feels now.

Adam reads her silence as affirmation.

'OK,' Adam says. 'Why not. You want to hear about

my background? I'll tell you if you really want to know. If you really think it will help.' He perches on the edge of Susanna's desk. His anger has vanished. 'It's funny,' he says. 'You know, *tell me about your mother.*' He gestures with his eyes to their surroundings. 'It's just a shame you haven't got a couch.'

Which is interesting. Not the couch part. The fact that when he thought about telling Susanna about his background, the first thing that occurred to him was his mother. The woman he implied earlier he barely knew.

And something else. He's pleased. He *wants* to tell Susanna his story. Meaning this is all part of the game he's playing too.

'So,' he says. 'Where to begin.'

11

I could do the whole biography thing.

You know, I was born here, on this date, and spent my early years blah-di-blah-di-blah.

But I always find that tedious. Don't you? Like with famous people, their memoirs. I read a lot, true stuff mainly. Not stories – I always think what's the point? There's so much stuff that actually happened, why would you bother with anything made up? Although I bet you don't think that at all. Do you, Susanna? I bet your bedside table's stacked with novels. I don't mean Mills & Boon or, I don't know, crime stories.

Definitely not crime stories.

What I mean is Literature. With a capital L. The type of stories that don't actually have any story at all but are all about feelings and finding yourself and *meaning*. I'm sure you love books like that. Am I right? I bet I'm right. I can tell from your expression that I am.

But I started to say: memoirs. Biographies. What I'm interested in when I'm reading about someone famous is the famous bit. The bit that made me take the book out in the first place.

My parents, then. Because that's the part you want to hear about. Right, Susanna?

As far as my mother goes, there's not a lot I can tell

you. Because I was five when she died, like I said, and to be honest I can barely remember her. She –

Her name was Catherine, by the way. Catherine Geraghty.

I know she was beautiful because I've seen pictures. And I'm not just saying that because she was my mum. She had this thick brown hair and these deep blue eyes, so objectively you would have to say she was beautiful.

But before she died . . . I don't remember her ever being around. All I can remember from when I was young are small things mainly. Unimportant things. Like, a jumper I had. A teddy bear. The first time I tried Coca-Cola, which was from a half-empty can I found on the street. Not because I was poor or anything, no poorer than anyone else. Just because I was gross. But anyway, things like that. Sitting in my bedroom. Reading. Lots of reading. Playing with my cars. Being lonely, there was a lot of that as well. I remember feelings too. Being sad or, I don't know. Angry. And then, when my mother died, what I most remember is feeling nothing at all, other than glad my father was so upset.

Stephen Geraghty. That was his name. My old man. My so-called father. And his middle name was Donald as well, by the way. It must have been a family tradition or something. I don't know for certain. And to be honest I don't much care.

The weird thing was my father being with my mother at all. Because whereas she was beautiful, my old man was . . . not *ugly* exactly but he was short and he was bald, balding, and he wore these thick black glasses.

But my mother loved him, I guess, or else why would they have been together? And for so long? Because they were childhood sweethearts. That's what *he* used to claim anyway. That they were together when they were young and then they moved apart and then something happened that brought them back together. Like in a movie. That's the way he made it sound. Which I have my doubts about frankly because how could anyone ever fall in love with *him*?

Twice.

He hated me from the day I was born. I say I don't remember much from when I was small but I definitely remember that. How? Just because of the way he used to treat me. He never hit me or anything but some of the things he used to do, for example, were . . .

Wait.

My mother's death. Let's go back to that.

It was sudden. Her illness. I don't even know what she had exactly but –

You know what?

That's a lie.

I do know what she had. What it was that killed her. It was her kidneys. She got ill when she was pregnant and didn't get the right treatment. Not in time. And it damaged her. Having me. Left her vulnerable. So there you go, Susanna. Therapize *that*.

But anyway, that's what happened. She got ill and then she died. And afterwards it was just me and him.

And it's obvious why. Right? Why he hated me. It was because he blamed me for my mother being ill all

153

the time, which I guess is why she was never around. She got pre-eclampsia, it's called. When she was pregnant. But it wasn't spotted, or not soon enough anyway, and although she got better, she also never really recovered. It can affect your organs, you see. Your kidneys in particular, which is what happened eventually with my mum.

And my old man . . . as much as he hated me is the amount he adored his wife. You'd say it was sweet, I expect. True love and all that. Me, I think it's pathetic. I *know* it was. I saw it. The way he fell apart. At the funeral someone had to hold him up. One of his friends or his brother or something. No one I knew. But literally, they had to physically stop him from collapsing to the ground.

So yeah, first my mother was ill and then, at the end of it, she died. Because of me. Because of what I'd done to her. So in fairness to my old man, I guess if I was him I would've hated me too.

Some of the things he used to do.

This is what you really want to hear, isn't it, Susanna? What my father actually did to me. Because this is like . . . what's that phrase? Grist to your mill. And the other thing, I bet you get all sorts of people in here whining about how their parents resented them, blah blah blah, and I bet half the time you're thinking, yeah right. Like, they *say* their parents hated them but the only actual evidence they can point to is the fact their dad sometimes shouted maybe and their mother could get a bit stroppy. But for some people that's enough.

Enough of an excuse, I mean. Because I bet that's what most people who come to you are looking for. An excuse, basically, for why their lives are such a mess. Can't get a job? It's all my parents' fault. Can't get a girl-friend? That's my parents' fault too. Too sad to get out of bed in the morning? To take a shower and pour your-self some cornflakes? Blame my parents for squashing my self-esteem.

Seriously, I bet you get that all the time.

So what I'm saying is you probably think I'm exag-gerating. I wouldn't blame you if you –

No.

Don't.

Don't interrupt.

You asked me to tell you, so I'm telling you. So why don't you sit there and just listen?

Where was I . . .

So this one time – and I remember this clearly – we were at the park. I don't know what we were doing there because my dad never took me to the park. But we were there, for whatever reason, and these older kids started giving me hassle. They were twelve, maybe thirteen. I was ten. They took my ball and I asked for it back. They said no, obviously, and started pushing me around. I guess we were round the back of the cafe or something, or some-where anyway that no adults could see. We were, because I remember I was kicking my ball against the wall. Just on my own. Just playing on my own. And like I say, nobody could see us – nobody apart from my old man. Because *he* saw. He was sitting on a bench. A way away but close enough that I remember watching the pigeons that were pecking at his feet. Which means he saw when the older kids stole my ball and he saw them surround me when I asked for it back. He saw the biggest one hit me. He saw another one kick me in the shin. He watched when they shoved me to the ground and he didn't even move enough to scare the pigeons away when, one by one, they took turns to lean over me and *spit*.

So, yeah. *He* never hit me. But he was happy enough when other people did.

That was the last time I ever asked him for help, by the way. The last time I physically called out. Like, if I had a nightmare or something after that, I never ran crying to my father's room. I just lay in bed and dealt with it myself. It was the same at school. I got hassled at school as well but there was no point telling anyone. I didn't want to give my father the satisfaction.

This other time I got a bad tooth. It was over Christmas, which was always when my father was at his meanest. So anyway I started getting toothache and normally what you'd do is go to the dentist. Right? But I was eight at the time, just turned, so I would have needed somebody to take me. Cue my father. But instead, what he did is, he let me suffer. And toothache for me is basically the worst kind of pain. It –

Look.

Do you see?

I'm getting goosebumps just talking about it.

And I don't know if it's because the tooth is part of your jaw, connected through your bones to all the rest of you, but what I find is that when your tooth hurts it's not just the tooth that throbs. You must have had toothache, you must know what I'm talking about, the way the pain gets channelled all around your body. It hurts to walk, to talk, to breathe, to *look*. It hurts when you're just lying still. *Especially* when you're just lying still. And obviously you can forget about eating or drinking.

My father must have known that too. He must have known how much pain I was in. In fact it's not even in question. He *did* know. I *told* him. But there was no school for me to go to, nobody else around who would have seen, so as far as he was concerned it was an opportunity, a chance to let me suffer. To punish me, basically, for something I didn't even know I'd done.

He took me to the dentist in the end but claimed when we got there that the ache had only started that morning. Three days he let me suffer with it. I was in my room for most of that time, living off milk and orange juice. Room temperature because if it was cold it was like someone had come at me with pliers.

But that's how it went. It was less that he actively hurt me, more that he did nothing to keep me safe. It was like he ignored me. Except not like that because if he'd ignored me I would have preferred it. If he'd ignored me I would have known where I stood. Because he could be nice. Not nice but normal. Like, he made me dinner most evenings, made sure I took a sandwich to school. He did the stuff other adults would have noticed if he hadn't. The stuff *kids* notice, though: my father did none of those things. He didn't hug me or kiss me or comfort me or *love* me. He made me feel small. Made me feel like I was a burden. Even the nice stuff he did, the normal stuff – he did it out of spite. To remind me how much I *owed* him. How much I'd ruined his life.

Because that's the thing. That's basically what it came down to. It was something I only found out when I was older. I didn't *find out*. Or I did but only because my father *told* me, which to my mind isn't quite the same thing. But what he told me was they never wanted me in the first place. Neither of them.

He was blunt like that, just spelled it out. This was after my mother died, when he was sure I was old enough to understand. He blamed religion. They were both Catholic, him and my mum. And it was because of the religion thing that they didn't get rid of me. When they found out my mother was pregnant. They weren't married then either, so that's like a double sin, isn't it? Or it would have been, if she'd had an abortion as well.

Whatever.

The point is they kept me and I ruined my mother's life. She had to give up work, my father told me. She had to sacrifice her career. Because of her health. That was one of his favourite words, by the way. *Sacrifice.* When he was talking to me about what he'd done or what my mother had done, for my sake I mean, it was all 'we sacrificed this' and 'she sacrificed that' and 'you, look at you, you've never said one word to show you're grateful.'

When he said that once – later on, this was – I remember I answered back, said I didn't know what he expected me to be grateful *for*, and that was the only time he *did* hit me. Slapped me, right across the face. Which, again, pathetic. Slapping me like that. Like a little girl would, not a man.

But when he told me about how they'd never wanted me in the first place, that's when it all started to make sense.

I remember I was in my dad's bedroom when he said it. My mum and dad's room, it had been, and I was looking through some of her things. There were boxes on the top shelf of the cupboard that I knew I wasn't supposed to look in but I'd done it anyway and I'd found a load of old photographs, just of my mum when she was younger, with friends of hers, relatives of hers, I guess, her mum and dad – people, basically, I'd never met. And that's when he found me. 'Get out!' he started yelling. 'Get your filthy little hands off your mother's things!' And I argued, said I had as much right to see them as he did. And my father was like, 'You have no right! None whatsoever!' And it went on like that until basically he just came out with it. 'She never loved you, you know. She never wanted you. You were a curse. You were a curse and in the end you killed her!'

And it was ... it was like one of those moments when suddenly you just get it. Why I was always so lonely. Why I can barely remember anything about my mother and why I wasn't upset or anything when she died.

I know what you're thinking, Susanna.

I do. Again. I know.

You're thinking you finally understand. Right? Poor Adam. His parents never loved him. It's no wonder he turned out the way he did. All angry, all *damaged*, all bursting into some random stranger's office. I bet you're even wondering whether you can help me. Whether you can *cure* me. And who knows? Maybe in normal circumstances you could.

The thing is, though, that's not the end of the story. I think you know it isn't.

The *real* end is: it was all a lie. A clever one because it was hidden in truth. Like, my father blaming me for my mother's death? Him saying they never wanted me in the first place? He did. They didn't. But that wasn't all. It wasn't even the half of it.

Was it, Susanna?

12

'Let's take a break.'

'What? Why?'

'Because I'm thirsty. It's all this talking. You're all right, you've got your bottle of water, but I haven't had anything to drink since I got here.'

'There's a jug of tap water on the table beside you. The glasses are clean if that's what you're worried about.'

Adam wrinkles his nose. 'I don't drink water. Can never really see the point.' He gestures towards the door. 'You must have a little kitchen area out back. Haven't you got any, like, juice or something?'

'Juice?'

'Come on,' Adam says, standing. 'You can show me around.'

'But . . .' Susanna is . . . disappointed? *Really?* She checks and finds that she is. She doesn't want to be here, would give anything to be somewhere else, but she was enthralled by what Adam was telling her. She supposes it is just as Adam said. Stories like his are grist to her mill. And even though she has heard variations of the same tale before, each time it is totally unique.

'I would have thought you'd be dying to escape this room,' Adam says. 'Aren't you feeling a bit claustrophobic? A bit, you know. Trapped?'

Susanna stands, wobbling slightly as she does so. Adam uses the knife to gesture for her to lead the way.

Geraghty. Adam Geraghty. Catherine Geraghty. Stephen Geraghty. Geraghty. Geraghty.

The name means nothing to Susanna. She hasn't spent a great deal of time dwelling on it until now because she has been assuming it must have been made up. There is still a chance it could have been of course (*it was all a lie . . .*) but she has seen Adam's driving licence, his bank cards, and anyway there's no telling what Adam meant. *What* was a lie? Which part? Not who his parents were, not the way he grew up. Susanna is convinced his story had the ring of truth. Besides which, she has seen his acting. And though he is better at it than he gave himself credit for, there are certain things, in therapy, that can't be faked. Adam's intensity once he started talking, for example. Susanna would have liked the opportunity to dig deeper, which is why she is so frustrated by this interruption. She is curious, yes, that's part of it. But also she remains convinced that the sooner she understands Adam, the sooner her daughter will be safe.

'It's just through here.' Susanna leads Adam along the landing. She can hear him behind her and she is trying not to think about the knife. It is levelled at her kidneys, she imagines, and if she were to abruptly stop moving, Adam would walk it straight through her.

She bears right and weaves past Alina's desk. 'This way.'

The kitchenette is opposite the staff toilet and isn't

actually much bigger. There are two cupboards and a sink, as well as a kettle, a mini fridge and, tucked in a corner on the counter, a tatty, soup-encrusted microwave. The soup is Ruth's doing. Even though Ruth's surgery is spotless, elsewhere in her life she is a self-confessed slob. 'When it seizes up I'll buy us all a new one,' she told Susanna when Susanna happened to mention the microwave's condition. 'Life's too short to be scrubbing minestrone.'

'I'm fairly sure there isn't any juice or anything,' Susanna says but when she looks across her shoulder she realizes Adam is no longer there.

'Just pick something for me,' he calls. From the sound of it he has continued along the landing into Ruth's surgery. 'Anything with flavour.'

Susanna is momentarily discombobulated. She is alone. How odd it feels to be standing here alone. Her heartbeat accelerates as once again she has the urge to run. Is Adam testing her, she wonders? Or is he taunting her, reminding her that she is tethered here no matter how much slack he gives the rope?

She opens a cupboard, retrieves the Nescafé from behind Ruth's tin of biscuits. 'You mean coffee or –'

'Not coffee.'

What is he doing? He sounds distracted, as though something has captured his attention.

Susanna turns to the mini fridge, which she insists they keep cleaner than the microwave. Even so it emits the smell of something curdled, which may in fact be embedded in the fridge itself. They bought it off eBay and it hasn't worked properly since they plugged it in.

163

Inside there is milk, an apple, a piece of cheese wrapped in cling film. Something pasta-y in Tupperware – Alina's, almost certainly – and, behind that, a can of fizzy drink.

'There's a Diet Coke in the fridge,' Susanna calls.

There is a pause. '*Diet?*' Adam responds.

Susanna waits.

'Fine,' says Adam at last, getting back to whatever it is he's doing. 'Just so long as it's cold.'

Susanna presses her palm against the can. It's not. It's basically the same temperature as her hand. But it will do. Susanna may have no choice other than to play Adam's games but she'll be damned if she's going to act like his waitress.

It is as she turns to leave that her eyes catch on the draining board. She freezes. Her gaze flicks up, towards the empty doorway, and then back again. There, beside the washing-up sponge, is a little paring knife. It is curved and viciously sharp. Susanna knows because she has a scar on her left thumb from the last time she used it. The knife would look like a toy, Susanna suspects, set beside Adam's but it would be just as effective against someone's jugular and this one would fit up her sleeve. Susanna wouldn't have imagined, even an hour ago, that she would seriously contemplate wielding a weapon but the longer this has gone on, the more she has come to realize how unlikely it is to end on her terms. She needs a back-up plan. Huh. She needs a *plan*, is what she needs, but where is the harm in having a contingency?

Adam could see: there's the harm. He could discover

the knife and decide there and then that this game of his has gone on long enough.

More than the fear, though, the thing that makes Susanna hesitate is Adam's story. It is ridiculous, she knows, but she cannot suppress her instinct for sympathy. It is ingrained in her the way that odour is ingrained in their little refrigerator. It permeates her very being, sits at the core of everything she does. It's like the lying. Since Jake she has done everything in her power to resist the urge to cast blame. First, always, she endeavours to attempt to *understand*. It was something about herself – one of the only things – of which she was proud. It gave her strength, she thought, although in these circumstances, clearly, it is a weakness.

She straightens. Honestly, she chastises herself, what did you expect? Of *course* Adam has a past. Of course he wouldn't have had a happy childhood. People who do the sort of thing he's doing, don't. It doesn't give him an excuse. Plenty of people go through worse and come out of it only wanting to do *good*.

And Emily. Think of Emily. Who is more important to you, your daughter, or this stranger who is effectively holding his own knife against Emily's throat?

Susanna checks the door again. She stretches out her hand. She feels dampness from the draining board as she clasps the knife and –

'*Boo!*'

Susanna spins and sees a monster at the door. It has goggling red eyes and a claw-shaped nose and teeth so prominent they could be tusks. She screams and falls backwards against the sink. There is the sound of metal clattering on the parquet floor. It severs the cackle of Adam's laughter.

'What was that?'

Adam removes the mask.

'What did you drop, Susanna?'

He looks and he sees.

'Oh no. No, no, *no*.'

He bends and he reaches, then stands up clutching what he has found. He looks furious, exactly like a spoilt child. 'It's going to be all fizzy,' he says. 'If I open it now it'll spill out everywhere.'

Adam examines the can in his hand. There is a dent in the rim where it landed.

Susanna attempts to shuffle sideways. The paring knife is pressed tight but visible against her wrist.

'Oh well. I suppose it was my fault as much as yours.' Adam looks at Susanna and grins. 'Sorry,' he says, waving the mask. 'I couldn't resist. I saw this hanging in your friend's office when I was here last time.'

'When . . . what?' Susanna tries to slip the knife into her sleeve. But it is awkward with her wrist bent backwards and the blade feels hooked around a thread. If she isn't careful she really *will* drop it.

'When I was here before,' Adam repeats. 'Last month, this was. I booked myself a check-up with . . . Ruth, is it? I liked her, Susanna. She was very complimentary about my teeth.' Adam flashes her another grin. This time it looks as much a growl. 'Although I admit that wasn't the real reason I came,' he goes on. 'I wanted a

166

chance to look around. To get the lie of the land, sort of thing. But anyway, that's when I noticed this mask. I've been dying to try it on ever since.'

The mask is Himalayan. Ruth went trekking there after her second divorce. It is a hideous thing but Ruth insists on hanging it in her surgery. 'If nothing else to set a good example,' she told Susanna, as she ran a finger along the monstrously impressive teeth.

'What have you got there?'

All at once Adam is moving forward, the mask dropping to his side. The knife is pressed tight against Susanna's arm. She is certain there's no way he could see it.

'What? Nothing. Where?'

'*There*, Susanna.'

Adam is frowning again. His arm extends forward and grazes hers.

'Biscuits?'

He has picked up the tin that Susanna took out to reach the Nescafé.

'They're Ruth's,' Susanna stammers. It is the only thing she can think to say.

Adam tucks the biscuit tin under one arm. He slips the mask back on his head, so that he is wearing it this time like a cap.

'I *like* Ruth, Susanna. I really do.'

Susanna swallows. The knife, finally, slides up her sleeve.

'Now, let's get back to it,' Adam says. 'Shall we?'

13

They are seated back in front of the fireplace. The room feels even smaller now than it did before, the air stale and fetid. The shadows are beginning to lengthen, like a crowd of figures closing in. Adam holds out the can of Diet Coke in the space between them – closer to Susanna than to him – with his fingertip curled around the ring pull.

'Brace yourself . . .'

He pops it open and the Coke bubbles up and over. He is hoping Susanna will flinch but instead all she does is watch.

Adam laughs even so, leans to slurp up the froth, then noisily sips from the can.

He makes a face.

'Eurgh.' He sips again, grimaces again. 'Seriously, what's the point of Coke without the sugar? I'm probably going to need some of that water after all, just to wash away the taste.'

He sets the can down beside the jug of water and dangles his Coke-covered hand as he checks around for some way to clean it. He looks at Susanna, then proceeds to dunk his hand in the water jug. It comes out dripping, and he wipes it on the fabric of his armchair.

This time Susanna cannot help showing her disgust. Adam has grown in confidence since Ruth left and though his antics have been juvenile at best, they have also felt surprisingly intimidating. It occurred to Susanna before that Adam's upbringing had damaged him and the thing she wonders about now is how badly. Maybe there *is* no getting through to him. Maybe the knife tucked up her sleeve really is Susanna's best chance of getting out of this.

'Your father . . .' she ventures, even so. Because to abandon hope like that would be to abandon the beliefs she's fostered for the past fifteen years. It would be to deny the single positive legacy left over from the life of her son. 'Is it possible you misinterpreted his feelings towards you?'

Adam is immediately on edge. 'What do you mean?'

It is a dangerous topic for Susanna to address and normally she would not attempt to do so this directly. She would come at it obliquely, attempting to steer the discussion so that the client raised the subject himself. But that would be in a normal session, with a normal client. Here, now, *normal* isn't a restriction that applies.

'You were very young, Adam. You said as much yourself. And your father . . . grief does very strange things to people. More than strange. It's one of the most powerful emotions there is. *Emotion*, in fact, doesn't begin to cover it.'

Adam is listening. At the very least, Susanna has got his attention.

'Believe me, I've experienced it myself,' Susanna goes on. 'When you lose someone . . . it's not that you change. It's that the world does. Your senses, your feelings – everything warps, becomes distorted. Colours seem tarnished, smells curdle, taste becomes almost non-existent. Grief: it's like a drug. It's so powerful it's almost . . . hallucinogenic.'

Up until this point Adam has been wearing the mask atop his head but he reaches up and slips it off. 'Hallucinogenic?' he echoes. 'Meaning you saw things, Susanna? Is that what you're telling me?'

Susanna remains completely still. Something about her reaction, though, convinces Adam that he's right.

'What did you see, I wonder? Did you see him, Susanna? Did you see *her*?'

Susanna stares. How long has it been since she pictured *her*? How long since she allowed herself to?

'Do you see them now, I wonder? Does Jake haunt you even now?'

He doesn't. He hasn't, not for a long time. But just for an instant, looking at Adam, his face morphs into Susanna's son's.

Susanna blinks and the effect is gone. In place of the vision, though, Susanna hears a voice – the same voice that whispered to her before.

You know him.

Susanna clears her throat, recovers her posture. 'It must have been very hard for your father,' she forces herself to say. 'The stress of your mother's illness. The way he must have felt after she died. Don't you think?'

From appearing pleased at his insight into Susanna's afflictions, Adam suddenly seems distinctly uncomfortable. He doesn't want to think about his father as a human being. As someone frail, fragile, a victim himself.

'To lose a partner like that, so early in life,' Susanna presses. 'Particularly when you have a young child.'

Adam bridles. 'You're saying it's my fault? The way my father treated me?'

'Absolutely not. What I'm saying is that maybe your father's behaviour was more complicated than simple love or hate. Maybe for him the two emotions got confused. Like crossed wires.'

Adam's expression doesn't alter. But it is at least fixed now, a wall Susanna can see she must find a way to breach.

'Most of us, when we imagine diametrical opposites, tend to picture a horizontal line. But maybe, rather than a line, what we should be thinking of is a loop, where each extreme threatens to overlap the other.'

There is a twitch of curiosity in Adam's eyes.

'Take, I don't know. Politics, for example. The far right and far left often end up being indistinguishable. And hot and cold. Have you ever had that feeling when you touch something freezing and you think at first you've actually been scalded?'

Adam shifts and Susanna knows he has.

'Well, maybe it's the same with love and hate. In fact I'm sure it is. And that's what I mean by crossed wires. It's no exaggeration to say that your father, in his grief, experienced an emotional earthquake. It's no wonder that love and hate for him became so confused. Probably everything else he was feeling did as well. And I'm not saying it's your fault and I'm not trying to claim the way he treated you wasn't his. But maybe it wasn't quite as black and white as you've come to believe.'

Susanna waits. She watches Adam, who sinks a fraction into his chair. He is scowling but it is as much an expression of concentration.

'There's that phrase,' he says at last. 'Isn't there? "There's a fine line between love and hate." Something like that, anyway.'

'Exactly. That's it exactly.' Susanna would like to say more, to drive the point home, but she knows that it will resonate more if Adam develops it himself.

'So are you saying my father loved me after all? That . . . that I got it all wrong?'

'I'm saying it's not easy being a parent, even in the most stable of circumstances. Just look at me, for example. At what happened to us. Jake had a father *and* a mother, and even so . . . Well. You know exactly how things turned out for Jake.'

It is an opening; a chance for Adam to switch the focus back to her. But he doesn't take it.

'I guess I've never thought about it that way. About my father . . . suffering . . . as much as I did.'

Susanna feels a rush of adrenalin. She has experienced something similar in session before, when a client appears on the verge of a breakthrough Susanna had given up hope was ever coming. This time, though, the rush is laced with fear, hope, doubt, dread: a cocktail of competing emotions that makes the whole sensation that much more potent.

She takes a breath.

'And remember, Adam, there's your own grief to take into account as well. To lose your mother, at the age you did . . . I simply can't imagine what that must have been like for you.'

Adam's expression hardens. 'I told you –'

'I know, I know. You said you didn't feel anything. You also said you can barely remember her. So what I'm wondering is, maybe some of those memories of yours have been repressed. Maybe your love for your mother got tangled the way your father's did, and since then, this anger you feel, maybe that's a reaction to the grief as well.'

'How do you mean?'

'I mean, grief has to go somewhere. It needs an outlet. Your father vented his on you. Yours turned into this fury you're feeling, which you in turn vented on your father. And on . . . Well.' Susanna doesn't finish. She doesn't need to.

'On you,' Adam says for her, and he sounds almost ashamed.

Susanna meets his eye. Her lips twitch as she raises a shoulder. Adam watches her for a moment, then turns his gaze, unseeing, towards the floor.

It makes sense. It genuinely does. That Adam should admire Jake, yes, because Susanna can see how to someone like Adam, Jake might seem a kindred spirit. Confused, angry, let down by everyone around him. And Susanna is the parent who failed her son, the very personification of everything Adam has taught himself to resent. If his mother is dead and his father is for some reason beyond his reach too, Adam's fury has to go somewhere. But if Susanna can show him that his rage is misplaced, that instead of feeling angry he might simply allow himself to grieve . . .

She feels that drumbeat of her heart again. She is scrutinizing Adam intently, trying not to show that she is. Is she right? Has she got through to him? *What is he thinking?*

In the end she can't resist breaking the silence.

'Adam?'

He looks up, giving the impression he had forgotten Susanna was there. 'Sorry. I'm trying to get my head around it, that's all. Around everything you've just been explaining.'

Susanna forces herself to stay quiet, to give Adam time.

'So . . . I mean . . . if you're right . . . what should I do?'

Let me go! Let Emily *go!*

Susanna wants to scream it. It takes all of her self-control to hold it in.

Instead, she says what feels like the hardest sentence she has ever had to utter. 'I can't tell you what to do, Adam.' She takes another deep breath to try to steady herself. 'I can only help you try to figure out why you're doing it,' she goes on. 'What it is you really want to achieve.'

She is on the edge of her seat, Susanna realizes. She is leaning forward, her elbows on her knees, her fingertips inches away from Adam. Susanna can't see his eyes but from the way his hand is positioned around his mouth, he looks like he is on the brink of tears.

Which is the first indication Susanna has that something is wrong.

'You know, if what you're saying is true,' Adam says, 'it changes everything. What I'm feeling, what I'm doing here. Just . . . everything.'

He peeks at Susanna through his fringe.

Susanna pulls away. She feels her fingers curl, her jawbone clamp and then tighten.

'All this time,' Adam says, and he gives a sob. 'All this anguish, and the only thing I needed, it turns out, was to find someone who'd listen. Someone who'd show me the way.' Adam peeks again. His expression is a parody of gratitude. 'Someone like you, Susanna,' he says.

'Stop.'

Susanna turns slightly away but not enough that she fails to see Adam grin. He sits straighter and pulls back his fringe, then leans to catch Susanna's eye. He winces, as though embarrassed.

'Was it the sobbing?' he says. 'Should I try it again without the sobbing?'

He doesn't wait for Susanna to answer.

He coughs, clears his throat, then leans forward, reassuming his position. 'All this time!' he intones, this time with melodramatic flair. 'All this anguish! The only thing I needed, it turns out, was to find someone like you, Susanna! Someone who'd listen!' He pauses, letting the words resonate, then collapses into a phony paroxysm of tears. His left hand flashes out and grasps Susanna's, gripping it so tightly it hurts.

'Let go of me.'

Adam, head down, continues his wailing. Susanna struggles to pull away.

'I said, let *go*.'

She breaks free, abruptly, and Adam's crying – his performance – dissolves into laughter. His amusement is genuine but his laughter isn't warm the way it was before. Rather, it is how she has always imagined Scott laughing. Pete and Charlie too. The delight is inflected with cruelty, the pleasure derived purely from having caused pain. Watching him, listening to him, Susanna has never loathed anyone as much as, right now, she loathes Adam. She is this close – *this* close – to taking her chances with the paring knife. In fact she would impale him quite cheerfully. With her knife, his, either, *both*.

'Sorry.'

Adam's laughter dwindles to a splutter.

'Sorry,' he repeats. 'I couldn't resist. You seemed so excited. So sure you'd *cured* me.'

Susanna was wrong, before. There is one person she hates more than she hates Adam. It is only the thought of Emily that stops her plunging the knife into herself.

Adam tilts his head, affecting disappointment that Susanna evidently can't take a joke.

'Don't be like that,' he says. 'Don't be angry. I said, didn't I? I *told* you. Everything you've been so busy analysing: it was all a lie. Not the way I was brought up. Not my mother and father hating me. But the *reason* they did . . .' Adam watches to see if Susanna has caught on. She still doesn't have a clue what he is talking about.

She can tell she's pouting but she's powerless to stop herself.

'Seriously, Susanna. You're being too hard on yourself. You can hardly be expected to fix someone if you don't know the reason they're broken.'

Give up, Susanna is thinking. *You're not going to beat him, so you might as well give up. This . . . hypothesizing. This* guesswork*: it's only making things worse.*

'Here, have a biscuit.' Adam is holding out the tin he stole from Ruth. He shakes it and Susanna hears a clatter of crumbs. 'No? Suit yourself.' Adam dips into the tin himself. He stuffs a digestive into his mouth, then resumes talking as he chews. 'How about this?' He chases the biscuit with a sip of Coke, which elicits another grimace when he swallows. 'How about I finish my story and then you can therapize away.'

Susanna settles back soundlessly in her seat.

'So . . .' Adam brushes his knees of crumbs. 'I ran away. That's how it ends. Or begins, I guess you could say.' His tongue probes biscuit from his teeth. 'I was sixteen by the time I did, so this was just last year. I would have left sooner but, honestly? I was scared. Of just about everything really. Of life. The world. I wasn't streetwise at all. I had no friends to teach me. There were kids I knew but no one I *talked* to. So I was scared and I was alone and, much as I hated my father, I didn't see that I had anywhere else to go.'

Adam is watching Susanna carefully, alert, she suspects, for any sign of ridicule.

'And the other reason I stayed?' Adam goes on. 'My

education. Because I was scared, I was ignorant, but I wasn't stupid.' He pauses and his gaze tightens. 'You can see that, can't you, Susanna? That I'm not stupid?'

Susanna looks back at him and nods.

'I wanted to finish school. My GCSEs, at any rate. And I did, I passed them all, and the moment I found out I packed my bags. Before I left, though, I needed money. I knew my old man had some in the house because he hated banks, hated any kind of *institution*. Probably because he'd spent some time in prison when he was younger but that's a whole other story. So anyway, I figured he owed me. Right? And he was always magicking tenners from somewhere, so I reckoned I was due basically whatever cash I could find.'

Adam carefully picks up his knife.

'Also, I needed ID. Documents of some kind, just to prove I was me. I knew I didn't have a passport but there had to be something. My birth certificate or whatever. And again, I knew all that stuff would be somewhere but it was like with the money: I had no idea where my father kept it.'

The knife in Adam's hand appears so much more threatening than Susanna's. It is bigger, sharper, meaner. Susanna's, against her wrist, feels no more menacing now than a toothpick.

'So I ransacked the house. Literally. Started with the kitchen, made as much mess as I could, and worked my way up to my father's bedroom. It was childish, I know, turning the house upside down like that, but it was fun. *Therapeutic*,' he adds with something like a wink. 'Hurling the bag of flour at the wall, slicing up my father's mattress. I got so into it, at one point I almost forgot what I was supposed to be doing.'

Adam's hand has tightened around the knife handle and somehow Susanna understands that it is the very knife he used to slash his father's bedding. And that he has been carrying it with him ever since.

'I didn't find anything, though,' Adam goes on. 'A couple of quid down the back of the sofa but that wouldn't have even covered my bus fare. But the thing was, I'd overlooked my mother's shelf. The one I told you about before? With her belongings? It was so ingrained in me not to touch it I guess subconsciously I must have considered it off-limits.'

Adam stops talking. His eyes sparkle with anticipation, as though he is about to draw back the curtain.

'So I got on a chair, and I pulled myself up so I could see into the cupboard . . . and guess what I found there? In a box tucked right at the back of the shelf, behind all those dusty old photos.'

Susanna, all of a sudden, doesn't want to know.

'Money, yes. Almost a grand, as it happened. But what else, Susanna? Can you guess what else?'

She shakes her head, as much a ward against what's coming as a response. 'The . . . documents,' she says. 'Your birth certificate?'

Even as she says it, Susanna feels herself sickening. There is a dread budding in her stomach.

Adam beams.

'My birth certificate. That's right. *Both* my birth certificates. The fake one . . . and the real one. And that's what I meant about it all being a lie. My mother's name wasn't Catherine Geraghty. It was Alison. Alison *Birch.*'

Susanna opens her mouth uselessly. She shakes her head once more, uselessly. It's not possible, she tells herself. It's *not.*

'You understand,' Adam says. 'Don't you? You get it. *Finally.*'

He lets go of the knife, reclines in his chair. He laughs on an exhalation of breath.

'To be honest, I was getting a little worried. And I'm disappointed that it took you so long. But I guess we got there in the end.'

Susanna's hand is wrapped across her mouth. She peers at Adam over her fingertips. *She knew him.* She told herself she knew him and she did.

And her theory. She was right. In spite of the lies, in spite of Adam's misdirection, *she was right.*

Adam watches her watching him.

'So,' he says, with that oh-so-familiar schoolboy grin. 'Now that we've got that out of the way, perhaps we can get back to the story.'

'The story?'

'*Jake*'s story, Susanna. We've discussed how adept he was at making friends. We've established that you never really loved him, not the way you clearly love Emily.'

Adam allows Susanna the space to interject. She

couldn't say anything coherent if her life depended on it. Which, quite possibly, it does.

'Now we just need to fill in the gaps,' Adam goes on – and he reaches into his messenger bag and pulls out a ragged stack of paper.

Emily

22 August 2017

I didn't think I'd ever feel this happy again. After yesterday and the day before and obviously that day on the common . . . I've just been so worried. I haven't slept and I've barely eaten and I've been ignoring Frankie when she's called. Like it was her fault. You know? And Mum too. I've been snapping at Mum. She's been trying to get me to leave my room, to come downstairs, to go for a walk, to sit in the garden in the sunshine, just *anything* other than lying on my bed staring at the ceiling and listening to misery playlists on Spotify.

Mum figures I've had an argument with Frankie, which is basically what it feels like times a thousand. What it *felt* like rather because today, guess what he did? Adam, I mean, obviously. He texted me and asked me to meet him at the park, the one round the corner from my house. He didn't say why, so what I'm thinking is he's going to break up with me. Not that we're even together at this point, not officially, but that just makes it even worse. You know, that's it's over before it's even really begun.

But when I get there, he's standing there with this single white rose.

'Hey,' he says, when I come up to him.

'Hey,' I tell him back.

There's a pause, and then we both start talking at the same time.

'Look, I –'

'I've been meaning to –'

And we laugh. Both of us. Together. And the best part is, we don't need to say anything after that.

He takes me to this place out of town. This big country house. We go on the bus and because it's busy we don't really talk much the whole journey, which in the end takes almost an hour. But it's nice, actually, just looking over at each other and smiling. Also, the *waiting* to talk. It's like walking home with a magazine and a bar of chocolate.

Adam pays and we go in. Not into the house, which is just this big old stone building that's half in ruins anyway. Instead we go to the garden, out back. And the garden at this place, it's like a whole other world. A *secret* garden, like in the book, which I always loved when I was a kid. Also, it's huge. Endless really, because at some point at the bottom of the hill the garden turns into countryside. But you can't see any of it from the front of the house, which is what I mean about it being secret. There are paths leading this way and that, and types of trees I've never even seen before, and this amazing variety of flowers. The smell is *incredible*.

'Wow,' I say when I see it.

Adam grins at me and takes my hand. 'I wanted to

bring you a whole bunch of those,' he tells me as we walk, gesturing to the rose in my hand. I've carried it all the way with me on the bus. 'But I figured you'd have to put them somewhere and your mum . . . Well. She'd see and she'd figure something was up.' He looks at me bashfully. 'So seeing as I couldn't bring flowers to you,' he says, 'I figured I'd bring you to the flowers.'

He stops as we come out into this meadow, and makes this grand gesture with his arms. And the feeling, what I'm feeling, is that everything in the garden has been planted just for me.

I turn away so Adam can't see me blush.

'Thank you,' I say. 'I mean it. *Thank you.*'

And Adam just gives this little smile.

We walk for ages. Just ambling along the paths, through the flowers, around the edge of this little lake. Just chatting.

'I had no idea this place even existed,' I say. 'I had no idea there were places like this in the entire *world*, let alone so close to home. I thought you only found them in, like . . .'

'. . . stories,' Adam says, as though he's reading my thoughts. Seriously, it's almost *biological* or something, we're so in tune.

'Right,' I say, grinning at him. I look around, out across the lake, taking it all in. The sun on the surface of the water is like glitter, sparkling in the ripples from the breeze. 'Honestly,' I say, 'my mum would *love* it here.'

'Yeah? Your mum likes flowers too?'

I bump him gently as we walk. '*All* women like flowers, silly,' I say. 'But yeah, she loves anything to do with nature. Trees, fields, flowers. And the sky, especially at night.'

'Yeah?'

'Yeah. And the whole nature thing, I think it feeds into what she does. She's a counsellor. I've told you that, right?'

Adam narrows his eyes like he can't quite remember. 'Maybe,' he says. 'I think so.'

'Anyway. Counselling, nature, the environment. She thinks it's all part of one big whole. Like, human nature is part of just, like, *normal* nature. You know?' I check to see if Adam gets it. 'I'm not explaining it very well,' I say. 'If you asked her, Mum would probably explain it better.'

'Maybe one day I will,' Adam says. Then: 'Tell me about her. Your mum, I mean.'

I shrug. 'There's not much to tell.'

'What about her job, though? The . . . counselling, did you say? That sounds interesting.'

I look at him to see if he's joking. 'Really?'

'Really. I mean, unless it's, like, top secret or something. Like, your mum's got some secret identity.' He pauses, looks at me. Grins. 'Like she's a spy, I mean,' he says, 'and the counselling thing is just a cover.'

'Ha. Right. Like anything in my life is that exciting.'

We walk on for a minute and then he asks me again. 'Seriously. Tell me. I'd like to hear.'

I'm still doubtful, still thinking he's humouring me,

but in the end I do. I talk about Mum, about what she does. And you know what? It turns out that counselling isn't as boring as I thought it was.

'Whoa,' Adam says, when he's finished listening. 'I bet as a counsellor you could really mess someone up. Put ideas into their heads, get them thinking there's something wrong with them when there isn't. That sort of thing.'

And yeah, it's a joke, but it's the one time he tries to be funny that I don't laugh. 'My mum would *never* do that,' I say. 'She's the most caring, most honest person I've ever met.'

And Adam, then, gives me this look.

'What?' I say, a bit defensive.

'Nothing,' he goes. 'Sorry. I wasn't taking the piss.'

I twitch a smile at him, embarrassed. 'S'OK,' I say. 'I know you weren't. It's just, she takes it so seriously, that's all. The counselling. I think she'd get upset if I didn't take it seriously too.'

Adam nods, like he totally gets it. 'It sounds like you love her very much.'

Which I guess I frown at. 'Course,' I say. 'I mean, she's a pain in the arse sometimes but only because she tries so hard to keep me safe. Why? Don't you love your mum?'

Adam shrugs then. 'To be honest I never really knew her. She died when I was young.'

Which makes me feel like a total idiot. You know, for bringing it up. I want to say something to make it better but I don't know what.

'What about your dad?' Adam asks me after a moment.

'My dad?'

'Is he around? You live with your mum, you said. Just you and her. But do you see him?'

'Nope. Never.'

'How come?'

'He ditched me and Mum when I was a baby. Which, as far as I'm concerned: good riddance. Right? If he's the kind of bloke to do something like that?'

Adam nods. 'I never knew my father either,' he says. 'My real father, I mean.'

I stop walking. We're back by the meadow, near where we started. 'Really? So who did you live with? After, like . . .' I trail off, wishing I'd never started the sentence.

'After my mum died?' Adam says, rescuing me. 'My stepdad, I guess you'd call him. Who, basically, was a fucking arsehole.'

Adam's expression goes sort of dark then, a bit like it did that day in the park when he first saw that little boy crying.

'Wow,' I say. 'Sorry. I guess that must really have sucked.'

Adam shrugs, like it did, yeah, but what can you do?

Poor Adam. Poor baby.

'He was a liar,' Adam goes, out of the blue. I mean, I'm not expecting him to say anything after that, not on the subject of his stepdad at least, but out of nowhere, suddenly, he does. 'A coward and a liar,' he says. 'He lied to me pretty much my whole life.'

'Lied to you? What about?'

He looks at me, opens his mouth, then shakes his head, like it's all too complicated to explain. 'Everything. Everything and anything.' We've started walking again but now Adam stops and turns to face me. 'Can you imagine, though? Not being able to trust your own parents? The people who are supposed to love you. Can you imagine how you'd feel if you found out they'd lied to you pretty much from the day you were born?'

And what I'm thinking is, Jesus. You know? Like, what could his stepdad have lied about that would make Adam that upset?

All I say is, 'No. I can't imagine it.'

Adam gives this little sniff.

'I'm lucky, I guess,' I go on. 'My mum can be a pain in the arse, just like I said. She always wants to know everything about who I'm spending time with, who my friends are, where we hang out. Just *everything*, you know? But she loves me. More than anything. And there's no way she'd ever lie to me. She always tries so hard not to lie to *anyone*.'

Adam's smiling now, sort of to himself, but I'm just pleased I've managed to distract him from thinking about his stepdad.

'You must be curious, though,' Adam goes, after a moment. He's looking out across the meadow. 'About your dad, I mean. I would be, I think. If I was in your position. Didn't you ever want to try to find him?'

I shrug. 'Not really. I used to want to. But not any more. I don't need him. Not when I've got my mum.'

Adam looks at me, then looks away.

'And anyway you are,' I say.

'Huh?'

'You *are* in the same position I am. With your real dad?' I grin at him, waiting for him to catch on. To realize how *perfect* that is, that our backgrounds are so identical.

'Oh,' Adam goes. 'Right. Yeah. I guess I am.'

I bump him again, to chide him or whatever for not realizing.

'So are *you*?' I ask him.

'Am I what?'

'Curious. About your real dad.'

He shrugs, smiles, but you can tell he's making an effort because the smile doesn't quite reach his eyes. 'A bit.'

'Do you think you'd ever try to find him?'

Adam stops. He pauses, just for a second, then turns to face me. 'One day,' he says. 'Maybe.' He tucks my hair gently around my ear. 'You know, if the opportunity were to ever present itself.'

I think – hope! – he's about to kiss me, but instead all he does is just stare. Like, *properly* deeply into my eyes.

It's so intense I have to look away.

'Come on,' I say, and I tug his hand.

'What? Where?'

I've startled him, I can tell, and I grin at him to try to get him to stop frowning.

'Come *on*,' I insist, and I start pulling him into the middle of the meadow.

'I think we're supposed to stick to the paths.'

'It's fine,' I say, 'don't be such a baby.' And once we're in the middle of the meadow I pull him down on to the ground. When we're lying like that among the flowers, we're completely hidden from view.

'Emily . . .' Adam says, in a voice a bit like one Mum would use.

'Re*lax*,' I say, 'no one can see us.'

'No, I know, but . . .'

'Kiss me.'

'What, I . . .'

'*Kiss* me.'

Adam swallows. He shuts his eyes. And then he kisses me, finally, and it's tentative, worried almost, but it's also about the most delicious thing I've ever tasted.

When I open *my* eyes, Adam's are already open too.

'We should go away somewhere,' he says.

'Go away?'

His expression has gone all dark again. What I figure is he's feeling a bit like I am, that he's annoyed the two of us have to hide.

I try to kiss him again but when I do he pulls away.

I prop myself up on my elbows. 'You mean a trip or something?'

'Right. A trip.' He smiles and it looks a bit weird this time but I guess it's just because he's so close.

I think about it. 'But where? *How?*'

'Could you get one of your friends to cover for you? Tell your mum you were staying over at their house? Without your mum checking up on you, I mean.'

I think of Frankie, obviously. And I feel a bit guilty about the way I've been ignoring her lately.

'I guess,' I say.

'When?'

'Huh?'

'When?' Adam says, and I smile because it's obvious he's suddenly all eager. Before, I thought there must be something *wrong* with me. You know? Because until today he hasn't even kissed me, has barely even held my hand, but all of a sudden he's talking about us going away together.

I'm trying not to think too hard about what that means but Frankie's had sex, like, four times and she's been going on at me that I need to have it too. And I've always resisted, always thought that I haven't been ready, but now, with Adam, I know I *am*.

'I don't know,' I say. 'Next week maybe?'

Adam looks all keen but then I remember something and I have to disappoint him. 'No, wait, that won't work. Frankie's going away with her parents on holiday. It would have to be after we go back to school. Which might actually work better because on Thursdays, during term time, I usually stay at Frankie's house anyway.'

Adam's eyes go narrow.

'Her mum has this evening class,' I explain. 'Meaning me and Frankie get the place to ourselves. It's the only time my mum lets me stay over anywhere. She reckons me and Frankie are studying, but . . . well . . .' I smile, shrug. Normally what me and Frankie do is eat ice cream and talk about boys. But obviously I don't tell Adam *that*.

'Well, I guess I can wait,' Adam says. 'You know, if I *have* to.'

I grin up at him. With him leaning over me I notice how broad he is, how *strong* he looks.

He says, 'So if you ditched school Thursday and Friday, we could be gone for two whole days.'

'Ditched school?' I've never ditched school in my entire life. Mum would *kill* me.

'Sure. Why? It's no big deal, is it?'

'No, I . . . no. Course not.'

And it isn't. It really isn't.

'How about Brighton?' I say.

'Brighton?'

'Yeah. I went there once with my mum and it was the best day out I ever had.'

But Adam's not keen. 'It's too far away,' he says, shaking his head. 'We'd get there and basically have no time. And anyway I already have somewhere in mind.'

'You do?'

He smiles at me. 'Sure.'

I grin back. 'Is it nice? As nice as here?'

He shifts so he can get a better view of me, then like before rolls my hair behind my ear. 'Nicer,' he says. 'You'll love it, I promise you. It's somewhere you can just . . . forget yourself. You know?'

'How do you mean?'

'It's kind of hard to explain. But when you get there, I promise you: you won't ever want to leave.'

6 p.m. – 7 p.m.

14

Dear Ms Birch,

I just wanted to thank you. For helping me with my English paper? I know I should probably have gone to Mr Williams but when I saw you sitting there in your classroom and you recognized me from that time with the bin, I thought to myself, she's smart, she's kind, she's not like the rest of the teachers here. Like Mr Williams, for example, who's basically only ever here because he has to be, not because he genuinely cares. So I'll just ask her, I thought. And you did, you said you'd help. In fact you said you'd be delighted to. And then, what you said to me about being intrigued by what I'd written? About how Piggy was lucky in a way, Simon too, because at least it ended quickly for them and they never had to live with what happened? I realized you think exactly the same way I do.

So thanks. For the encouragement, I mean. And for taking the time to help me in the first place.

The other thing I wanted to say, and that I wish I'd said to you face to face, was that I think you handled things extremely well. The other day. With the bin. I mean, those boys were only messing about. They didn't mean anything by it and anyway it was only a bin.

But you dealt with it in exactly the right way. Not dobbing them in, for example. Not reporting them to the headmaster. Particularly seeing as you're new and that. And to be honest that's kind of what I mean. You don't seem like other teachers. You don't seem like other people full stop. Most people, practically everyone I've ever met, they're all floating through life in their little bubbles, not even caring that most of the stuff they do, there isn't even any point. They can't tell the big stuff from the small stuff, the stuff that doesn't even matter. But you can, I think. I think you can.

So anyway, that's all I wanted to say. That, and also that you've got a really nice smile.

Yours,
Jake (King)

Dear Ms Birch,

It's Jake again. I just wanted to apologize for that note I sent. The other day. It was stupid and I shouldn't have sent it.

Jake

Dear Ms Birch,

I'm writing again and I don't even know why. I don't even know if you got the other ones. I should have put them in plastic bags or something instead of sticking them under the windscreen wiper of your car because they probably only got wet in all the rain. You probably didn't even read them. They didn't really say anything anyway so it doesn't matter. I don't even know yet if I'll even send you this one. I wouldn't want to leave it under your windscreen wiper again because of the rain, partly, but also in case someone saw me and got the wrong idea. Like Scott or one of the others, who take the piss enough as it is (they're basically OK, by the way. Not the same as you and me but at least they recognize all the bullshit in the world too).

Why I'm writing again is just to tell you about something that happened. So I was walking the other day by the river. I go there a lot. Nobody knows. I get these, they're like headaches, but it's not an ache and it's not really in my head. So not headaches really, more just this sense of things pushing down on me, crowding in, and walking along the river helps me forget. So anyway, I'm walking, on my own, I spend a lot of time on my own because other people – well, you know. I don't have to tell you. But I'm walking and the river isn't exactly the prettiest place to be. The water's nice, if you don't look too closely, don't notice all the junk that people have dumped in it. But the bank is basically just mud and gravel. The odd shopping trolley here and there, stuff like that. And I'm walking and the sky's all grey, the river's brown, and the world is basically just *colourless*. You know? But then I see it. Right in the middle of this patch of nothing. A flower. Just one. It was blue. I don't know what kind it was. But anyway, that flower? Whatever it was? It reminded me of you. It was the exact same colour as your eyes. And I smiled when I saw it for the first time in what felt like weeks. I was going to pick it, to show it to you, but I didn't want to ruin it. I guess you'll just have to imagine it. I hope you can imagine it as clearly as me because it's not something I'll ever forget.

So that's it really. That's all I wanted to say. You don't have to write back. You don't even have to answer. Maybe I won't even send this. Or maybe I will. If I do, maybe I'll leave it on your desk or something. In your drawer maybe would be safest.

Yours,
Jake

Dear Ms Birch,

Sorry about the coffee. I'm such an idiot sometimes. And you startled me, coming into the room like that. I know I shouldn't have been inside at lunchtime and I shouldn't have been in your classroom but I was just look-ing to see if Charlie was there, that's all. I don't know why he would have been but he said he was going inside and I'd basically looked everywhere else. But he wasn't in there obviously, so what I was doing was I was trying to work out where to look next. I swear I wasn't going through your things. It may have looked like I was but I wasn't, honest.

But anyway, that's how I spilled your coffee. When I turned round. When you came in. I didn't notice the cup. I didn't realize it was full. I guess you forgot about it too, which is why it was cold but that's a good thing probably, seeing as what happened. I'm sorry it went over your jumper, the one that smells like perfume. You can send me the bill for cleaning it if you like. I've got enough money to pay for it. I could even buy you a new one.

So yeah. Sorry. And let me know what you want to do about your jumper. Don't throw it out or anything, will you?

If you don't want it my mum does these like, charity collections, for refugees I think. So if you gave it to me I could make sure she got it. I wouldn't do anything else with it, I promise.

Yours,
Jake

Dear Ms Birch,

This is the last time I'm going to write to you, I swear. I just wanted to say I think you're beautiful. That's all.

Love from,
Jake

PS I've never said anything like that before. Not to anyone. Ever.
PPS Please don't tell anyone I did.

Dear Ms Birch,

I know I said no more notes but I wondered why you hadn't responded to the last one. Did you get it? I'd appreciate it if you could just let me know whether you got it or not and then I promise I'll leave you alone.

Jake

Dear Ms Birch,

So you probably know what this is about. I can't believe you came to my house!

Mum said this teacher showed up and she said it was you and she said you said something to her about me having a crush. I can't believe you would even say that! It isn't true, for one thing. I said to Mum, I said I have no idea what she's going on about. She meaning you. I admitted I wrote you a note thanking you for thanking me and that, and maybe another one to say sorry for the coffee but that you'd basically got completely the wrong end of all the sticks. I mean, how old are you anyway? Like, 20? 21? And I'm coming up to 16, in just like 10 months or whatever, so there must be, what, like 4 years between us? Which actually isn't that much but that isn't even the point. What I'm saying is I'm not stupid. I realize you're way too old for me and I don't have a crush on you anyway!

So thanks. Thanks a lot. For getting me in trouble with my mum and for basically starting stupid rumours that I just know are going to be all around the school.

Jake

Dear Alison,

Can I call you that? Not at school obviously but here, when I write to you? I realized I said I wouldn't do that any more but I had to in case you thought I was angry. Which I was, I guess, because I still can't believe you spoke to my mum. Why would you do that? Come to my house like that? When basically I haven't even done anything wrong?

But what I'm sorry about mainly is if I sounded cross. Which I did, I know I did. I'm a total idiot sometimes and when I'm angry I say things I don't even mean. And then, what I do is I worry. I worry a lot. And it helps writing things down, writing to you, because basically there's no one else who'd understand. There's Scott and that now but I can't talk to them obviously, not about the kind of stuff that's on my mind, because they'd just call me a . . . You wouldn't want to know what they'd call me. And if I try to talk to Mum it's always pointless because she never gets what I'm trying to say. The problem is she doesn't listen, just hears whatever it is she wants to hear. She'd say I was depressed or something probably. Take me to see some doctor, who'd make me take some stupid drugs. And anyway, she's never around. It's like she's purposely trying to avoid me, I sometimes think. And Dad . . . Dad's 'busy' too. Dad's got his 'own' problems. Like how to finish level 98 or whatever of *Tomb Raider*, mainly. And he's definitely avoiding me on purpose. He's avoided me basically since I was small.

So instead, writing to you, I find it helps. So sorry. About being angry. Even though I wasn't. Much.

What I'm angry about more, now, is about you ignoring me. Because is that what you're doing? Like, the times we walk past each other in the corridor. Or my notes. You never respond to my notes. I guess you're busy with schoolwork and that, marking homework, and I realize it's not allowed for you to talk to me the way I think you want to but maybe if you gave me a sign or something instead? Like, in code or something? And then I wouldn't worry so much. I wouldn't even get angry when really there's no actual need.

J

Dear Alison,

I get it. I do. Our 'chat' or whatever, it really helped. At first I thought you were being serious. When you caught up with me after morning lessons and asked me to step into your room? Your face was like it was that time you caught Scott and that melting the bin. Just like a teacher's. A proper teacher's, I mean. You fooled me, anyway, and Scott and that afterwards, they were all like, what the bloody hell did *she* want, like you were telling me off for something I'd done.

But our 'chat'. Even when we got into the classroom, I thought what you were telling me was really real. The things you were saying about it being unhealthy, that you were worried it was going too far? There was that bit when you said you would have to consider talking to the head-master, and I kind of figured you'd never do *that* but I wasn't *sure* sure, you know? Because of that time you spoke to my mum. And finding interests. What you said about me trying to develop interests? Even that part sounded real, even though I know that you know that hobbies are basically total bullshit, just ways of killing time until you die.

It was only when you touched my arm that I realized what it was that was actually happening. That I realized you were doing it all for show. Because obviously you listened to what I said. About code? About signs and that? And that's what I'm saying: I get it. I get that you figured some-one might have been watching/listening/spying and I get you couldn't say what you really feel. And I probably looked pretty upset. I'm sorry if you thought I lost my temper. I can actually picture my face, the way I would have looked to someone peering through the door. Which is pretty embarrassing when I think about it but I honestly really don't mind. Not now anyway. I'm just pleased, that's all. More than pleased. It's like, touching my arm like that? Giving me a sign? It was the nicest thing you could have done.

All my love,
Jake

Dear Alison,

The flowers were from me. Just in case you didn't guess.

J
x

Dear Alison,

Did you get the flowers? Sorry they were squashed but I had to carry them in my bag just to make sure no one saw. Like Scott or any of the others, for example. But they should have been OK if you put them in water. (The lady in the shop said to cut off the ends.) ((Of the stalks, not the ends with the flowers, which is what I thought she meant when she told me!))

Anyway I just hope you liked them.

J

Dear Alison,

Have I done something wrong? You haven't mentioned the flowers is all, and when I was walking down the corridor today and you saw me coming it looked like you turned the other way. And I realize I'm probably being paranoid but on the other hand did you? Turn the other way? Because I get that you need to be careful but there was hardly anyone around and anyway there's no need to be rude.

Jake

Alison,

That's the second time now. The second time you saw me coming and turned away. And this time it was definite, it wasn't my imagination. I know because you looked me right in the eyes. I even called after you but when I got to the corner you'd disappeared. So this time why I'm writing is, please don't ignore me like that.

Jake

Dear Alison,

I'm sorry. I really am. I keep losing my temper and I don't mean to and the whole point of writing things down is that it gives me time to think about what I say. But sometimes the way I'm feeling just gets the better of me and I say things, send things, before I've got time to take them back. Can you tell me what I've done though? Why you're

208

ignoring me? Because that's the hardest part, not knowing what it is I've done wrong. I thought you understood. In fact I know you do, so that's the part I don't get. I promise you that if you want to you can tell me anything. I'll understand, I swear, just like you do. I know you can't write to me, because of your job, because of you being my teacher, but what about if you did it just this once? You don't have to sign it or anything. I'll know exactly who it's from.

I sent you some chocolates, by the way. Sort of like a peace offering. I didn't know what type to get, like whether you like milk or dark, so what I did was

15

'Where did you get these?'

'You haven't finished reading.'

Susanna flips from page to page. The letters are written on thin blue airmail paper and form a messy pile in
her shaking hands. One of the pages escapes her grip
and floats delicately – innocently – to the floor. 'But,
there are so *many*.' She rifles ahead in the stack Adam
has given her. Words leap out at her as she scans.

Jake

Alison

love

why

angry

please

hurt

It is too much for Susanna to absorb. She feels lost,
bewildered, so she starts again, shuffling her way back
to the top of the pile. *Dear Ms Birch, I just wanted to
thank you . . .*

'There's more, you know. I only brought a selection.'

'More?'

'Twenty-seven in all. It's a shame they're not dated
but it doesn't really matter. He would have sent them in
the space of about six months, between the day he first

spoke to her in the driveway that time and the 17th of May 1999.'

17 May 1999. The day the world ended. Whenever Susanna hears mention of that date, catches sight of it looming on the calendar, she always imagines it emblazoned on a tombstone.

'How far did you get?' Adam reaches for the letter Susanna has bookmarked with her thumb. He pulls it partway from the stack and only needs a glance to work out what it contains. 'There's only four more after that from what I can work out. Then they stop.'

Susanna flips to the letters she hasn't read yet. She can tell without reading the notes line by line that the remaining letters follow the same theme: Alison is ignoring Jake, Jake wants to know why. He switches between pleading, chastising, then pleading again, and all the while the notes get more intense. It is subtle, and more than once Jake attempts to rein himself back, but knowing her son – knowing what happened – Susanna can see the signs are there. And the parts where Jake talks about leaving the notes under the windscreen wiper of Alison's car, the suggestion he was going through the things in her desk. It was like he was stalking her. Not *like* stalking, in fact. Stalking is exactly what it was. Did he follow Alison too, Susanna wonders? Did he go to her *home*?

'Where did you get them?' Susanna asks Adam once again. What she means is, *how do I know they're real?* But she does know, categorically. Apart from anything, she would recognize her son's handwriting anywhere. The longing, the obsessiveness, all the more. And she can hear the creeping humiliation, the yearning for Alison to take him seriously. For *anyone* to take him seriously – Susanna included.

'My mother's shelf,' Adam answers. 'Her stash of lies.'

Susanna looks up. 'She kept them?'

'Wouldn't you?'

Susanna isn't sure how to answer. She thinks of her 'junk' drawer in the wardrobe in her bedroom, the one containing her own stash of lies. And Emily, when she was young, rummaging through it and pulling out the photograph of her dead brother. 'No one you know,' Susanna said to her when Emily asked who that little boy was. Meaning, *no one you need to know. No one I will ever tell you about.*

But that's different. Isn't it? What Susanna did

(is still doing)

to Emily isn't the same as what Adam's parents did to him.

Is it?

'Why are you showing them to me?' Susanna wants to toss the letters back into Adam's lap but she can't let go. Through the Braille-like imprints Jake's biro has left on the paper, it feels almost as though her finger-tips are in contact with her son. Touching him, stroking him, the way she used to when he would sit beside her on the sofa when he was young, the reading light on and the television babbling in the background.

Oh Jake. Oh my sweet, silly, stupid boy. What did you do?

'I thought you'd be interested,' Adam says. 'Aren't you interested, Susanna?'

She shakes her head, a rebuttal rather than an answer. 'Here.' She thrusts out the stack of letters. '*Here.*'

Adam relieves her of the letters. 'Tell me about her,' he says.

'Who?' Susanna responds, stalling. She sniffs. Almost reaches into her sleeve for a tissue before she remembers what else is up there that she might unwittingly displace.

'Alison Birch. My mother. Tell me about her. What you remember.'

Once again Susanna shakes her head. This time it's a rebuttal and a refusal both: I can't, I won't. It's a plea too. *Don't make me.* Alison Birch is the woman Susanna cannot bring herself to think about. She is the sixth person on Susanna's list of people she cannot help but blame.

'Tell me about the time she came to see you,' Adam says. He taps a fingernail against the blade of his knife. It is a reminder, as though Susanna needed one, that ultimately she has no choice.

'It was late when she knocked. After dinner one night, in the middle of the week.'

It was a Thursday, in fact. Susanna remembers because Neil was home when he shouldn't have been. On Thursday evenings he had his 'boys' night', which as far as Susanna had ever been able to ascertain involved Neil and three of his old school mates sitting around playing video games, drinking lager and smoking hash. Just as though they were still a bunch of teenagers. But that Thursday, Susanna recalls, the boys' night was cancelled. Steve, the host, was recovering from a knee operation and wasn't up to having everyone over. Susanna remembers Neil's imperviousness to the irony, that their adolescent get-together was cancelled because one of their gang was so decrepit, bits of him were having to be replaced.

So Neil was home. Grumpy, on his way to being pissed, it was Neil who opened the door.

'I recognized her,' Susanna tells Adam, 'but I couldn't place her. I was watching over Neil's shoulder. I couldn't see my husband's face but I could tell from the way his posture changed that he was . . . impressed, let's say, by what he saw. He brightened immediately, as though someone had delivered her just for him.'

Susanna recalls how a line from her favourite movie, on seeing her husband's reaction, flashed into her head. *Thin, pretty, big tits. Your basic nightmare.*

'What did you think of her?' Adam says. 'You said you recognized her. Had you ever spoken to her before?'

'Never. I thought she was . . . attractive. You couldn't help but think she was attractive. Dainty too. And I thought she looked awfully young.'

Alison Birch was twenty-four, as it happened. Older than Jake had assumed, going on his letters. But it was true she might have passed for eighteen. In contrast to her delicate bone structure, she had thick toffee-coloured hair that she wore – that night, and every other occasion Susanna saw her – pinned up loosely in a bun. It wasn't her fault

(it *wasn't*)

but Alison Birch's hairstyle was oddly, unwittingly alluring. Even Susanna could see it. Neil was practically drooling into his beer can. And to a teenage boy, that thick cushion of hair, one clip from cascading on to her shoulders, would have been as enticing as a missed button on a blouse.

'What did she say? About Jake, I mean. How did she raise the subject?'

Susanna blinks. 'She started by asking whether he was home. I think she knew he wasn't. And she was embarrassed, you could see. In retrospect, anyway. At the time I thought she was being snotty. The house was a mess, and there was Neil with his beer can, and her expression when she looked around the lounge . . .' Susanna shakes her head and it turns into a shiver. She isn't cold, it's not that. 'She was worried, obviously, about broaching what she'd come to us to say. But me being me, I assumed she was passing judgement.'

'So you didn't like her,' Adam judges.

Susanna wriggles. He's right, she didn't. Not when she first walked in, not after she'd said her piece and left. And it wasn't just because of what she told them about their son, which no parent would particularly want to hear. Admit it, Susanna, if only to yourself. You didn't like her because she was young and she was *pretty*.

'Did she spell it out for you? The extent of Jake's feelings towards her?'

'No. Absolutely not,' Susanna replies. 'She said she was concerned, that's all. She was worried that Jake was becoming "distracted".'

At which point Neil had coughed to conceal his laugh, Susanna recalls. She could tell exactly what he was thinking. *Who can blame the lad? He's only human!* And, naturally, *boys will be boys* . . .

'It took a bit of back and forth before she spelled out what she meant,' Susanna says. 'She said she thought Jake was "infatuated". That was the word she used. She said she thought he was lonely and that rather than cultivating friendship groups, he was focusing his attentions on her.'

And Susanna immediately recoiled, she remembers. She saw Alison Birch try to cover her mortification with a smile and she chose to read it as self-conceit. She thought she was *boasting*, for pity's sake.

'I asked her what evidence she had,' Susanna goes on. 'And all she could come up with were . . . vagaries. The way Jake looked at her, she said. His "behaviour" towards her. And again I asked for specifics but she became cagey, said she'd rather not go into details. She said she'd prefer it if we talked to Jake directly, that we got the full story from him.'

'And that's it? That's all she said?'

Susanna hears Adam's question but finds herself entangled for a moment in the memories. Not of the conversation with Alison Birch so much, which can only have lasted five or ten minutes. It is after, rather, that she is thinking of. Of Neil, in particular. He *laughed*,

Susanna recalls. 'Jesus Christ,' she remembers him saying after Alison had gone. 'I thought it was going to be about something serious.' And then, after another swig of lager, 'Good on the lad, I say. I mean, she's a bit out of his league but at least we know now that he's batting for the right team.' He shook his head, drained the can he was holding, then popped open another. He was *celebrating*, Susanna realized.

'Susanna? Are you with me, Susanna?'

'What? Yes. What?'

'I said, was that it? She said she was worried about Jake, asked you to talk to him. Did she say anything else? Did she tell you about the notes?'

'The notes?'

Adam rustles the pages impatiently. The flimsy paper makes an angry sound, something between a flutter and a hiss. 'The notes, Susanna. The *letters*.'

'I . . . no,' Susanna says. Then, more categorically, '*No*. She didn't say a thing about Jake having written to her.'

She can hear it in her tone: the urge to blame is creeping in again. Looking back, Susanna can see that Alison Birch was trying to be tactful. She didn't want to embarrass Jake in front of his parents, hence the reason she neglected to show them the notes. Yet if she had, would Susanna's reaction have been different? Would the outcome have changed?

Would Jake, in other words, still be alive?

This is Susanna's problem, the difficulty she has with the issue of blame. It is a noxious thing, as stealthy and shadowy as a poison gas, to the extent that without anyone realizing, it is able to surround and contaminate us all. Susanna knows, for example, that it wasn't Alison's fault that she was pretty. She can see as well how her behaviour was motivated by an instinct to be kind. And the notes . . . maybe, probably, they would have made no difference. There would have been only a few at the time for one thing and, more importantly, Susanna can imagine all too easily how she and Neil would have shrugged their existence aside, just as they did every other aspect of Jake's behaviour they considered out of character.

But still. *Still.* In spite of everything, Susanna can't help wishing Alison had been uglier, more belligerent, less *her*. She does: Susanna blames Alison Birch. She cannot help it. And though there are worse things Susanna has kept hidden all these years, the fact she does remains one of her most shameful secrets.

'Did she go to the headmaster, do you know?' Susanna hates herself for asking but she does it anyway. 'In his letters Jake says Alison threatened to talk to the school's headmaster, to ask him to intervene. Did she?'

Adam appears amused. 'You're asking me?'

'I thought you might know. That's all. I wondered why I hadn't heard about Jake's letters before.'

'There's your answer,' Adam says. 'You hadn't, so I guess she didn't. Or if she did, then clearly the headmaster took her about as seriously as you did.' He watches for a moment as Susanna squirms. 'But anyway, what does it matter? The point isn't who saw them back then. The point is that he wrote them at all.'

She *should* have shown them to someone, though. Shouldn't she? Twenty-seven letters. It was more than infatuation. It was an obsession. *Evidence* of an obsession, moreover, meaning something could have been done. Except yet again it comes back to Susanna. The blame remains thickest around her. Because what were Alison's options? She tried talking to Susanna; Susanna opted to ignore her. And as a young, female teacher, where else was Alison supposed to go? If she'd gone to a colleague, a superior, she would have seemed weak, ineffectual, which, given her looks and her stature, is probably what most people would have assumed her to be anyway. The notes, if anything, would have counted as evidence that she'd fail to deal with things the way she was supposed to. And she would have got Jake into trouble, when in her mind Jake was just a confused adolescent. He was harmless. That's what Alison Birch would have told herself.

Perfectly harmless.

'What about Jake?' Adam says.

'Jake?'

'She asked you to talk to him. Did you?'

'Of course I did!'

'And?'

'And . . .' And there are two accounts Susanna could give. The uncensored version would probably only make Adam angrier, because Susanna recalls some of the things Jake said. That Alison Birch was a fantasist, effectively; that she was basically making it all up. What he said, actually, was that Alison Birch was a lying cow. Which Susanna had chastised him for, naturally. But she'd been more focused on what it was Jake was telling her. Sure, he knew Alison Birch, Jake admitted – everyone did – but she was just one of those people who insist on being the centre of attention. 'She thinks she's God's gift,' Jake said. 'Always going on about how she looks like Kylie. And she flirts, Mum. Leans over the desks so you can see her cleavage, touches all the boys on the arm. I mean, how old is she? Like, thirty? Seriously, it's embarrassing.' Which simultaneously didn't quite ring true and chimed with everything Susanna wanted to believe herself. Hadn't she already decided that Jake's teacher was looking down on them? That she was as vain and self-absorbed as she was attractive? Which is another reason not to tell Adam.

'He denied it,' is what Susanna says. 'Just the way he said he did in his letters.'

Adam responds with a knowing smile. It would seem sympathetic if it wasn't so sly. 'I suppose he was bound to,' he says.

He thinks for a minute.

'So that's that, then. As far as Jake's relationship with Alison Birch went, you didn't hear anything more about it?'

Relationship? The word seems offensive somehow. Obscene.

And the way Adam is referring to his mother . . . he's said more than once that he can barely remember her but that doesn't explain the absence of emotion when he speaks of her – particularly given that his mother is so obviously now the reason Adam is here.

'No,' Susanna says. 'I didn't hear anything more about it.'

Adam rustles the letters. 'But it was simmering,' he says. 'Wasn't it? All the time you say you weren't aware. Just like their "plan". Scott's plan. That was simmering in the background too.'

Again, *simmering* doesn't seem the right word. Susanna thinks of something on fire, a fuse lit from both ends.

There is a pause.

'And so we get to it,' Adam announces, leaning back in his chair. 'The day itself. The 17th of May 1999. Let's talk about that now, shall we?'

16

It was the opportunity the boys had been waiting for: the evening of the big school performance.

Susanna was there herself that night. Only by chance. Jake wasn't involved in the production, of course, but Susanna was on the PTA and she'd been a bit slack of late in terms of her participation, so she'd thought she had better show her face. The irony being that because she was caught up with the crowd at the show, she was among the last to find out what happened. She can see it all vividly as she recounts it to Adam but only because she has watched it playing so often in her dreams. And not just her dreams. It haunts her in her waking hours too, to the extent it feels almost like a memory of her own. But really, her knowledge of what actually took place came mainly from Jake himself, who, the day after his arrest, confessed with unblinking eyes every detail of what he had done.

'This way. Quick.'

Scott led. The way he and the others had planned it, they would be the only ones in the main building. Everyone else would be in the school's gymnasium, which doubled as the assembly hall and stage. And it was, it was perfect. Not only would teachers' attentions be elsewhere, there would also be so many people on the grounds, suspicion would be too thinly spread to ever narrow in on them.

Plus, they wanted an audience, didn't they? What would be the point of starting a fire if nobody was around to witness it? No one would be hurt. The gymnasium was in a corner of the grounds, and was linked to the main building by a single corridor, meaning the parents, teachers and pupils would all have plenty of time to evacuate. Maybe a few would get a singed eyebrow or two but again, so much the better. At least then people would remember it. Far more than they would a shitty school production of some lame-arsed musical.

'Hurry up! Shut the door behind you. The *door*!'

They'd rigged the window in the boys' changing room that afternoon so that it didn't close properly, allowing them to enter the building undetected. But they still needed to get from the changing rooms past the gymnasium without being seen. If they were caught in the corridor, they would be able to explain their presence easily enough. But then the game would be up before it had even begun and, almost as bad, they'd be forced to endure two hours of smug-faced parents tapping their toes and clapping along as some little Year 10 homo crooned 'Oh, What a Beautiful Mornin''.

That was assuming whoever saw them didn't also spot the matches and the can of lighter fluid sticking out of Scott's pocket. If they did, it wouldn't only be the game that would be up. They would be kissing their school careers goodbye as well. No bad thing in itself but their parents would go fucking *mental*. Scott's old man in particular would beat him so badly, he'd be pissing blood until Christmas.

'Shit, wait up! My shoe!'

Scott stopped and Pete and Jake ran into the back of him. They turned and saw Charlie limping along behind them, one trainer dangling off his foot.

'For fuck's sake,' Scott hissed. He glanced ahead to check no one was coming, then spun round to face Charlie. 'Why didn't you just wear your own shoes?'

Charlie caught up. 'I told you why.' His foot was back in the trainer but Jake could see how both shoes, when Charlie walked, slipped almost to the bottom of his heels. 'Forensics.'

It was actually kind of smart, Jake thought, at least in theory. Rather than wearing his own trainers, Charlie had 'borrowed' a pair of his older brother's. That way, he'd maintained, if they left any footprints, the police would be looking for someone with feet two sizes bigger. Pete had thought it pretty smart too – and, looking at Jake's feet, had suggested to him that the two of them swap shoes for the same reason. Jake's shoes were bigger, Pete's smaller, meaning the police would be confused in exactly the same way. Right?

Jake had simply stared back at him, waiting for Pete to spot the flaw in his plan.

But Charlie's idea, it made sense. Or it would have, if on a dry May day, indoors, there was any chance they would actually leave any footprints at all. And if wearing shoes two sizes too big didn't mean Charlie was left struggling to walk, let alone to run should it get to the point they might need to.

'*Forensics*,' Scott scoffed. 'Maybe you should of hopped all the way instead. That way the cops'll concentrate on looking for a suspect with only one leg.'

Jake laughed. Charlie scowled. Pete, looking at his feet, seemed to be genuinely thinking it over.

'Come on,' said Jake, 'let's go.' He was eager to get on with things, he told the police, though he didn't fully explain why. Susanna understood, though. She pieced it together, and it is all the clearer now she has seen Jake's letters. Jake, that night, was running mainly on rage. His feelings of frustration, of self-loathing, of humiliation – they were all bubbling below the surface, fuelling him in everything he did.

Susanna recalls how markedly Jake's behaviour had deteriorated in the month or so before. At home he had become so moody, so monosyllabic, that Susanna had begun to question whether Jake wasn't suffering from something more than severe adolescence. Only to question it, mind you. Nothing more.

Needless to say, Susanna had no inkling at that point about Jake's obsession. So blind was she, so self-involved, that even those letters wouldn't have revealed to her the depth of her son's despair. Love for a time had filled the hole in him, if love indeed was what it was. Maybe Jake thought it was that but even love, Susanna suspects, had in her son's mind morphed into something darker. An infection, almost. Something else to eat away at his insides – all the more so when he realized his love was unrequited. Unacknowledged, in fact. Belittled rather than offered back.

'Shhh. Don't move.'

There were sounds of people heading towards them. The corridor connecting the gymnasium area to the main building was just around the corner, and if whoever was drawing near came their way, they would be caught in the no man's land between the gym and the changing rooms. It sounded like kids rather than grown-ups but nevertheless they would be *seen*. And the idea was that nobody would even know they'd been in the building that night at all.

'. . . see what she was wearing? Apparently her mum made it for her. Out of tinsel?'

'I know. It was so gorgeous. I wish my . . .'

They heard snatches of the approaching conversation but it faded then cut off completely, meaning whoever had been talking had entered the staging area behind the gymnasium rather than continuing towards them. There'd been a brief burst of noise as the doors backstage had cracked open.

Scott had been pressing Jake against the wall. His arm slackened, then fell away.

'Are you sure this is the best way to go?' asked Pete from behind them.

'It's the *only* way to go,' Scott muttered back, leaning forward to peer around the corner. 'It was come in this way or through the main entrance, and you can bet the headmaster will be standing at the door, just waiting to kiss everyone's arse.'

Charlie sniggered in Jake's ear. When Jake turned to look at him, he saw how broad and black his friend's pupils were. It was the coke, probably. Charlie, Pete and Scott had each done a railroad track before they'd set off: a line in each nostril, from the gram filched by Scott from his old man's stash. He'd get a beating for that no doubt too but at least that one would be worth it. They needed some Dutch courage, Scott had insisted, and unlike weed coke wouldn't dull their senses. Just the opposite, in fact.

They'd offered Jake some as well, tried to taunt him into snorting at least a line, but Jake wasn't interested. He'd tried it before. He'd tried everything they'd offered him before. Coke, weed, pills, acid. He didn't mind pills, except for the comedown. Acid he never wanted to experience again, and as for coke and weed . . . Weed just made him paranoid, to the extent that one time he'd locked himself in the toilet and wouldn't come out again, for fear of what was waiting behind the door. And coke was the worst of all. It made him agitated, angry, when most of the time these days he was agitated and angry enough.

Besides, he wanted to keep his head clear. Tonight, this thing they were doing: he wanted to be able to enjoy it.

'Anyway,' Scott was saying, 'Jakey-boy here insisted we start the fire in Miss Bitch's room. I was all up for setting it beneath the stage.'

That was bullshit and Jake knew it. None of them would have risked starting the fire where there was a chance someone might actually get hurt – and, more importantly, where they might very easily get caught. Scott was only saying that now because they'd already settled on a plan, and he was free at this stage to say anything. To *claim* anything. Probably the coke was a factor in that too.

It was true, however, that Jake had been the one to push for starting the fire in Ms Birch's room. Again, he hadn't told the others why. They knew nothing about his fixation with her, nor about the way Alison Birch had rejected him. Although in fact she hadn't even had the guts to do that. She'd teased him is what she'd done. Led him on. Made him think she liked him when all along she was just pretending. *Faking*, just like everyone else, practically, Jake had ever met. As far as he was concerned, setting the fire from her desk was the least she deserved. And Scott was never going to argue. Technically it had been his idea in the first place, and in Scott's mind he still owed Alison Birch for having given him that week's detention.

'Ready? Make sure those shoes are laced up tight, Charlie.'

Scott was on point again, his hand raised to give the signal for them to move. The babble of the audience was dying down, meaning the show was about to start. This too was part of their plan. If there was ever going to be a time when the corridor was completely empty, it would be right at the beginning of Act One. After that, there was no telling who they might bump into. A teacher rushing to some backstage emergency, some parent taking a little brat for a piss . . .

There was applause and Scott gestured for them to go. Walk, he'd briefed them before, don't run. But don't go slow. You know? Move like you've got somewhere you need to be.

But as they started along the corridor, they couldn't help but break into a sprint. It was the buzz of it. The fear, the thrill, the sheer *fuck you* of what they were contemplating. And not just contemplating, not any more. They were doing it. Actually fucking *doing* it. That was why Scott and the others, in Jake's opinion, were so cool. They talked a lot of crap, sure, but they followed up on a lot of it as well. Other people were full of so much bullshit. Like his mum and dad, for example. Dad was constantly like, yeah sure, son, just as soon as I have time, which he did, always, just none he was willing to offer Jake. Mum was no better. She had her work and her book group and the PTA and yoga and *something* going on every night of the week – which, actually, suited Jake these days just fine. If they didn't care about him, why should he give a toss about them?

And there was Alison, of course. Ms Birch. Miss *Bitch*. Jake thought she was different but it had turned out she was just like all the others. Worse, because as well as being a fake she was a coward. A prick-tease, in fact. A *slut*.

As they hurtled along the corridor they could hear the headmaster droning away on stage. Jake caught a glimpse of him through a window as they flashed past, a phoney welcome grin plastered across his face. *Go on, keep smiling*, Jake found himself thinking, and he realized he was grinning himself. Not only at the prospect of the headmaster's face when it was half illuminated by flames but at his own impending sense of triumph. They were all grinning: Charlie, Pete, even Scott. They were bouncing off each other as they ran, bouncing off the corridor's walls, and by the time they'd bypassed the entrance hall and veered deeper into the main building their grins had burst into outright laughter.

'Stop!' Pete was laughing so much he couldn't breathe, and as he stumbled to a halt he clutched his stomach. 'Ow,' he gasped, still battling laughter. 'Fucking *ow*.'

The others came to a standstill beside him, panting for air and hinging towards their knees. 'Fucking A, you mean,' Charlie managed, and this creased them up all the more.

Pete sniffed and swiped at his nose, and slowly his laughter sputtered to a halt. 'I'm bleeding,' he said, and then he laughed again. Nervously, though.

'Huh?' Scott got a hold of himself and stood up straight. He turned Pete towards the light, then grinned and pushed him playfully away. 'It's just a nosebleed. From the coke I 'spect. Wipe it on your sleeve.' Scott peered along the corridor, back the way they'd come. 'You've probably left a spatter trail as long as my old man's rap sheet. So much for Charlie's forensics.'

They all looked at Charlie, who was in his socks now and wearing his brother's shoes like gloves. Charlie smiled at them and shrugged, and the sight of him was all it took. They were off again, laughing again, until Jake could barely see through his tears.

'Come on, you homos.'

Scott shoved Jake until he started forward. The others followed, and after a few steps they were moving in silence. Without anyone having to say it, they understood that the time for laughing was at an end.

It didn't take them long after that to get to where they were going. Ms Birch's form room was down a short flight of stairs, midway along the corridor that dissected the main wing. That was another reason Ms Birch's room was so perfect: it was slap bang in the middle of the building. The fire, once lit, might spread anywhere, *everywhere*.

They gathered around the young teacher's desk, one of the boys standing at each corner. A reading light had been left on in the classroom, and the four of them could see one another's expressions quite clearly. This was the moment from which there'd be no turning back. Once they struck that match (those *four* matches, for again this was part of the plan: a match each, so that no one, afterwards, could claim they'd only been along for the ride) they would cross the line into being fully fledged criminals. And it wasn't like possession or shoplifting or anything. Arson was *serious*. As in, life-sentence-level serious. Which they wouldn't get because they were minors and more to the point they had no intention of getting caught . . . but even still.

It was Jake who started spraying lighter fluid first. He admitted it, never tried to deny it. The can was in Scott's hand and Jake reached out and snatched it from him. It was just a squirt, initially, but that squirt led to another, and then a spray, and soon Jake was upending the can all over Alison Birch's chair, across the surface of her desk, on the jumper she kept there for the days it turned cold, which was stained on the sleeve by spilled coffee. The others watched, waited, and then the four boys simultaneously struck their matches. And this part . . .

. . . this part Susanna cannot help but view from Alison Birch's perspective. Partly it's because Susanna doesn't *want* to see it from Jake's standpoint. That she can't, in fact. She simply cannot put herself, at this point in the story, in Jake's mindset. It would be like trying to use reason to explain madness, heaven to extrapolate hell. Her empathy doesn't extend that far.

But Alison . . .

This is the paradox Susanna has never been able to reconcile. She blames Alison Birch but at the same time there is no one in the world for whom Susanna feels more sympathy. Because she can imagine what happened next from Alison's point of view all too clearly. She can literally see it through her eyes. The moment she came through her classroom doorway and saw those four shadowy figures gathered around her desk, their features warped by the flames from their matches. And Jake's face, as it occurred to him why the reading light had been on, that they weren't alone, that rather than triumph this was his moment of utmost shame. The others turning, seeing it too, and realizing they'd been caught red-handed.

As one the matches were extinguished.

'What's going on here? What on earth do you boys think you're doing?'

It was an echo of the first time the lives of Jake, Alison, Scott, Pete and Charlie had collided, and Susanna wonders if, for Jake, it registered.

'What's that smell?' The tang of lighter fluid would have been thick in the air. (Susanna, ever since, cannot fill her car up at the petrol station without first wrapping a scarf across her face.) 'Is that petrol? Lighter fluid? Are those *matches* you're holding?'

The boys looked at each other. Apart from Jake, who didn't take his gaze from Alison.

'Answer me. One of you. Explain to me what the devil's going on.'

It was at this point Alison switched on the overhead light. Susanna wishes that she hadn't because that one simple action, as Susanna understands the sequence of events, had the effect of firing a starting gun.

'Switch that off!' Scott moved with astonishing speed. He moved so quickly that Alison had no time to get out of his way, and he had to shove her bodily aside to reach the light switch.

'Hey! Turn that back –'

Alison got as far as grabbing Scott's shoulder before, perhaps meaning only to shake her off, Scott's hand whipped out and hit her jaw.

She staggered and stumbled on a chair. She tripped, the clatter of her fall drowned out by Scott's curse.

'Shit!'

When Alison focused her eyes she could see Scott

233

looking down at what he'd done. She saw him turn to the others, who were gaping, immobile, back at him – other than Jake, who hadn't looked anywhere but at Alison since she'd entered the room. He was staring at her legs now, and Alison couldn't work out at first what he was looking at. But then she saw her skirt had ridden up when she'd fallen, exposing the bare length of her thighs. She tried to wriggle her skirt down but her movement released a jarring pain in her jaw. It pinned her.

'*Shit*,' said Scott again. He looked over at the shortest one – Charles, was it? Charlie? 'Don't just fucking stand there!' Scott barked. 'Shut the door or something! And Pete, switch off that fucking desk light!' He glared down at Alison. He appeared afraid, a bit, but mostly just angry. 'Why the fuck did you have to stick your nose in?' he said. 'Why do you *always* have to stick your nose in!'

Alison swallowed, wincing once again at the pain this caused. She propped herself up, tried tugging her skirt towards her knees.

'What were you doing in here?' she said. She was trying to sound firm, authoritative, but to her ear she sounded exactly how she felt. She sounded scared.

She tried again. 'Jake? Tell me what it was you were doing in here.'

Jake's eyes were locked on Alison's legs. His gaze crawled higher.

'You shouldn't be here, Alison,' he said.

Alison was so outraged she almost missed it: the fact

he'd called her by her Christian name. She caught the others noticing it too.

'*I* shouldn't be here?' she heard herself saying. 'This is my classroom! I was *working*!' Her choice had been either to do her marking here, taking advantage of the fact the school was open this evening, or cart thirty sets of school books all the way out to her car and then back again. And school books were *heavy*, particularly for someone of her size and strength. 'You're the ones who need to explain yourselves,' she insisted. The anger was helping, she found. She felt like she was regaining control, at least of herself.

She focused again on Susanna's son.

'This has to stop, Jake. This fixation. This *obsession*. You've crossed a line. You crossed it a long time ago and I should have taken action sooner but this, setting fire to my desk, as – what? Retribution? *Punishment?* Don't you understand that I'm your teacher? That you and I can never be more than friends?'

Pete stopped short of the desk light, which was still casting its ashen glow across the room. Charlie turned, the door into the classroom now closed behind him. He took a step back towards the others. 'What's she talking about, Jakey-boy?'

Alison looked at Jake, who was blooming red.

Charlie repeated his question. 'Jakey-boy? What's she going on about? And why did you call her Alison? Just now. Have you two got, like, a *thing*?'

Alison saw Jake swallow. She saw the redness of his cheeks turn puce.

'No, we don't have a *thing*,' Alison said. She was still afraid. Not of Jake, not at that stage, nor even of Pete or Charlie. It was Scott, rather, who most frightened her. She could see his mind was racing, scrabbling to find a way out of this mess he'd blundered into.

But as well as afraid, Alison was also furious. Here she was, lying on the floor, her jaw throbbing and her skirt stuck halfway up her belly, while four pupils – *pupils!* – stood menacingly over her. She was a grown woman. A *teacher*, for heaven's sake. This shouldn't be happening! 'Jake thinks there's something between us but there's not,' she said. 'He doesn't understand that it's entirely inappropriate for a boy his age to –'

'SHUT UP!'

Jake, if it was possible, moved quicker than Scott had. In the time it took Alison to turn her head he had crossed the ground between them and was leaning over her, forcing her back towards the floor. 'Just shut your mouth!' he yelled, his finger raised in warning. 'Do you hear me? Just stop!' He grabbed Alison's jaw, squeezing so Alison couldn't swallow.

Charlie moved into Alison's field of vision. He was grinning but cruelly. 'Who'd've thunk it?' he said. 'Who'd've thunk our Jakey-boy had it in him? *Jake and Alison, sitting in a tree* . . . You're probably wasting your time, you know. We're not even sure Jakey-boy here can get it up.'

Someone tittered – Pete? – and Alison could see Jake wanting to round on his friends. Instead, he focused his anger on her. Except . . . it wasn't just anger. There

236

was rage in the blackness of his eyes, yes, but humiliation too. His pupils glittered unnervingly, fixedly, and Susanna, imagining this, doesn't doubt that Alison caught a glimpse then of his lust.

And now it *was* Jake she was most afraid of. This, whatever *this* was, it was out of control. She needed to get out into the corridor. And, when she got there, she needed to run.

She shuffled backwards. She tried to stand. She might have said something about going to the headmaster, she might have said nothing at all, but it wouldn't have helped by this stage either way.

'Stay where you are!' Scott's voice, bearing an authority Alison had never truly felt able to do more than mimic. 'Jake, stop her. Don't let her move!'

Jake dropped lower. His knee came to rest on top of Alison's, and his hand bore down on the front of her shoulder. She felt his palm press uncomfortably into her bra strap.

'Scotty?' said Pete. 'What are we doing, Scotty?'

'We can't let her leave,' Scott spat. 'She saw us with the matches. I just accidentally fucking *hit* her! My dad'll slaughter me if he finds out!'

'Yeah but . . . she's a teacher. Maybe if we make her promise . . .'

Charlie stepped forward. 'She's not gonna *promise*. And even if she does she's not gonna keep it.'

Alison looked at Jake. She saw his lips part, his tongue flicker nervously between his teeth.

'Get off me. Jake? Do you hear me? Get off me.'

Her voice was quiet at first, preternaturally calm. But then, steadily, she began to panic. 'Get off me,' she repeated, louder now. 'Get the bloody hell *off* me.' She wriggled, started to kick. 'Do you hear? Are you listening to me? Get off me!'

'For Christ's sake, Jake, make her shut up! Someone'll hear!'

So Jake hit her. Hard. And Alison's head rebounded against the floor.

'Shit,' said someone. '*Fuck.*'

'Let's go.' This from Scott. 'Jake! Do you hear me? Let's go!'

If Jake had turned, he would have seen Scott with a lighted match ready in his hand. He would have seen Pete and Charlie bundling towards the door.

'Leave her, Jake! We've got to *go*!'

Scott didn't wait for Jake to respond. He tossed the match on to Alison Birch's desk, which burst into silent flames. Without another glance at Jake, Scott ran the way his friends had. They were gone, fled . . . leaving Jake and Alison alone.

Alison recovered from her daze and saw Jake staring down at her blackly. He was deathly still, despite the fire, the concrete mass of him haloed by a hellish glow.

'Jake? What are you doing, Jake?'

He was on top of her, the whole of his body weight bearing down. The little crucifix Alison wore around her neck had caught on Jake's hand and was being pressed jaggedly against her windpipe.

'Jake? Jake, please. Get off me.'

Something ripped. *Was* ripped. A noose tightened around her ribs and Alison realized with horror that it was the waistband of her skirt.

She started to flail. She sensed Jake recoil and the pressure that was trapping her ease – but then it redoubled and all at once there was a hand around her throat.

'Don't . . .' she heard herself saying. 'Please . . . stop . . . don't . . .'

Because she knew what was coming. The fear was like nothing Alison had ever experienced. Perhaps in a dream, a nightmare, where you are powerless to fend off the approaching terror, but in a nightmare you always wake up. And when you sleep your senses are dulled. Here, now, Alison saw, heard, smelt everything. She felt Jake's clawing hands and the ugly press of him through his jeans. She could *taste* his hunger for her, a bitter tang that made her want to gag. She did gag, when Jake released her throat and moved his fingers over her, under her, into her.

She froze, after that, and her eyes, through it all, remained locked on the open door. *Help*, her gaze said. *Someone*. But no one came, no one saved her, and there was nothing Alison could do to save herself.

17

'And then the fire.'

The fire. The crime Jake and the others had set out to commit, reduced in the end to a postscript.

Susanna is weeping. She feels like a fraud for doing so but she cannot help it. Imagining what Alison went through – reliving the experience through her eyes – is almost more than she can take.

'And then the fire,' she manages to say.

It wasn't quite the conflagration the boys had planned but the damage it caused was extensive enough. The school was closed afterwards for over a week, the main teaching wing for almost three months. They had to erect temporary classrooms on the playing field, which when the rain came turned into a muddy bog.

'You were there? You saw it?'

Susanna sniffs. It crosses her mind she must appear a pathetic mess. She doesn't care what she looks like; it's the pathetic part that bothers her. For Emily's sake.

'I saw it. The alarm went off and we were all ushered out on to the street. The school didn't have a sprinkler system, though, so by the time we were all outside the flames were up into the roof. And it was chaos. Most people, most parents, they wouldn't leave the gymnasium until they'd located their children. And others, if they couldn't find their kids outside, they went back in. Through the fire doors if they could fight their way past. Otherwise around and up along the drive.'

Susanna, at the time, thought that was the worst of it. The frightened children, the panicked parents. But as well as the fire, it later turned out, there'd been an inferno of another kind. A rage of frustration and desire, as cruel and destructive as any blaze Susanna could have envisaged.

'But no one was hurt.'

'No,' Susanna says. 'Not from the blaze.' She recalls what Adam asked her before. *Do you wish it had happened as they'd intended?* The plan, he meant, the fire. And her answer: *More than anything.* Because if a building burned had been the worst of it, Alison would have been untouched, Jake would still be alive and none of this, now, would be happening.

And then it strikes her. Reverberates in a way it hasn't so far had a chance to.

Her grandson. Sitting across from her, threatening her daughter, is Susanna's *grandson.*

'That must be a relief for you,' Adam says. 'The fact that there are no other ruined lives you're responsible for.'

Susanna says nothing. She cannot.

'Tell me about Jake,' says Adam, changing tack. 'You were with him when he told the police what happened. Right, Susanna? How did Jake seem, did you think?'

'How did he seem?'

'Was he confused, would you say?'

'Of course he was confused,' Susanna answers,

making an attempt to tidy her eyes. 'He was in shock. He . . .' She struggles to find the words. How to explain how Jake *seemed* after what had happened? He *seemed* at first to be unrepentant, as though he barely registered the horror of what he'd done. And rather than confused, he *seemed* in perfect command of his memory, recalling the sequence of events with barely a need for pause. He didn't remember getting out – how, after what he did, he escaped the burning building, nor how Alison got out after him – and that should have offered Susanna a clue to his mental state. Perhaps the way he recounted the events should have too. Jake's tone, his mannerisms: they were robotic, utterly devoid of emotion. Sitting beside her son as Jake voiced his confession into a camera, Susanna found she had to turn to face the wall. *He's a monster*, she told herself. *I've raised a monster.* She couldn't touch him, couldn't have held his hand if he had asked. Which he didn't. He just kept his hands folded in his lap, not even reaching to take a sip of water.

But of course it was exactly as she told Adam. Jake was in shock. Profound, paralysing shock. The emotion was there but it was balled inside of him. He was denying it, repressing it, squeezing it tighter, tighter . . . until eventually that bubble inside him burst.

'Jake was confused, afraid, bewildered,' Susanna tells Adam. 'He was struggling to comprehend what he'd done.'

And Jake wasn't the only one. There remains a part of Susanna that continues to disbelieve any of it ever really happened.

Adam is contemplating her response. Susanna can't tell if he is satisfied with it or not.

'But you just accepted it? You didn't doubt anything Jake admitted to?'

'What do you mean?'

'He was in shock, you say. He was confused. And yet you didn't question whether he'd done the things he said he had?'

'I didn't *believe* it, if that's what you mean. I *couldn't* believe it. But the evidence was there. Jake's statement, Alison's statement . . .'

'But you accepted he didn't start the fire. Even though they eventually pinned that on him as well.'

'That was different,' Susanna says, not quite understanding where this is leading. 'Alison verified Jake's version of events, that Scott was the one to throw the match. But Scott, Pete and Charlie all claimed Jake was the one who started the fire as well. And Alison . . . in the end she admitted she wasn't certain, that she couldn't even recall how she'd first ended up on the floor. The police had no choice except to blame Jake, particularly in light of what he admitted to.'

Adam's lips twist sideways.

'What about my mother?' he asks. 'She got out. She escaped the fire just as Jake did. How do you think that happened?'

'It was instinct, I suppose. Just instinct, the same way it must have been for Jake.'

Susanna pictures Alison stumbling into the corridor, her clothes singed and torn, her lungs hacking out smoke. She's seen a photo of her that was taken soon after the paramedics found her: Alison wrapped in a blanket and hunched on the ground beside an ambulance. 'A survivor' the newspaper captioned her, before anyone reading the story could have known how much she'd endured.

Adam has risen from his chair. He taps the knife against his leg as he talks.

'How did you feel when you found out Scott and the others would get away with it?' he asks. 'They claimed they'd only been along for the ride. Right? The lighter fluid they brought, the matches: they said they hadn't really intended to use them. They'd been joking, they said, just messing around, and it was Jake who in the end lost control. And the police believed them.'

'They didn't!' Susanna says. 'They didn't have any way to disprove what they said, that's all. It was three against one. Scott and the others, they should have been punished for what they did. The fire, hitting your mother. And in the end they left her to *burn*!'

Adam turns to face her. Incredibly, he is smiling.

'You know Scott eventually went to prison?' he says.

'What?'

'I looked into it. I mean, I don't know if he's in prison any more but he was. Lots of times. For lots of things. So in the end I guess he got his dues. And Charlie . . . I couldn't find out what happened to Charlie. Nothing good, I think. And Pete – get this – Pete's a fireman.'

'You're kidding,' Susanna says.

Adam shows her his dimples. 'I am, actually,' he

admits. 'Wouldn't that be great, though? But no.' He raises the knife to study the blade. 'What actually happened to Pete is that he died.'

Susanna swallows. She wipes the sweat from her palms.

Adam notices her unease. 'It wasn't me, if that's what you're thinking. It was an accident. Something at work. Involving fire, predictably enough.'

Susanna sees that Adam, this time, is completely serious.

'Look,' she says. She rocks to shuffle forward on her seat. She leans towards Adam, as near as she can get without rising. This, right here: it is the closest she has come to outright begging.

'Look,' she says again, 'I'm sorry. So, so so sorry. About what happened to your mother. About what my son did to her.'

She reaches a hand and then forces it down. It joins the other and the fingers of both hands interlock. And now she is: she is actually begging.

'It was awful. Just horrendous, and I can only imagine how it's impacted on your life. I can *see* how much it's impacted, how angry and upset you clearly feel. And you're right. You're right to be angry, particularly at me. And I will, I'll do anything you say. Just please – *please* – let Emily go.'

Susanna doesn't know what she's expecting. For Adam suddenly to accept her apology? To pick up the letters and his bag, and perhaps to hand over Emily's phone, and then to go merrily on his way? *Oh, all right.*

Like she was a child and he was tired of her constantly asking. *Go on then, I forgive you. Let's let bygones be bygones.*

Instead, 'You're sorry?' he says. And then he laughs. 'You're sorry,' he echoes, 'for what happened to my mother.' He looks at her. 'You still don't get it, do you? After everything I've said, after everything *you've* said.'

Susanna stares back at him blankly.

Adam starts pacing around the room.

'Talk to me about the letters,' he says. 'You haven't told me yet what you think of them.'

'What I think of them?'

Adam is waiting but Susanna doesn't know what for. She shakes her head. 'I'm sorry, I –'

'The *letters*,' Adam emphasizes. 'The notes your son wrote to my mother. They prove he loved her. Don't you think?'

Love? Susanna is thinking. *Really?* 'They show he was infatuated, certainly. That he *thought* he loved her, maybe.'

She has said the wrong thing. She catches the glint of irritation in Adam's glare.

'Would they have made a difference, though?' he presses. 'At the trial, I mean.'

'But there wasn't a trial. It never . . .'

Adam, swooping, is across the room. He levels the knife. 'I *know* there wasn't a trial, Susanna! I *know* that! I'm asking *if. If* there'd been a trial. Would the letters have made any difference?'

Susanna forces herself backwards in her seat. Her hands are tight around the armrests. 'What kind of difference? I don't know what you mean!'

'To Jake! To the verdict! To whether or not he was found guilty!'

'No. *No.* He raped her. What does it matter if he wrote to her first?'

Again, it is not what Adam wants to hear. He spins away, disgusted.

'What about in your eyes, Susanna?' he says, with his back to her. 'What do they alter in your eyes?' He turns to look.

Susanna shakes her head. She doesn't know what to say. 'What do *you* think they alter?' she counters. 'Why did you show them to me in the first place? What is it you think they prove?'

'Do you really need me to spell it out for you?'

'Yes! *Please.*'

Adam slams the knife down on Susanna's desk. He strides until he is once again in Susanna's face. He counts on his fingers as he talks.

'The letters. They prove Jake loved her. That's *one.*'

Susanna knows better now than to demur.

'*Two,*' Adam continues, wiping away spittle. 'It never *did* come to trial. My mother, so called, dropped the charges.'

'Yes, but . . .'

'But what, Susanna? But *what*?'

Susanna shrinks. 'Nothing,' she mutters.

'Three! Not only did she drop the charges, she changed her story. Said that Jake didn't actually rape her after all.'

But . . .

It is there again at the back of Susanna's throat, tussling to get out. She wants to object even though she doesn't understand what Adam is saying, what it is he's trying to contend. Because the points he's made, *one, two, three*, they're all so familiar. So sickeningly, maddeningly familiar.

'Four: you just admitted Jake was in shock, that he was confused about what actually happened. Meaning his confession doesn't count. No one *saw* him rape my mother. There weren't any witnesses, remember? And anyway he took it all back, every word of what he said!'

'But . . .' It slips out. This time Susanna cannot stop it. Jake only recanted his statement as a response to Alison recanting hers. And anyway, it wasn't even Jake, not really. It was Neil, their solicitor, *her* – because the truth is Susanna went along with the solicitor's advice just as Neil did. 'Jake was only doing what everyone told him to do,' Susanna says. 'That's the reason he changed his story, not because what he first said wasn't true.'

'Five! Even the newspapers said Jake was falsely accused. They called *him* the victim, said it was a travesty what he'd been put through. And I know you mock them, Susanna, and I know you mock me for reading them but the papers can't print these things unless there's some truth in them. They can't! There are *laws*!'

It is – it's like listening to Neil. The desperation, the naivety. The sheer bloody *wrongness*. What Susanna can't work out is what these words are doing coming out of *Adam's* mouth.

'Are you saying . . .' Susanna shakes her head again,

with incredulity this time. 'What *are* you saying, Adam? That it never happened? The assault, the rape, what my son did to your mother.' She gestures wildly in Adam's direction. 'You're standing there! You're living proof!'

'No, that's not what I'm saying! I'm not saying they didn't have sex. Clearly I'm not saying that.'

'Have *sex*?' Susanna stares, and as she does some of the phrases Adam has used come back to her. He's spoken of Jake's 'feelings' towards Alison, of their 'relationship'. He's talked about *love*, for pity's sake!

And sex. *Sex!*

'It wasn't *sex*, Adam. It was rape. *Rape*. Sex is beautiful, joyous. Rape is ... it's the opposite. It's vile. It's violent. It's about the most awful thing you can do to someone and afterwards leave them still alive.'

'Oh, *please*,' Adam responds, and as far as Susanna is concerned, he might as well have slapped her across the face. 'Sex, normal sex, can be rough too. It can be forceful. Even inappropriate. And I admit their relationship was inappropriate, Susanna. But what I'm saying is, maybe, based on all the evidence, it wasn't actually rape. Not really. Maybe what happened is that he and my mother had sex and it was *Jake* who saved my mother from the fire. *That's* the only story that makes sense. He loved her, remember? He practically says as much in his letters!'

And there it is: evidence, as if Susanna needed it, of how damaged Adam really is. Deranged, even. His judgement is as twisted as his logic.

Susanna, watching him, is aware what she must look

like. Adam sees her staring at him, the disbelief in her eyes, and he looks back at her with outright contempt.

'You see,' he says. 'This is exactly what I'm talking about.'

Susanna forces her mouth closed. She watches as Adam resumes pacing around the room, faster this time, like there is something he is trying to escape.

'Your mother . . .' Susanna starts to say. Adam gives no indication he is listening but Susanna forces herself to continue even so. 'Your mother, Adam: she dropped the charges because she was ashamed. Rape, for a woman . . . it's not just the act itself that's so hard to bear. It's the humiliation. It's the prospect of having to live it all again. In police interviews, in court, in cross-examination. And that's before you even consider how to explain it to your friends and family. How you can hope to get across that it wasn't – even partly – your fault. Because that's what other people invariably think, you know. That a woman who's been raped, she must have done something to encourage it. To *deserve* it, in fact.'

Susanna speaks as though from experience. And though it's true Susanna has never been a victim of such a horrific crime herself, she feels as passionately about the subject as she would if she had been. How could she not?

'*That's* why she dropped the charges, Adam. That's why she changed her story. She said she'd lied, then ran away, *disappeared*, because it was easier to do it that way than to relive what happened to her in court, and every day of her life after that. To subject herself to –'

But then it strikes her: she was pregnant.

Of course.

Alison was *pregnant*.

Susanna has always assumed that the reasons Alison changed her story, why she withdrew the accusation she'd levelled at Susanna's son, were those she's outlined to Adam. Shame, humiliation, *fear*. But the real reason she ran is because of her baby. Because she found out that she was pregnant. She was Catholic. She was a woman, for heaven's sake; an expectant mother. And she wanted to protect her child.

Adam.

Adam is the reason his mother ran. He's the reason they had to let Jake go. Public enemy one day; a victim himself the next. All because of Adam.

'You don't understand. I knew you wouldn't and you *don't.*'

Susanna didn't notice Adam moving so close. He is looming over her, a silhouette against the window in the darkening room. The knife flashes in his hand.

'What do you mean?' Susanna manages to say.

'I *mean*, my mother changing her story isn't the *point*. Whether it was rape or not doesn't even *matter.*'

'So what is the point? If you don't think it was rape, why are you so angry about what Jake did? Why are you even *here*?'

Adam shifts and his smile, when Susanna sees it, is all fury.

'*This.* This is the reason I'm here.'

For a second Susanna assumes he is talking about

the knife – that they have come to it, finally: the bitter end – and it is all Susanna can do when Adam moves to stop herself screaming.

But then he tosses a sheet of paper into her lap. The same thin blue airmail paper, the same slipshod scrawl. One final letter – which, when Susanna reads it, explains everything. What Adam thinks, why he's here, how he *knows*. Because it is all right there, written down in front of her: every detail of Susanna's darkest secret.

Emily

13 September 2017

It's weird. Somehow, when I heard the knock on our front door this morning, I just knew it would be Adam. Even so when I opened up and saw him standing there, I couldn't help looking a bit alarmed. Just because of Mum. Because of the whole sneaking around thing, what she'd say if she found out me and Adam have been seeing each other, let alone the fact we're going away together tomorrow morning. (I still don't know where Adam's taking me, or how we're getting there, or anything really, other than it's finally happening!)

But anyway that's my point: I panic when I open the door because I don't want to ruin it, our secret trip, not when it's getting so close. Plus, the other thing is, I've got to leave to get to school in like ten minutes, otherwise I'm going to miss my bus.

Adam laughs when he sees my face. 'You look almost disappointed to see me.'

'What? No!' I say. 'I'm surprised, that's all.' I can't help peering across his shoulder.

He smiles again. 'Don't worry. I saw her drive off.'

'What? Who?'

'Your mum. I hid over there, behind that van, until I was sure she was gone.'

'No, I know. It's just, she might come back.'

'Doesn't she work today?'

'I guess.'

'Then she won't come back. Trust me.'

I want to ask him how he can be so certain but the fact is he's right. Mum left twenty minutes ago, just before eight, which means if she hasn't come back by now – like, if she's forgotten something or something – then she won't be home at least until lunchtime, probably not till gone six.

'Aren't you going to ask me in?' Adam goes, and now he's the one who's peering past me.

'Right. Of course. Come in. Sorry.'

I get out of his way and he squeezes past me. I take a quick glance at our neighbours' house but the windows are empty and their car's gone from the drive, so they've probably all headed off to work too.

I try to relax.

'So what are you doing here?' I say, making an effort to sound pleased this time.

I turn and see Adam's already disappearing down the hallway. He's looking left, right, up, down, like he's just stepped into some museum or something rather than our totally dull 1980s semi.

'Adam?'

I shut the door and hurry after him. He's heading towards the kitchen, at the back of the house, and I can't remember what state it's in.

'What are you doing here?' I ask again when I catch Adam up. Then, because it suddenly strikes me, 'How do you even know where I live?'

'What?' Adam's leaning through the doorway to check out the kitchen. He turns to face me. 'Oh. You told me.'

'Did I?'

'Sure.'

I frown. I remember telling Adam *roughly* where I lived but not the exact address. But I guess I must have, and anyway I don't get a chance to think about it because Adam's off again, into the kitchen.

'Wow, this is *nice*. Really spacious. Your mum's doing pretty well for herself, huh?'

Our kitchen's just a normal kitchen. Frankie's is way nicer. They've got this island where you can sit and have breakfast and this humongous American-style fridge that shoots out ice through the door, plus this, like, pan rack or whatever, which dangles from the ceiling in the centre of the room. Sort of like art, or a chandelier or something. Ours is just, you know. Your basic kitchen. White cupboards, grey surfaces, crappy laminate floor. And yeah, there's space for a table but only just, and to me it always feels kind of poky. Me and Mum, we're always bumping into each other around the sink.

And that's the other thing: there's stuff all piled in the washing-up bowl. I was supposed to clear up the breakfast stuff before school but I got distracted upstairs (packing, in theory, which basically involved piling everything I owned on my bed. It's like, how are you supposed to pack for a trip away when you don't even know where you're going?).

But the kitchen, it's a bit of a tip, is the point. There's even washing hanging on the airer. Sheets, thankfully, no knickers (!), but even still.

Adam sees me watching him and there must be, like, an expression on my face.

'What's wrong? Should I have taken off my shoes? God, sorry.' He bends to untie his laces.

'No, no, no, it's not that. I wasn't expecting you, that's all. It isn't always such a mess in here, I promise.'

'Mess?' Adam checks around, as though he's missed something. He looks at me after that like I'm crazy. 'Trust me, this isn't messy. Not in my book, anyway. It's nice, actually. It looks real. You know, like a proper family home.'

I remember about his childhood then, his upbringing. His mum dying and his stepdad being such an arsehole. And I realize, what's the big deal? So there are a few cereal bowls in the sink. So what? So finally I *do* relax. I smile, properly this time, and I remember: it's *Adam*. As for school, thanks to my failed attempt at packing I was probably going to be late today anyway. Plus, if I'm ditching the next two days, what difference will an extra hour make this morning?

So what I say is, 'Would you like a tour? Of the rest of the house, I mean.'

And Adam, he smiles back at me. 'You know what?' he says. 'I really would.'

*

Half an hour later we're in my bedroom. It's taken that long to show Adam around, even though there's basically nothing to see. That's what I thought, anyway, but I guess . . . I don't know. Maybe it sounds all big-headed to say this but I guess I underestimated how much Adam's into me. You know? He was acting the way I would if I'd been looking around *his* home. All interested in every detail. Even Mum's room. Especially Mum's room. Although I figure that's another part of his whole mum thing. You know, being . . . not jealous exactly, but . . . envious. Sad and that. About his own mum. So he was looking at Mum's stuff, where she slept, the books on her bedside table, just everything really. He wasn't obvious about it. He made out like he was looking at the view. Because he was embarrassed, I suppose. One thing I've learned about Adam is that he's not exactly open with his feelings. So it was kind of sweet, I thought. Which is why, even though I knew Mum wouldn't have liked it much, I let Adam look for as long as he wanted.

But after that we're just sitting in my bedroom.

'Whoa,' Adam goes, when he sees my bed. Not my bed so much as the stuff on it. I told you, I'd pretty much emptied out my entire wardrobe. Jeans, dresses, tops, shoes, it's all on there, like I've spent the morning building an indoor bonfire. Which is pretty much what I feel like doing with all my clothes because basically I can't stand *any* of them. Some of the dresses in particular, I don't even know what I was thinking.

'Is this all for tomorrow?' Adam asks me, which when he says it I have to return his grin.

'Not *all* of it, obviously,' I say. I spot some underwear (clean!) on the floor by my feet and I kick it under the bed. 'But it's hard, you know? Deciding what to take when I don't even know what we'll be doing.'

And what I'm hoping is Adam will give me some sort of clue then, just a hint even, but instead what he does is he keeps grinning.

'I wouldn't sweat it,' he says. 'Just take whatever you feel comfortable in. Maybe a jumper. It's possible you might get cold.'

Which is odd, a bit, because the forecast for the entire country is sunny and twenty-five degrees. But I guess he's just thinking of at night.

'You sound like my mum,' I say, which, again, he just smiles at.

'But you're all set?' Adam asks me. 'Not with the packing clearly. But with Frankie? That's really the reason I came round. Just to check we're all systems go.'

'Yep,' I say proudly, 'all set. Mum thinks I'm staying at Frankie's, as per, and Frankie thinks Mum's making me stay at home.'

I don't know how much Frankie believed me but as long as no one starts looking for me until I get home on Friday evening, that's basically all I care about.

'What about music?' I ask Adam. 'I've got this little speaker for my phone. Should I bring that? And what about Wi-Fi? Should I download some playlists before we go? What kind of stuff, do you think? Like, acoustic maybe?' Romantic, is what I mean.

'Sure,' Adam goes. 'Whatever. Although to be honest I doubt we'll have that much time to listen to music.'

'I just thought when we're . . .' In bed, I almost say! '. . . chilling out or whatever. Maybe in the evening?'

'There's not going to be much of that, either,' Adam says. 'Chilling out, I mean. The next two days: they're going to be pretty exciting. For both of us.'

'Really?' I'm smiling so much at this point I can hardly get my mouth wide enough.

'Really.'

'Oh,' I say, remembering. 'What about money? I was going to head to the cashpoint after school. How much do you think I'll need?'

'Don't worry about it,' Adam goes.

'But . . .'

'Seriously. Don't worry about it. Forget about music and forget about money. Just bring yourself. That's really all either of us is going to need.'

I drop on to the bed beside him. 'So where are we meeting? What time?'

Adam seems pleased to be getting down to business. He angles towards me.

'You know where the station is, right?'

'Like, the train station?'

Adam nods.

'Course,' I say. 'Why, are we going by train? I *love* train journeys, like . . .'

'Emily . . .'

'. . . but seriously, this one time, when I was young, me and Mum took the train all the way to Brighton.

I told you about our day in Brighton, right? But the journey, on the train, it –'

'*Emily.*' He says it sharp. 'Just listen. Will you?' I guess I jerk back or something, because it is, it's like getting snapped at by a teacher. 'Sorry,' he says. 'It's just, this is important. You know?'

I do know. It's my fault for prattling on like some excited little kid.

'Of course,' I reply. 'Sorry. Go ahead. I'm listening, I promise.'

Adam takes this deep breath. 'So tomorrow,' he says. '*Behind* the station there's that old warehouse. Do you know the one I mean?'

'The old perfume place? With those big faded letters on the wall?'

'Right. There.'

'What . . .' I start to say but I catch myself. I wait for Adam to explain.

'There's a hole in the fence beside the gates where you can squeeze in,' he says. 'And then, around the back, past the entrance to the main building, there's a row of lock-ups. Like, garages almost. Meet me there. Outside the unit with the yellow door.'

'The yellow door?'

'Right. And make sure no one sees you. The lock-ups are all empty, and obviously the warehouse is abandoned, so there won't be anyone around anyway. But technically no one's supposed to be there, and anyway you don't want anyone to recognize you. Come early, like for eight-thirty or so, and you'll be fine.'

'Er . . . OK,' I say. 'Got it.' I salute, and Adam likes that, I can tell. It's an odd place to meet but I don't say so because I don't want Adam getting angry again. And anyway he explains in the end without me even asking.

'Don't tell anyone,' he says, taking my hand, 'but it's kind of where I've been staying lately. Just until I get a job.'

'You've been sleeping in a garage?' I say. It just blurts out of me, before I can stop it. And to think I was worried earlier about what Adam would think of the way I lived here!

Adam just smiles this lopsided-looking smile. 'Just for the past few weeks. I had a room in this house for a while but it fell through. And it's not that bad, actually. It's dry and secure and no one bothers me. Plus, best of all, it's totally free. There're even showers at the leisure centre round the corner. You can use them and nobody stops you.'

Oh Adam. Oh you poor, poor thing.

I stop myself saying it this time but it's there in my head even so. My free hand covers the top of his.

'Hey, it's cool, I promise,' Adam insists. 'And next week . . . Well. I'm pretty sure I'll be moving on anyway.'

'Moving on? Like . . .'

'I don't mean leaving.' He raises my hands to his lips. They're cold and kind of dry but even so I go all tingly. I shiver in fact, and Adam grins. 'Trust me,' he says. 'You'll be stuck with me for a good while yet.'

I smile then, and this time I kiss *his* hand.

'Tomorrow, then,' I say.

'Tomorrow,' he says back, and I can tell he's just as excited about it as I am.

7 p.m. – 8 p.m.

18

The aftermath.

Susanna recalls precisely how it played out.

The first she knew that something had happened – something worse than the fire – was when she got home that evening. There was a police car parked in the driveway and lights burning throughout the house. She'd lost track of Jake's sleeping habits of late but it would have been unusual for him to be out of his room at this time of night. Neil too should already have been asleep. Either that or locked away in his 'playroom', where the only illumination would have come from his computer screen and the fag smouldering in the ashtray on the arm of his chair.

Susanna assumed the police were there because of the blaze. It was gone midnight and she'd just spent the last several hours attempting to help the teachers, the headmaster, the police shape some sort of order from the overspill of panic. Although, in fact, once a cordon had been established and all the children and parents accounted for, she had mostly stood around watching like everyone else. It was like bonfire night in the end but without the festivity. Some of the older kids, inevitably, were laughing and cheering but mostly the mood was sombre, the crowd muffled by a blanket of shock.

Other than those pockets of celebrating children, the only sounds were the shouts of the firemen and the whip-crack rage of the fire itself. It was astonishingly loud, far louder than Susanna would have imagined. The noise was almost more alarming than the sight of the flames dancing on the roof. Every snap, every bang, was another body blow, an audible reminder of how much damage was being done inside the building. In contrast the flames appeared almost graceful. If it hadn't been for the sound and smell of the fire, you almost wouldn't have believed that anything so beautiful could inflict any damage at all.

So, yes, when Susanna saw the police car in her driveway, she didn't doubt that they'd come about the school. Initially she had simply assumed the blaze had started by accident but, while she had been standing outside the building, rumours of arson had spread as quickly as the flames themselves. So probably the police were looking for witnesses. What they imagined Susanna would be able to tell them, however, and why they were so prompt in coming to her, she couldn't have said.

She remembers getting her key ready before she had even reached the front door. She remembers stepping into the hallway, through to the kitchen, without taking off her shoes or coat. Her handbag was still in her hand when the male constable, surprisingly old given his rank, deferred to Neil to establish Susanna's identity.

'Is this your wife?' he asked him, as though – what? She might just possibly be his mistress? She was too female to be able to answer for herself?

Neil, uncharacteristically silent, only nodded.

'Can I help you?' Susanna asked, out of irritation addressing the male policeman's colleague, a young woman in a constable's uniform as well.

'There's been an incident, I'm afraid,' the male policeman said, before his colleague could respond. 'You and your husband will want to come with us.'

'The fire, you mean? I know, I was there, I saw it. I've just –'

And then it struck her: why was Jake not downstairs too? With the police here, and all the lights on, why had she not seen her son eavesdropping from the stairs at least, or passed him loitering in the hallway?

'Oh my God, has something happened? Has something happened to Jake? Was he there, at the school? He said he wasn't going to be there!'

In her panic she was casting from face to face. Neil continued to avoid making eye contact. The male policeman remained impassive. And the young policewoman, unless Susanna was imagining it, stared back at her with outright hostility.

And so it began.

Jake: her baby: her sweet, loving little boy: sitting all alone in a prison cell.

It is an image, a motif of that period in her life, that has stayed with her more than any other. More even than the day Susanna walked through the front door to find her son hanging from the banister. She's relived that moment innumerable times too, of course she has, but the *visuals* of it, the optical imprint on her brain . . . it's blurred. Her brain has shrouded it, hidden it from her the way a nurse might draw a curtain. Instead it is her emotions from that day that have scarred her more than anything. Her grief, shock, panic, which threaten to boil over whenever she has cause to recollect.

But Jake sitting alone on that bench, his face shadowed by soot (and something else, Susanna remembers thinking, which rendered his features even darker – unless that only appeared in retrospect): Susanna sees that image almost every time she shuts her eyes.

She recalls as well how long it took her to find out exactly what had happened. At first nobody would tell her anything, not even Neil. The drive to the police station had elapsed in silence. And then, once they'd arrived, the story emerged only gradually. Even when it had she couldn't comprehend it. These words she was hearing –

assault
incident
complaint
victim
rape

– she understood them. It was just, in the context of her son, they made no sense. None whatsoever. *Rape*, for heaven's sake? How? When? *Who?* There'd been a mistake, clearly. A mix-up. Mistaken identity, that was the phrase that kept recurring in Susanna's mind.

Except: Jake. The way he was refusing, like Neil, to even look at her, to say a word in answer to her prompts. For that entire first night Susanna couldn't tell what was real. Was she asleep? Dreaming? What about the fire? Had *that* happened?

And then Jake's confession the next morning, when the facts of the matter became inescapable.

As Susanna sees it, what happened next can be split into two distinct phases. The period in which the world hated Jake. And then, harder to bear, the period it didn't.

His identity emerged almost immediately. The newspapers couldn't reveal it because of Jake's age, obviously, but everyone knew that Jake was the boy involved. The street, the school, the community, everyone who mattered. And so when the media reported the 'facts' of the case – a (young, idealistic) teacher raped by one of her (wicked, loner) pupils, the scene of the crime (a school!) set ablaze to cover the assailant's tracks (all 'allegedly', of course) – it was an open secret that Jake was the boy responsible.

There was outrage, inevitably. The newspapers might not have been able to point the finger at Jake specifically but they stirred up enough moral indignation that those who knew who the guilty party was (Susanna has never been quite sure what happened to the 'innocent until proven' part) took up the cause with vigour. At Jake's remand hearing the van he was being transported in was almost toppled. Bricks, eggs, faeces, all were hurled at the windows of Susanna's house. What Jake had done, at the age he was: it summed up everything that was wrong with modern society. And modern society, in response, was about ready to lynch Susanna's child.

So that was the point she thought it couldn't get any worse. Or, more accurately, the point she thought she could tell exactly how things, from here, would deteriorate. Jake had confessed everything to the police. Alison had told her side of the story, as had Scott, Pete and Charlie. The other boys' accounts differed from Jake's, yes, but the important thing was that everyone by this stage knew what had really happened. And so the course of their lives was laid out in front of them. The recriminations, the reprisals, the retribution. Susanna thought she knew exactly what was heading their way.

But she was wrong.

Alison Birch, six weeks after Jake's arrest, changed her story. Not only that, she disappeared, as suddenly and completely as Susanna would attempt to after Emily was spat at in the street. Susanna assumed that Alison was as repulsed by the furore around what had happened as she was. In theory her identity was protected, just like Jake's, but in reality – in the community – Alison was about as anonymous as Susanna's son. And with the prospect of a fully fledged trial coming up, there's no doubt she would have been afraid. Ashamed as well, probably, in precisely the way Susanna framed it when she explained it to Adam. Susanna had tried to contact her soon after Jake's arrest (knowing it was a terrible idea, knowing her lawyers would object if they found out), to explain to her how sorry she was but, understandably, she was rebuffed. So she had no way of *knowing* why Alison ran. It stood to reason, that was all. It was the only thing in the whole sordid situation that in Susanna's mind made any sense whatsoever.

The papers, though, saw it differently. That was their job, apparently. Not just to see things differently, to present them differently too, irrespective of the facts. They wanted blood, that was the problem. Their readers *demanded* it. And when the Crown Prosecution Service was obliged to drop Jake's case, to declare that, without a complainant and after Jake had recanted his confession, they had had no firm basis on which to proceed, the baying crowd found itself deprived of its prey. Which obviously wouldn't do at all. So the press did the only thing it could do. It found a new prey.

The news cycle turned at such a rate that Susanna was left feeling spun-dry. Not only was Jake not guilty, the papers declared, he was innocent. Wronged. Falsely accused. Jake was the victim in all of this, not Alison. And Alison Birch – whom the newspapers could now name and shame with impunity – was the criminal. To think, not only had she accused a child of rape – a *child*, dear reader! – she'd stood by her perverted fiction for over a month, wasting police time, misleading the public and coming close to ruining a young boy's life. And why? Because she was a fantasist. An attention-grabber. A *whore*, they might as well have said. Indeed, to Susanna that was almost the most shocking thing of all – that this was the outcome the newspapers seemed secretly to have been hoping for all along. Boy rapes woman? Huh. Not exactly man bites dog. But a *false* accusation of rape, where the *woman* is really to blame . . . Well. There are your op-eds for the next two weeks at least, your Sunday supplements for a solid month. Even better, there was no counter-argument to contend with. No pesky lawyers crying libel, no perplexing shades of grey. With Alison not around to defend herself, it was a story that could run and run and run.

Susanna recalls her arguments with Neil. Arguments/ argument – there were a string of them but really they were just that: a single looped and twisted thread, with each flare-up contributing another knot.

The rape was forgotten, the arson all but forgiven, and Jake – their *son* – was off the hook. What the *fuck* was Susanna's problem, her husband demanded to know?

'Nothing's been forgotten!' Susanna insisted. 'Nothing's been forgiven! They're calling the fire an accident, a prank gone wrong, but he'll still face charges. And Jake's not the innocent victim they're all claiming. You know he's not! He's *guilty*. He did it, all the terrible things they're accusing him of!'

'But they're not accusing him. That's the point. They're *not* accusing him, not any more. Why can't you just be happy for him? Glad that it's all gone away? The way any normal mother would be!'

'*Normal?*'

'Yes, normal! It's your duty to stand by your son, no matter what. It's your *responsibility*.'

Susanna couldn't believe what she was hearing. 'You,' she said. '*You* are talking to me about responsibility?

The man who spends every spare hour he has hiding from his family? Whose idea of fathering is to act like a teenage boy?'

Neil scoffed and waved a hand, would have walked away if doing so wouldn't have proved Susanna's point.

'And what about *taking* responsibility?' Susanna pressed. 'At what point do we teach our son about that? Jake *did it*. He *confessed*. He raped someone – *rape*, Neil! – and then he set fire to his school.'

'That wasn't even him! Jake didn't set fire to anything!'

'He was about to! You know that as well as I do!'

'Lower your voice, for Christ's sake.'

'What, are you worried your son will hear what his parents really think? Are you that afraid of showing him what's right?'

'*Your* son now, is it?'

'Ours. I meant ours.'

'And what the hell do you mean, *what's right*? It's out of our hands. *She* ran. *She* decided to withdraw the charges, to claim she made it all up. What are you or I supposed to do? What's *Jake* supposed to do, other than be grateful he's been given a second chance?'

And that was the thing.

Susanna didn't know.

All she knew was that it *wasn't* right. None of it. Yes, Jake was her son and she understood that above all she should be grateful, in precisely the way Neil argued. Jake was just a kid, he'd made a mistake, and everyone who makes a mistake should be given a second chance. That was the reasoning, the line Neil was toeing. But it was the *magnitude* of Jake's mistake that Susanna stumbled on. Plus, how can you call something like rape a *mistake*? A mistake, in sexual terms, was . . . making an advance at a party and being rebuffed. Having sex with a stranger without protection. But rape, a mistake? Knocking a young woman to the floor, pinning her there, forcibly penetrating her, *violating* her, and then saying, what? *Oops*.

No.

No.

Rape wasn't a mistake. It was a travesty. It was the antithesis of every value Susanna held dear, had always assumed she'd instilled in her son. Compassion. Kind-heartedness. Consideration. Respect for others and oneself. Without which we would none of us be any better than animals.

No. Rape wasn't something to be forgotten. It wasn't something so easily forgiven. Rape, in Susanna's mind: it was inhuman.

She couldn't pretend. She just couldn't. But what else in the circumstances was she supposed to do?

People knew, of course. Not the public at large, who swallowed every fabrication the press fed them. But friends, family: they knew. Some chose to allow them-selves to be deceived, and sided with Neil. That's how Susanna saw it. There was Neil's side, and there was hers. Except her side, the people who knew what Susanna knew, even if they weren't privy to all the facts: they weren't really on Susanna's side either. There were the people from the school, who, in deference to what Jake had ostensibly been put through, had allowed the arson charge to be downgraded but also made clear that Jake would need to find somewhere else to complete his studies. There were Susanna's neighbours, who thereafter refused to look her in the eye. There was her brother – her *brother*, her only surviving close relative – who, barring the time Susanna turned up on his doorstep with Emily crying in her arms, never spoke to Susanna again.

Shunned on one side, confounded by the other, Susanna didn't know what she was supposed to do. Betray your son or everything you believe in. That was the choice. Was it a surprise that she so utterly failed to make one?

And Jake. All the while there was Jake.

Susanna can't imagine how he must have been feeling during those weeks after he was arrested. And when he came home, when the charges were dropped, he was as quiet and insular as Susanna had ever known him. He barely left his room, and when he was up there he never opened the curtains. He slept with the duvet over his head, the way he had when he'd been young, when he'd been afraid of what was waiting in the dark. Now, when he ate at the kitchen table he wore his hood up, with his headphones covering his ears. Susanna wasn't even sure they were playing any music.

She tried to speak to him but not very hard. It was Neil, to be fair, who tried hardest. Except Neil's approach seemed to be to attempt to convince Jake that none of it had ever really happened. That the story the press was spinning was the truth. Susanna wasn't even sure Neil didn't actually come to believe it himself: that Jake really *was* the victim in what had happened, and Alison deserved all the vitriol that was flowing her way. Susanna watched him frowning at all the newspaper stories. Not because he found the reports so difficult to reconcile but because he was concentrating so intensely on trying to persuade himself they were true. Maybe that *had been* what really happened. Susanna could practically hear the thoughts in his head. Maybe Jake *hadn't* done anything wrong. And he left the newspapers splayed out for Jake to find.

One time Susanna found the two of them in Neil's playroom. She came home from . . . somewhere, a walk probably, which she'd taken to doing a lot by then, just walking, always away from town rather than towards it. But she came home and she heard the sound of Neil's computer and she found them up there seated side by side. Neil was the one with the controller, his eyes fixed on the screen. He was playing some stupid video game in which the central character was a buxom young woman running around in hot pants. Susanna found herself staring at the screen in disbelief – until she noticed Neil had also given their son a beer.

She exploded. 'What the hell do you think you're doing?'

She was talking to
(shouting at)
Neil, she thinks, but it was Jake she hit. Only on the

top of his arm but it was enough of a slap that it would have hurt. Jake barely even flinched.

'Jesus Christ,' Neil blurted.

Jake's beer can had toppled to the floor and there was a frothy puddle forming on the carpet. There were two more beer cans – empty – at Jake's feet, and Susanna instantly understood that the promise of alcohol was the only reason Jake was in here. He hadn't even been looking at the video game.

'You gave him *beer*?' Susanna said. 'Our fifteen-year-old son. You got him *drunk*?'

Neil forced Susanna out on to the landing. The two of them were so intent on tearing at each other's throats, they almost didn't notice Jake slip out behind them.

'Calm down, for fuck's sake,' Neil said.

Susanna struggled from his grip. 'It's times like this I wonder what I ever saw in you, Neil! Whether our entire marriage wasn't some calamitous mistake! What the hell were you thinking?'

'We were just hanging out!' Neil countered. 'Spending some time together! I thought that's what you wanted!'

'I wanted that fifteen years ago! Now it's too late!' she said. 'Don't you understand? It's too late!'

'That's bullshit! You're the only one who's given up. Who's turned her back on her son. Don't you understand he –'

But he got no further. Their argument was cut short by the sound of the front door slamming, and the echo of its reverberations in its frame.

*

So Jake knew. He understood the way his mother was feeling. It must have been so confusing for him. His father, on one shoulder, preaching bygones. His mother, on the other, saying nothing but in such a way that she positively crackled, distorting every other sound in the room.

Because the fact was she could barely look at him. She couldn't look at Neil, she couldn't look in the mirror, and her eyes came no closer to her son than the floor at his feet, the empty space just over his shoulder. She loved him, she loathed him. He needed her but he disgusted her. And all the while Alison was being flayed in the press. Raped *again*, violated *again*. Susanna couldn't do it. She couldn't let the enduring lesson she imparted to her only child be how to hurt someone and then get away with it. That wasn't her and she wouldn't let it be him.

And so that's why she did it. That's why she went to Jake's room that night, when Neil was off yet again with his friends, trying to reclaim his lost childhood; to pretend that his failure as a husband, as a father, had never happened. Although isn't that precisely what Susanna has been doing ever since? Pretending that what she did, what she said, that night never happened?

But there's no pretending any more. No more secrets, no more lies. All these years working as a counsellor, Susanna should really have understood. No matter how hard you try to escape it, the past has a way of catching up.

19

Dear Alison,

I hope you get this. I'm going to send it to your home, which I know you've left now, but maybe there's someone taking care of all your things. Checking your post, forwarding letters, all that.

The other thing is, if you do get it, I hope you read it. Because I know you get hate mail now and probably this will just get put straight in the bin. Or maybe you'll open it and see who it's from and then put it in the bin, without even reading what I've got to say. So probably I should just get right to it. You know, before you get a chance to throw this away.

So why I'm writing is to tell you goodbye. I know when I've written to you before I've said it will be the last time but this time I genuinely mean it. You'll see I do, I promise. Because basically there's no point carrying on. If I could I would run away the way you did but I don't even know where I would go. It would have to be somewhere else, somewhere different, except the way I see it there is nowhere different. Everywhere is just exactly the same. And anyway the whole world hates me. Scott and that. My parents. Everybody.

Even you.

And that's the thing that's been tearing me apart.

What I've been searching for is a way to make you understand. How I feel, I mean – about everything. But all I could think was there was no way you ever would, not after what happened. So I have to show you. That's what I figure. So really that's what this is all about.

How I decided was, I was sitting in my bedroom. That's where I've been, mostly, since they let me out. There or down by the river. And mostly my parents leave me alone. My dad comes in sometimes with his stupid newspapers, trying to get me to read what they wrote. He doesn't get that I don't care what they say because none of it changes a single thing. And Mum. She's just the same. She probably thinks worse of me than you do. She can barely look at me most of the time. I sometimes wonder how she'd react if I tried to touch her.

Although that night, what happened was, my mum came into my room. She knocked and I didn't answer but she came in anyway and she asked whether we could talk. I just shrugged or something I guess. And Mum, she came inside and she sat down at the end of my bed, which is the closest she'd got to me in weeks. I was just lying on my side, staring at the wallpaper, which has these swirls you can follow round and round. I used to do that when I was a kid, trace the swirls with my finger.

Can I turn on a light? she goes, and I say, Whatever. So she does, she turns the light on, the little side light, and I'm waiting for her to say what she has to say. It doesn't matter what it is, I just want her to say it so it's over with and then she'll leave me alone.

But, Listen, she goes. We need to talk, Jake. Properly talk. Don't you think?

And my mum is the last person I want to talk to but there's something about having her there beside me that feels different from all the times before. So I don't say no. I just lie there and I don't say anything.

Will you answer me something? she goes. If I ask you a question? She takes a breath then, like she's getting herself ready. Are you sorry? she says. About what happened?

And I don't know what it is but after all these weeks of trying to explain, of other people explaining, of no one getting close to understanding and me not being able to see a way out, it's like finally somebody's asked the only thing that matters. You know? Because I am sorry, about everything. I'm sorry you never really understood me, not the way I always thought you did. I'm sorry I messed things up so badly, that I never really understood anything either. I'm sorry I fucked up my life, basically, and that I fucked it up for everyone around me. And what happens is, I start crying. Just like a little kid. All quietly, just sort of shaking, but there are tears running down my face.

And Mum, she sees. Oh Jake, she goes. It's OK. To feel sad, to feel regret. That's how you should be feeling right now. It's normal. Healthy. If it was me I know I'd be feeling that way too. I don't know how I'd be able to live with myself.

I look up then, just as my mum looks down.

She starts crying herself then and moves a little bit closer. Not touching me, not quite, but almost.

I wasn't sure what you were thinking, she says. With everything they've been writing in the papers, all the things you've been hearing from your dad . . . I was worried, that's all. I didn't know what was going on in your head.

Then, what she says is, I'm glad, Jake. It might sound cruel but I am. I'm glad you're feeling the way you do. Because if you're sorry we can find a way past this. If you accept it we can find a way through.

Which is typical Mum. You know? Always looking to solve things when some things there's no way they can be solved. I turn to face the wall.

Jake, listen to me, she says, and she puts a hand on my arm. But slowly, testing, like I'm hot or something. Like she's worried she might get burnt. But then she sort of pulls me round. It may not feel like it now, she says, but there's always a way forward. Always. A way to overcome the past.

I don't answer. I just lie there and try wiping away my tears.

The first step is to accept responsibility, Mum says. Pretending this thing never happened, the way we've all been doing? It doesn't help anyone. It doesn't solve anything. Do you agree?

I do, I guess, so I nod, which just gets me crying all the more. What I don't say but what I'm thinking is that accepting responsibility doesn't help either. I tried that. It didn't work.

Then, Mum goes, the next thing is, you need to find a way to make amends. Do you understand what that means? To prove how sorry you are. What I think is, if you don't do *something*, you'll never be able to move on. You'll be feeling this way for ever, never getting past the pain you're living now.

Which is basically the way I've been feeling. Like there is no way forward, no way back even, just this being trapped inside my head.

And you. All the while there's you. Thinking I hate you probably, that I'm angry at you, when the only person I'm angry at is myself. Like, it's not your fault you didn't understand me. It's mine for not being able to make you. I failed basically, the way I've failed at everything my whole stupid life.

It's just such a mess, Mum suddenly goes. All of it! I don't understand, Jake. I don't understand any of it. What happened, what you did . . .

She shakes her head, wipes at her tears. But I can tell she's furious. I can tell exactly how much she blames me.

Alison, she says, squashing all her anger down inside again. I mean, I know she's gone but maybe there's a way of conveying to her just how sorry you really are.

She looks at me then, all meaningfully. And that's when I see it. The way out Mum's been talking about. I realize what it is she's trying to tell me. She even spelled it out for me: *I don't know how I'd be able to live with myself.*

Whatever it is, she goes on, however you choose to do it – it has to come from you. Do you understand, Jake? Do you understand what it is I'm trying to say to you?

Something else pops into my head then, one of my dad's stupid sayings. Actions speak louder than words, is what he says, which I'd never really got until then.

So I put my hand on top of my mum's, which takes her by surprise, I guess. She jerks back, which only makes me think what I'm thinking all the more. And it's like a relief, you know? Like someone's had their hands around my throat but now, finally, I can breathe.

I sit up. I say, I get it, Mum. I do. I understand what it is you're trying to tell me.

And Mum, what happened was, her face just crumpled. She hugged me then, and I sort of let her, because I knew it would be the last time she ever would.

So that's why. That's how I came to understand. It just seemed obvious, really, in the end. The way I feel, how I feel about *you*: I'm going to show you. Just like my mum showed me.

Love, always,
Jake

20

As Susanna stares down at Jake's letter, the ink here and there begins to bleed. She wipes away her fallen tears, smudging the handwriting further, but hoping her son will somehow feel her caress.

'You killed him, Susanna. You told him to do it and he did.'

'What? No!'

'You did! Look at the letter and tell me you deny it. That you deny putting the idea in Jake's head!'

Susanna stares again at the words on the page. She cannot help staring. She cannot stop her tears either, nor hold back the knowledge that Adam is right. If he's wrong, then why for all this time has she tried to hide it? Why has she never told *anyone* what she said, not even the man she was supposed to love – the man she did love, once, and who cared for Jake as much as she did?

'Oh Jake. Oh my boy . . .'

'You killed him, Susanna,' says Adam again. 'My father! My *real* father. He's dead and he's dead because of you!'

'But . . . I . . . Your mother. I thought this was about what happened to your mother?'

Adam looks at her with undisguised contempt. 'My mother? I don't *care* about my mother. Didn't I tell you that already? *She* never wanted me in the first place. And then she went and died and left me all alone to live with *him*. So why the hell should I give a damn what happened to her?'

It is cruel, unforgiving and utterly logical.

'This is about Jake, Susanna. All of this, right from the start: it's been about Jake. He was the only person in the world who would have wanted me. Who would have loved me the way a parent should. He was my only chance, Susanna. And you took him from me!'

'But he was a boy. Just a *boy*.'

It seems incredible to Susanna that anyone might think of her son as anything but the child he was, yet it strikes her how distinct Adam's perspective is from hers. It's as though they are looking at the same point from opposite horizons. For Susanna, Jake is a boy in stasis. A beautiful, lost, broken boy, who threw away his chance of ever growing up. For Adam, he is the man – the father – who never was.

Susanna can see it now. She understands every one of Adam's questions, everything he in turn has been saying to her. All his talk about how Jake loved Adam's mother, about how he cared for her. And Adam's suggestion that what happened wasn't rape, not *really*. The fire too, his obsession with whose idea it was, who started it, how Alison escaped the burning classroom. Adam has been doing exactly what Susanna accused the newspapers of doing; exactly what we *all* do when the truth is too appalling or upsetting or inconvenient even to bear. He has been seeing things differently;

288

manipulating the facts to construct and then reconstruct the narrative until it's the story he really wants to hear. More than that, he has been constructing a father: the parent he wished for but never got to have.

And as for Susanna . . .

In Adam's mind – in Adam's story – it is Susanna who stole his father from him, who dictated the shape of Adam's life.

And not just in Adam's mind, as it happens.

'You know I'm right,' Adam says. 'Don't you, Susanna? I can see you do. You've always accepted Jake died because of you. That's why you ran. You had to. You couldn't live with what you'd done. You couldn't live with the *shame*.'

There were so many reasons Susanna ran, in the end. She told herself it was because of Neil. After Jake's death, Susanna's husband took their private sorrow to the press. He even let them publish Jake's picture.

He was acting out of grief, Susanna knew. He was angry, lashing out, and he wanted the world to know the tragic fate of their son. Except Neil's version of events in the interviews he gave affirmed every lie the newspapers had allowed to take root. The abdication of their family's anonymity not only reignited the campaign of vitriol against their son's victim, therefore. It also exposed their future daughter in a way that Susanna convinced herself was unforgivable.

Particularly when Neil threatened to do it all over again. This was later, after the incident with the spitter. 'I've been thinking,' he said. 'Journalists are always asking us to give more interviews. We should talk about this, the hate there still is out there in the community. For Jake's sake. And Emily . . . with the money the newspapers offer, we'll be able to give her a decent education. A holiday now and then too.' It *was* unforgivable, Susanna decided.

And Neil: she suddenly realized it was only the paralysing weight of her grief/guilt, guilt/grief that had kept her at his side, which she hoped having another baby might help to lift. How she'd loved Neil when they'd first met. She'd been very young, admittedly, they both had, but his looks, his easy manner . . . once upon a time Neil had been exactly what Susanna needed. And she'd hoped having Emily might somehow save them; might bring them back to how they'd been when *Jake* was first born. She even managed to convince herself that the distance between her and Neil had only developed *because* of Jake – and that it had nothing to do with the fact that they had grown up into diametrical opposites, coexisting out of expediency and habit. But then, when Emily came along, the love Susanna felt for her daughter put her feelings towards Neil in starker relief. Having another child wasn't about saving their marriage, Susanna realized. It was all about saving herself.

And there was the incident with the spitter itself, of course. That was another reason Susanna ran.

No matter how Neil and the newspapers tried to spin things, there were people who *knew* what had really happened. *Scum*, the woman had called Susanna.

Meaning she was a traitor: to women, to common decency. There were others like her, Susanna knew, just as there were countless so-called 'fans' who, thanks to Neil, now knew exactly where to send their poisonous tributes to Jake.

Perhaps if it had just been her and Neil, Susanna might have accepted the world's attentions as her penance. Certainly she put up with the way she was portrayed in the press for long enough. It was as Adam said: they never liked her. She was too cold, too aloof, too reluctant to criticize Alison and not ready enough to cry in front of the cameras for the loss of her son. But the problem was, it wasn't just her and Neil. Susanna had to try to protect Emily, to give her daughter a future that wasn't tainted by what had happened in the past.

So Susanna had good reasons to run. Ultimately, though, and underpinning them all, wasn't it exactly as Adam said? Wasn't it *shame* that caused Susanna to flee? To *hide*, moreover? Wasn't the real reason Susanna became Susanna that she could no longer live with her old self? Adam asked her right at the beginning: *Do you deny you're responsible for what Jake did? For how it all ended?* Susanna thought he meant the rape, the fire, but really he was talking about his father taking his own life. And Susanna's answer?

I am responsible.

I *am*.

For what happened to Alison, for what happened to the school and for what happened to Jake. Susanna blames herself for *everything*.

And at last Adam can see she does too.

'You sit there crying,' he says to her, spits at her, 'as though crying will make everything go away. You sit here hiding in your little hole and you think no one will ever find you. But I found you, Susanna! *I* found you!'

Susanna is forced to listen then as he lays out how he did. By following the signposts online, initially; all the clues collated by Jake's fans or by those who simply made it their business to know. There was a rumour she was working as a counsellor, started by someone who claimed to have been one of her patients – and *that*, Adam says, was just too apposite – too *perfect* – not to follow up. A counsellor? How predictably *pathetic*. From then on it was easy. He didn't have a name but he had a location, and all counsellors have to register on the central directory that serves their area – assuming they want to get any clients at all – meaning in the end it was a simple process of elimination. Susanna was right to be afraid of the Internet, as things turned out. But she should have known that just because you cover your eyes doesn't mean the danger goes away.

Oh Emily. Where are you? What has Adam done to you?

'You think this makes up for it,' Adam says. 'Don't you? Doing what you do. You think by acting like you're helping people you can erase all the damage you inflicted in your former life. What was it you said earlier?' His voice goes higher. '*My life isn't about me any more!*' he mimics. '*I've made it so it's not about me!*'

He looks at her with all the hatred he's only shown so far in flashes.

'You don't even realize, do you? You don't get that this, all of this, it only makes things worse. You're a hypocrite, *Susanna*,' he says, mocking her name, the very person she thought she'd become. 'You ask people to tell you their secrets and all the while you're hiding behind your lies. About who you are. About what you *did*.'

Adam stands, so abruptly he dislodges his chair. It knocks the side table, and one of the water glasses tips and smashes on the floor. The sound is like a splash of cold water and it jolts Susanna from her shock.

'What are you doing?' she says, panicking. She presses herself deeper into her chair.

Adam levels the knife at Susanna's chest. His fingers adjust themselves around the handle. 'You're guilty, Susanna,' he declares. 'I said I'd judge you and that's my ruling: guilty as charged.'

'No, wait, I –'

'It's too late,' Adam says. 'Anything you say to me now, you're eighteen years too late. You're guilty – and it's time you were finally made to pay.'

21

Ruth has drunk too much wine. In the end she and Alina opted to share a bottle, which was always going to end badly – for Ruth, anyway – because Alina rarely drinks more than a single glass. She had two this evening but, even so, that left two-thirds of a bottle for Ruth, which she can take, no problem, and still be safe to drive – but being *legal* to drive, that's a different story.

It's a good job they ordered that plate of food. Ruth has nine points already, for speeding, a traffic light, not drinking, but even so she is flirting with a ban and if she lost her licence she doesn't know what she would do. Take to sleeping on her dental chair, probably, because how otherwise would she be at the surgery in time for work? But at least with something in her belly there's a chance, if she does get breathalysed, she might, *just*, sneak under the limit. Christ, those chicken goujons were so dry they no doubt soaked up all the alcohol anyway. If Ruth had wanted to, she probably could have stayed for another glass.

But that would have been a mistake. She was later leaving than she'd intended to be as it was, and although she's had a fairly decent time there is only so much of Alina's company that Ruth can take. It would have been different if Susanna had been there. Then Ruth really *would* have drunk too much, because it was turning into one of those evenings where the wine was slipping down like water. Unfortunately/fortunately, however, Susanna *wasn't* there, meaning Ruth managed to tear herself away.

She wonders how her friend made out with her client. Made out – ha! There's a double entendre if ever there was one. A double entendre or a Freudian slip? Susanna would know. Just as she knew exactly what she was doing earlier when she gave Ruth and Alina the brush-off. Ruth quizzed Alina at the pub and though this client of Susanna's might not have been a Leonardo DiCaprio, he apparently wasn't that far off a young Johnny Depp. 'Doubling up', my arse, Ruth tells herself. Her friend was flirting – *lusting* – pure and simple, and why the hell not? She knows Susanna is far too much of a professional to ever act inappropriately with one of her clients but that doesn't mean she can't permit herself the occasional harmless fantasy.

Ruth smiles as she totters towards her car. And she is, she is definitely tottering. One glass, Ruth. Two glasses maximum. How many times does she really need to tell herself?

And look: she's heading up the wrong street. There's a parking space right outside the surgery, which usually Ruth thinks of as hers, but this morning she arrived later than usual and the space had already been taken. So instead she had to park in the next street over, meaning she should have turned *left* outside the pub, the way Alina went, not *right* and back the way they'd come.

Cursing with more colour than is really justified, Ruth turns on her heels. But as she does so she manages to drop her car keys, which she knocks with her foot into the gutter. There's no drain, thank goodness, but even so. Ruth casts her eyes heavenward. Honestly, how is it she can pull a molar from a ten-year-old and barely cause them to flinch but in the real world is an Olympic champion at tripping over her own feet? And it's *not* the wine. Not always. If anything, mostly, alcohol actually makes her coordination better.

Yeah, right, says a voice. Save it for the policeman in the lay-by, old woman.

She is just about to bend to retrieve her keys when something catches at the tail of her eye. Movement, in the window across the way. Their window. *Susanna's* window. Which must be a mistake because the window is dark and if Susanna were still up there she would have turned on a light. As it is the glass reflects back at her blackly, just like every other window in their little mews. The street is empty, the buildings too. And as Ruth looks again she is certain: there is nothing, no movement of any kind. There is only the flicker just above her from the solitary streetlight, which glows a warm, shadowy pink that could have been plucked from the horizon of the dying sky.

Ruth picks up her keys. She doesn't totter this time. The sudden spookiness of the cul-de-sac has sobered her. She feels an urge to hurry off to find her car but before she does she takes a final look around. She checks the doorways first, the little alleyway that funnels towards the parade of shops, just in case the movement she thought she saw was closer than she assumed. It is only after she is certain there is no one around that she lifts her gaze once more towards Susanna's window . . . and that's when she sees it once again.

Movement. Unmistakable this time. The quick, back-and-forth tussle of shadows scuffling in the dark.

And that's not right. Whatever it is that's going on up there – whatever was going on up there earlier – Ruth is all at once convinced: it isn't right. Susanna doesn't *flirt*, for pity's sake. Ruth doesn't know what she was thinking. And doubling up? When has Susanna *ever*? Really, Ruth should have known better. More than that, she should never have left her friend alone.

22

It doesn't come. The pain – the release Susanna is expecting: when she opens her eyes Adam is past her and heading for the door. He has the knife, his bag, everything he arrived with bar Jake's letters. And incredible to Susanna as it seems, the fact of the matter is inescapable. He is leaving.

'Wait . . .'

Adam doesn't stop, doesn't turn round. Susanna stares helplessly at the back of him, and all the fear she was feeling before transforms abruptly into rage.

'STOP!'

Susanna finds herself on her feet. It is only the fact that Adam turns this time that prevents her lunging and hauling him back.

'You're just . . . you're *going*?'

'It's over, Susanna. Our little therapy session? There's nothing left for either of us to say.'

'But you can't just go!'

Adam sniffs. 'You've made your bed, Susanna. I suggest you lie in it. See how cosy it feels now.'

'But what about Emily? Where she is? What have you done to her? *Tell me what you've done to my daughter!*'

Adam smiles. And this time when he turns away Susanna knows he will not be turning back.

For a moment it is all she can do to stand and watch. She is pulsing, raging, to the point she isn't sure what she is capable of. On the one hand she is aware that any moment she could collapse on to the floor. On the other she is convinced that, if she wanted to, she could shoot electricity, lightning bolts, from her fingertips.

He is *not* leaving.

Susanna will not let him.

Not until he tells her about Emily.

Almost before she realizes she is doing it, she has freed the paring knife from her sleeve. The knife that, the last time Susanna used it, slipped and cut her almost to the bone. It is in her grip now, pointing down, but as she steps she raises it above her head. It is as before: Susanna doesn't know quite what it is she intends to do. Threaten Adam? Stab him? She needs to keep him here, is all she knows. *Pin* him here if necessary.

He is reaching for the door handle when he hears her coming. The room is so dark now it is mainly shadows and it is possible when Adam spins he doesn't immediately notice the knife. Susanna catches the anger on his face, the surprise too. But then he notices Susanna's raised arm, the glint perhaps of what is in her grip, and he drops everything he is carrying as his hand shoots up and grabs her wrist.

'What the . . .'

Susanna makes a sound somewhere between a shriek and a scream. She is driving downwards with all her strength and for a second she has a dreadful premonition that she will win. The knife will plunge into

Adam's shoulder, deeper, towards his heart, through it, and Susanna will have killed him.

Her own blood. Once again she will be guilty of spilling her own blood.

Perhaps it is this insight that makes her waver. Possibly – probably – Adam is simply stronger. Either way the tussle is over in a few short moments. Susanna feels her wrist bend, and then something explodes into her stomach. A fist, a knee, a foot. Whatever it is that has hit her, it drives her back, away, and she staggers and stumbles to the floor. Her head whips backwards and hits the wooden panel on the front of her desk, and for several seconds she lies sprawled where she has fallen, stunned.

When the fog lifts, Adam is laughing away his fury.

'You *lunatic*.' Somehow Susanna's knife is in his hand, replacing the one he dropped. He tosses it so it skids towards her feet, and Susanna yelps and does her best to draw away. It hits her anyway but if it pierces her skin she doesn't feel it.

'You were going to *stab* me?' Adam splutters. '*You* were going to stab *me*?'

Susanna, in response, gives a whimper.

'Is that what you've been waiting for all this time? For me to turn my back? You fucking *bitch*.'

Adam takes a step towards her, his hands clenched. There is no sign any more of his laughter.

'Where did you get the knife, Susanna? Do you keep it in your drawer? In your desk? Just in case . . . what? You ever get a client like me? Or do you carry it around with you, sleep with it tucked beneath your pillow?' Something occurs to Adam and his expression warps into something like a smile. 'I wonder, is it just for protection? Or do you get tempted sometimes to use it on yourself?'

Adam kicks her feet and the knife lying next to them clatters away. Susanna cries out again, at the pain this time that shoots up from her ankle.

'Unless . . . you got it from the kitchen. Didn't you, Susanna? What was it, just lying there? I'm surprised you had the guts to pick it up, snivelling coward that you are. Just look at yourself. Look at how pathetic you've become.'

Susanna does. In her head, she looks down at herself lying on the floor, broken in too many ways for her to count.

'Please,' she says as Adam leans over her. What light there is left coming from the window paints his face a ghoulish white, the colour of dug-up bones. '*Please*,' Susanna persists. 'Emily. Just tell me what you've done to Emily. Did you . . . is she . . .'

'Is she . . . what? *What*, Susanna? Is she dead? Is that what you're asking? Whether your daughter is as dead as your son?'

The words explode like another kick in Susanna's gut.

'Maybe if I don't tell you, you'll *never* find out,' Adam says. 'Because there's a chance you won't, you know. There's every likelihood you'll have to finish up this second life of yours without ever knowing what became of your second child.' He smiles again, horribly. 'I must say that appeals to me: the thought of you having to live with not knowing. The way *I* lived for so long. The way I was forced to live because of *you.*'

Susanna does her best to sit up. 'They'll find you,' she says. 'They'll catch you. If you leave without telling me, the police, they'll *force* you to tell them where she is.'

'Ha. One thing I'm good at is disappearing. Maybe because I've never really existed.'

The sound Susanna makes isn't quite human. It is a keening sound, something between a whine and a wail.

'Please,' she says. 'Please just tell me where my daughter is. You've made your point. You have. I understand now, I do. But don't punish Emily for something that isn't her fault. She wasn't even alive when any of this happened!'

Adam's features darken. 'Neither was I.'

He glares, and then his lips twitch out a narrow smile. 'You realize that even if you do find her, you're never going to get her back?'

'What? What do you mean?'

'There were so many options, that was the problem,' Adam says. 'She was just so *willing*, you see. So desperate to follow wherever I led. I thought of keeping her in a basement somewhere, like that girl on TV. I thought of pushing her in front of a train. Best of all, I thought of gutting her with one of the knives from the rack in your kitchen and leaving her body for you to find.'

Susanna moans.

'But in the end the solution I chose was the simplest. The most obvious. The most painful too, I'm afraid.

It's almost a shame I won't be there to see your face when you finally discover what I've done. If, of course, you ever do.'

Adam retrieves his bag and slings it across his shoulder. He finds the knife he dropped and picks that up too. He looks at Susanna one last time, the wreckage of her on the floor.

'Adam, wait, I –'

'Goodbye, Susanna.'

She watches his back as he walks towards the door. Her mouth opens, shuts, opens again. 'Your mother,' she finds herself saying.

There is a glitch in Adam's movements.

'I've been thinking about your mother, Adam,' Susanna says. 'And what I think is, you got it all wrong.'

Adam's head turns before the rest of him.

'You said she never wanted you. But think about what she did. Think about what she went through just to try to keep you safe.'

'Don't,' Adam answers. Just that.

'She changed her name,' Susanna presses, because what more has she got to lose? 'She got married to her childhood sweetheart, the only person I imagine she could trust. Probably she didn't even love him, not the way he loved her. But both of them: they went away, hid away, left their families. For you, Adam. She was protecting *you*.'

All at once Adam is upon her. 'I said, *don't*.' He points the knife at Susanna's left eye. 'We've done this before, played this game before. You already know how it ends.'

She does. They have. But last time Susanna was wrong. This time, she feels it, she is right.

'Your mother didn't choose to get ill, Adam. She didn't choose to leave you alone. What she chose is to give up her life for you. Her career. Her chance of justice, her reputation, everything.' Susanna swallows. 'If it's true she didn't want you, that she only had you because of her beliefs, then why didn't she just give you up? She fought so hard for you. She fought so hard to keep you.'

There is something running down Susanna's cheek, and she cannot tell whether it is water or blood. Adam's knife is so close the blade is nothing more than a blur.

'Even your father protected you from the truth. He may have hurt you,' Susanna adds hastily, when she notices Adam give a twitch, 'but he never betrayed your mother. He never betrayed her love for you. He knew how much you really meant to her, which is why he never told you the truth. Because if he had it would have betrayed her faith in *him*.'

It is the first time Susanna has seen Adam so still. Throughout their session he has been pacing, twitching, fiddling, as though movement were a pressure gauge for his anger. It is a good sign? Is he listening? Or is he simply coiling and readying to spring?

'Your mother loved you,' Susanna tells him. 'The way I love Emily.'

Adam jerks at this, flinches almost, as though for once he is ashamed to hear Emily's name.

'The way I love Emily,' Susanna says again, 'and the way I'll always love Jake. I never wanted him to die, Adam. *Never.*'

She watches Adam closely for his reaction. He is listening. She is not imagining it. Something she has said, somehow, has got through.

'I thought maybe . . . I don't know what I thought,' Susanna goes on. 'But you helped me realize, Adam. You helped me see. What happened to Jake was my fault, I know that, but that doesn't mean I wanted it to happen. I didn't intend for him to take what I said to him the way he did. I was trying to help him. To *save* him. The way, if you'll let me, I want to try to help you.'

Susanna blinks, her eyelashes tickling the knife blade, and when she looks she can't believe what she is seeing. Adam is scowling, hating, but there is a tear slipping down his cheek.

He draws the knife away from Susanna's face.

'Adam,' Susanna says, softly this time. 'Let me help you. Please. Tell me where Emily is. Tell me where I can find my daughter.'

There is a moment when time seems to teeter.

Susanna does not move. But something stirs, just inside her: the faintest shiver of hope.

Adam pulls back, just a fraction, and the hand holding the knife falls to his side.

His eyes meet Susanna's, and for the first time since this began Susanna sees the part of him he fought so hard to conceal. Lost, frightened, alone: she could be looking at Jake.

She is crying now too, Susanna realizes. Not in fear, this time. With *relief*.

'Adam,' she says, daring to smile –

– but then there is a sound Susanna is not expecting, and the door into her office bursts open. It takes Susanna as much by surprise as it does Adam. Incredibly, Susanna is the first to realize what is about to happen.

She feels her eyes go wide, her voice welling from her aching stomach.

'No! Ruth, don't!'

But Ruth is already in motion. She has taken in the scene before her and she lifts the fire extinguisher she is carrying above her head. It is on its way down by the time Susanna emits her cry.

There is a scream – Susanna's? – and then a crack: a sound like the snap of breaking shell.

And then, just like that, it is over. Ruth drops panting to her knees – and Adam slumps lifeless to the floor.

Emily

14 September 2017

15 September 2017

16 September 2017

17 September 2017

18 September

There is a chill in the house that has nothing to do with the shifting seasons. She has been carrying it with her for days, since before the summer finally died. It seems to emanate from deep within her, from the place that contains her broken heart.

Emily's bedroom is the coldest room of all, yet Susanna finds herself drawn here. Three days since Adam – four days since Emily went missing – it feels as though she is no use anywhere else. She has told the police everything she can, which they all know is frustratingly little. She has called everyone she can think of, on a Pay As You Go the police provided, in order to keep her regular mobile clear. But she has found out nothing, contributed nothing, and all the while the phone has remained obdurately silent. Susanna's only comfort has been Ruth, who – despite being under threat of prosecution for manslaughter herself – has sat stoically in Susanna's kitchen, making cup after cup of extra-strong tea. In her way she has been more useful than Susanna has, serving refreshments to the flow of police officers until that flow slowed to a trickle. Eventually – yesterday? The day before? – the flurry of activity moved on somewhere else, and now even Ruth has gone – to see her solicitor, at Susanna's insistence – leaving Susanna in the house by herself.

She waits.

It is all she can do.

She can't eat, can't sleep, won't drink unless someone forces a glass of water into her hand. Her right, because her left clutches her mobile and nothing short of a crowbar could force her to let go of that.

Emily's room isn't how it should be. Susanna sits at the end of the narrow single bed and surveys the leftovers of her daughter's life. She perches lightly, tentatively, wary of disturbing anything that might yield a clue. But of course the police have already been through everything, including Emily's computer, and have found no hint as to where she might be. Hence the disarray. The room isn't messy as such. No messier than it is normally. But it is a different type of mess – a subtle shift in familiarity that betrays the recent presence of strangers. Cushions out of place, books returned to their shelves in the wrong order, a desk drawer left slightly ajar.

All the police found of any relevance, however, were Adam's fingerprints. Which by themselves told them nothing, other than at some stage he'd been there. In Susanna's *home*. In her bedroom too apparently, and Susanna recalls how casually Adam mentioned the books on her bedside table, judging her choice of reading and gloating at her surprise at his supposed insight. But he cheated. Of course he cheated. It isn't a shock, shouldn't be, but even so it makes Susanna angrier. That is, when she has the space to feel angry. Most of the time she can't think about Adam at all, nor about anything other than her missing daughter.

Susanna looks at her phone, and the black, bottomless screen. She presses the home button to ensure the phone is working, and that she hasn't somehow missed a call – from the police, from *Emily* – but of course she hasn't. The volume is set to maximum and anyway she would have felt the vibrations in her aching palm.

She runs a hand across Emily's bed covers, smoothing them flat. Once she starts she finds she cannot stop, and soon she is also fluffing the pillows, as though preparing Emily's bed for her imminent return. Even at fourteen years old, her daughter has a special soft toy – a bug-eyed, multicoloured thing, as close to being a kitten as anything, won that day Susanna spent with Emily on Brighton pier – and Susanna tucks it beneath the head end of the duvet. She straightens the items on Emily's nightstand – a hairbrush, a tub of hand cream, a well-loved copy of *The Diary of a Young Girl* by Anne Frank – and then casts her eyes around the rest of the room.

Her clothes. Susanna should refold Emily's clothes. There are some in a heap on the chair, and Susanna knows the police have been through Emily's chest of drawers as well. Emily wouldn't care what state her clothes have been left in but Susanna does. All of a sudden she *does*, and is almost frantic that she hasn't thought to set her daughter's room straight sooner.

She places her mobile on top of the chest of drawers, checking the display again first, making sure the volume is still turned up, then starts with the chair, hanging the assorted jumpers, tops and pairs of jeans in her daughter's wardrobe. She tidies the bottom of the wardrobe too, straightening Emily's innumerable pairs of trainers. After that Susanna turns to the chest of drawers itself. She begins at the top, folding underwear, T-shirts, hoodies, until she kneels to address the final drawer. She is just about to pull it open when she notices the rings in the carpet: depressions where the chest of drawers has been moved.

Odd. Not necessarily that the chest of drawers has been moved. Rather, that it appears to have been moved more than once. Fairly regularly, from the look of things. One of the rings is deeper than the others – the place where the piece of furniture has been positioned most often – but both to the left and the right there is another mark that is almost as deep.

Susanna stands, her eyes never leaving the rings in the carpet. She turns, to check the marks left by Emily's bed, but here there is nothing unusual. It is just the chest of drawers that has lately been wandering.

She moves to one end of the unit and gives a push, and the feet of the chest of drawers slide easily into their accustomed position: the deepest of the overlapping rings. But as they shift there is a *thunk* – swiftly followed by the drumbeat of Susanna's heart.

This time she pulls, heaving the chest of drawers towards her. But it is too heavy, or she is too weak, so she dips and uses her shoulder. It takes all of her strength – all of her hope – but she manages to drive it fully towards the window, uncovering the patch of carpet beneath it and revealing . . .

318

Nothing.

Just dust, a marble, a forgotten hairclip – and, beside the skirting board, a loose thread of wool. There are scratch marks on the skirting as well, so light Susanna might easily have missed them.

Emily has been prising up the carpet.

In her scrabble Susanna breaks a nail. It rips to the quick but she barely feels it. She is pulling, tugging, her fingers repeatedly failing to find purchase, until finally the edge of the carpet comes free and lifts so suddenly Susanna almost topples backwards.

She hears that *thunk* again, and this time she sees what caused it. A floorboard. A *loose* floorboard. And as she gropes to pull it up, Susanna is sobbing in anticipation and despair.

Ten minutes later she is in her car. She runs a red, has her mobile to her ear and is drunk on a sudden surge of hope. Susanna has never driven this way in her life. It is as though she is making up for years of obeying the traffic laws by breaking as many as possible in one go.

'Pick up,' she mutters. 'Pick up, pick up, pick up.'

But Ruth's mobile goes to voicemail, and Susanna yells out in frustration.

The police then, even though explaining will take longer.

With one eye on the road, the other on the screen, she fumbles to bring up the call list, and scans for the number the detective inspector who is charge of Emily's case gave her. His personal mobile. Call me any time, he told her. Day or night. But just as her busy eyes pluck the number from the list, the screen changes to indicate an incoming call.

'Ruth! Thank God.'

'Susanna? What is it?'

'Listen, Ruth. I need you to do something for me. I need you to call . . . everyone. The police. Detective Inspector Bannon. Everyone.'

'Why? Is it Emily? Has something happened?'

Susanna tells her. About the warehouse, the old perfume place. About the lock-ups. About the unit with the yellow door. All the details Susanna discovered in Emily's diary. It was there all along, in its hiding place beneath the floorboards, only ever inches from sight. And Susanna had *bought* it for her. She didn't know Emily even used it but she should have *thought*. She should have looked!

The diary is on the passenger seat beside her now and, once Ruth has hung up, Susanna tosses her mobile down beside it. She is not a confident driver and she needs to concentrate. She needs to get to Emily in one piece.

As she drives she attempts to make sense of the story she read so frantically in Emily's diary, to fill in the gaps where her eyes hastened on. How Emily and Adam met. How she fell for him. How, in the end, he planned to hurt her.

Was this what Adam was about to tell her, Susanna wonders? The lock-up. The trap he set. Was that what he would have revealed to her before he died?

Susanna tries to quell the voice inside her head that

insists it was actually something else. That Emily was in the lock-up at first but now she's gone. That she *is* there but Susanna is already too late.

She takes a wrong turn. There is a one-way system around the train station, and in her impatience Susanna has veered right too early. If she follows the road she is on now, she will be funnelled back the way she came, wasting minutes she knows she doesn't have.

She doesn't hesitate. She jerks the car into reverse and slams her palm on the horn. There is another car behind her but Susanna puts her foot to the accelerator as though the road were clear. From reckless driving, Susanna has graduated to a high-speed game of chicken. Fortunately the other driver senses her resolve and steers his own vehicle on to the kerb. He is too shocked to even gesticulate as Susanna hurtles past.

She backs on to the main road, ignoring the blare of horns behind her, then arrows the car towards the turning that will take her where she needs to be.

The gates of the perfume factory are old but they look solid. Susanna brings the car to a ragged halt right in front of them and doesn't bother to close the door when she gets out. She runs straight up to the gates, rattling the bars like a prisoner desperate to escape her cell. There is a thick chain binding the gates together, and Susanna knows there is no way she can break it. Could she climb over? But the gates must be fifteen feet high, with a roll of barbed wire at the top and no discernible footholds to help her up. Maybe she should have driven her car at the gates after all.

And then she remembers. The diary.

She has to search for a moment but soon enough she finds what she is looking for: the gap in the fence Adam told Emily about. Susanna shoves her way through it, ignoring the undergrowth that scratches her cheek and the jagged wire that claws at her clothes. She half falls to the other side, and then she is up, running, following Adam's directions to the letter. Around the back, past the entrance to the main building, towards the row of lock-ups. The yellow door. The unit with the yellow door. The yellow . . .

There.

'Emily!'

She is screaming her daughter's name even before she is certain she is heading for the right lock-up. There are dozens of storage units all in a row, maybe forty in total, half on one side of the alleyway, half on the other. The door Susanna has spotted isn't yellow as such – it is the brownish hue of French mustard – but it is more yellow than any of the others. And even before she reaches it, Susanna can see the padlocks. Most of the other doors are broken, crumbling, rusting. The lock-ups, like the factory itself, have clearly long been abandoned. But on Emily's door – *please, God, let Emily be behind it* – the padlocks are a freshly minted silver. Even the bolts have recently been renewed.

'Emily!'

Susanna hammers on the heavy wooden doors. She pauses, holding her breath, alert for a response from within. A voice, a cry, a whimper – anything.

But there is nothing.

She hammers again. She tugs the padlock, uselessly, and works her fingertips into the gap between the doors.

'Emily! Are you in there?'

It's no good. She cannot break the lock and she cannot prise the doors apart. If Emily is in there, she might as well be a thousand miles away.

'Madam?'

Susanna spins. At the end of the alleyway, striding towards her, are two police officers. One male, taller; the other female, broader. It is the man who spoke.

'Madam?' he repeats. 'May I ask . . .'

Are they here because of Ruth? Or because of the way Susanna was driving? She doesn't care one way or the other. She interrupts the male police officer before he can finish speaking.

'Please!' she insists. 'My daughter. She was kidnapped. She's in there. I know she is. Behind those doors. But I can't . . . they won't . . .' She turns back to the doors and pounds on them again. She wrenches at the lock with all her might, only letting go when her hand slips and blood flows from something slicing into her palm.

'Madam!'

The policeman rushes forward, alarmed, and attempts to draw Susanna away. His female colleague, meanwhile, hasn't once moved her eyes from Susanna's.

'Stand back,' the policewoman says. She dips and picks up a piece of concrete, the size of a misshapen football. Susanna sees what she intends to do and allows the policeman to pull her to one side.

The first blow on the padlock has no effect. On the second the block of concrete breaks in two, and the pieces tumble from the policewoman's grip. But she retrieves the larger portion, her determination matching Susanna's, and on the third blow the padlock visibly buckles. On the fourth it clatters to the ground.

Susanna is free in an instant. She slips from the male police officer's hands and is past the policewoman before either of them can stop her. She yanks open the lock-up door, bursting through it as irrepressibly as a breaking wave. Briefly the stench knocks her back, the darkness too, but her eyes adjust quickly to the lack of light.

And then she sees.

Adam's plan. Emily's body.

Susanna, in that instant, sees it all.

After

The sky is the colour of Susanna's soul now: not grey exactly, not white, but blank. It extends unbroken to every horizon and it reminds her how big the world is, how lost it is possible to feel so close to home.

The ground is soft underfoot and a mist lies shimmering across the grass. Ordinarily this would be Susanna's favourite time of year. As the leaves turn and the days shorten, she's always had a sense of the world snuggling up. She even likes the spiders, the nets they build to catch the falling dew. And here, high on a hill overlooking the town, the view of the roofs, the roads, the graceful machinations of everyday life would ordinarily stop her short. Ordinarily.

She walks past the row of headstones, towards the grave that cradles her child.

She carries with her a single sunflower. She didn't know what to choose but the flower's vivacity, the connotation of light – it seemed appropriate. Others have brought flowers recently too, she can see, for loved ones buried near her own, but today it seems she is the first. It is still early and there are no tracks showing on the sheen of grass, no footprints for her to follow along the path. As she walks she thinks she hears movement beside her but when she turns it is just a sycamore bowing to the breeze.

The grave is ahead of her.

It has changed, inevitably, since the day of the funeral. The pain is the same, though. The sorrow, the grief. And that, for Susanna, is all that counts now.

She lays the sunflower on the earth and turns to check she is still alone. There is nothing, no one, and for a moment she allows her eyes to close. She is so tired. So, so tired. And it is a tiredness she knows sleep, if she could catch it, wouldn't alleviate. Is this it now, she wonders? Is this the way she will feel through the postscript to her life? She should know, given what she's been through. But the reality is nothing she can predict.

'My poor child,' she says aloud. 'My poor children.' And she kneels on the cold, damp ground and runs her finger across the name written on the headstone.

Her son's name.

Her little lost boy, who Susanna prays will help bring back her little girl.

It is hours later when she comes.

Susanna has retreated to a nearby bench, and sits watching from the cover of shadows. The sun is peering through the clouds, its pool of warmth reaching as far as Susanna's ankles. She has been sitting here for so long, her trousers – sodden before from when she was kneeling – have almost dried.

The graveyard has remained empty all morning, and so at first when Susanna hears movement she assumes it is the wind once again worrying the trees. But when she glances her gaze sticks. She finds herself tucking her feet beneath her, physically trying to make herself small. She is like a hunter who has stumbled across a deer and for several moments as she watches she forgets to breathe.

Emily is following the same path Susanna did. She moves slowly but it is clear she has been here before, just as Neil said she had. According to Susanna's ex-husband (*husband*, Susanna corrects herself, because the truth is they were never divorced), Emily has been coming here every morning since the day she came to stay with him. Susanna had to navigate her way to Jake's grave, reminding herself of the markers on the way. But then, it is her first time back here since the morning of Jake's funeral eighteen years ago. Emily, in contrast, knows her route across the graveyard precisely, her eyes fixing on Jake's headstone long before she reaches it.

She looks exhausted, Susanna thinks, as though she too hasn't had a good night's sleep in the whole of the past fortnight. Although it's no wonder. A strange bed, in a stranger's house. Her father's, yes, but still a stranger. And more than that there is everything Emily has been through. Five days she was in that lock-up, with just a single water bottle in her bag and nothing to eat but a pair of Snickers bars she'd brought with her for the journey.

The journey. The trip away Adam had promised her, when all he'd ever intended was for Emily to wither in that room, and to be tortured as she did so with Susanna's lies. When Susanna barged her way inside and her eyes adjusted to the darkness, the sight of her daughter was bad enough: Susanna's certainty, in that instant, that she was too late. Emily lay motionless on a blanket, too weak even to raise her head. And when Susanna stumbled to her daughter's side and discovered Emily was still breathing – that was when she saw it. The wall behind her. The pictures, the notes, the newspaper stories: the shrine Adam had erected to Susanna's past. All for Emily. That was what Adam meant when he claimed the 'solution' he chose for Susanna's daughter was the simplest. The most obvious. The most *painful*. She would die, but first she would suffer – and effectively at her mother's own hand.

When Susanna thinks about *that*, she cannot help but be glad Adam died himself. Except . . . would he have told her? At the last. Was he about to? And was Adam responsible for what happened, *really*? Was he not a victim as well? He paid a price for what he did, certainly, one Susanna can't help thinking was too high. Does that excuse him, though? *Can* what he did be excused? Or is Susanna getting confused now between what can be excused and what can be explained?

All she really knows is that it is her fault as much as it is anyone's. She failed her grandson. She failed Jake. She failed Emily. But her daughter, Susanna is determined, might yet be saved.

'No.'

'Em? Emily, wait.'

Her daughter has spotted Susanna approaching from the shadows. Neil told Susanna it was too soon, that

Emily still needed time to come to terms with things, but Susanna could no longer keep away. She'd absorbed Emily's rage once her daughter had become strong enough to voice it; she'd accepted Emily's insistence that she wouldn't be coming home after leaving the hospital, and even facilitated her moving two hundred miles away to stay with her father. And she's kept her distance. For over a week, almost two, she's stayed away, granting Emily the space she'd demanded, not even pressing her daughter to give her the chance to explain. That hadn't been easy, any of it – least of all facing up to Neil. And in the end it had become too hard. Life without her daughter: it wasn't something Susanna could accept.

'No,' says Emily again. 'You shouldn't be here. I told you not to come!'

'I had to, Emily. Don't you see? I had to. The way we left things, without even talking things through . . . I couldn't live with that, Em. I couldn't.'

Emily rubs at her arm. It was badly sprained, Susanna knows, where Adam seized hold of her when she tried to run. When, confronted with those pictures on the lock-up wall, Emily had finally realized the truth. Adam had grabbed her and held her in place, forcing her to see what he wanted to show her – to listen as he told her his tale. The injury should have healed by now, though, and Susanna has to wonder how much of the pain is actually in her daughter's head. Not that this makes it any less real.

'Does it still hurt?' Susanna says. 'Your arm? Because I've got some paracetamol in my bag if you –'

'It's fine.' Emily lets her arm fall to her side. 'Just leave me alone, Mum. Please. Just *go*.'

That word. *Mum*. Susanna almost weeps when she hears it. It is the first time Emily has said it to her since Adam. And though it is clear Emily does not want Susanna there, she has at least stopped backing away.

'Please, Em, I –'

'Emily! Call me Emily! I'm not a kid, you know. Why do you always have to treat me like some little kid?'

'I'm sorry. Emily? I am. About that, about *everything*. That's what I needed to tell you. I was wrong. Completely and utterly wrong. I lied to you and that's unforgivable. I know that. I do. But I'm asking you to forgive me just the same.'

Emily has forced herself tall. And for the first time in her life, Susanna sees it. How grown up her daughter is. How much stronger she is already than Susanna ever was herself.

'Why should I?' Emily answers. 'Why should I even *listen* to you? You lied to me. My entire life, you *lied* to me. I have a father. I had a brother. *Jake*. I mean, that was my brother's name. Right, Mum?'

Susanna can do nothing but nod her head.

'And Jake's grave,' Emily presses. 'That's it just there in the ground behind you. *Right?*'

This time Susanna closes her eyes.

'It's like I don't even know who I am any more,' Emily says. 'I don't know who I was. I don't know who it is I'm supposed to be!'

'But . . . nothing's changed, Emily. You're exactly the same person you always were.'

'I'm not! And neither are you! All this time, Mum. All these years I used to boast about how honest you were. Can you imagine?' Emily makes a noise like she can't believe it herself. 'I don't get how I could have been so *stupid*.'

'No!' Susanna blurts. 'You mustn't do that. You mustn't blame yourself. I'm the one who lied, Emily. I'm the one who should have told you the truth.'

'So why didn't you?'

Again it is a question Susanna should be prepared for. And she's thought about the answer, of course she has, but the logic has become so tangled over the years it is impossible to tease it into words.

Emily talks into the silence. 'You always said that being truthful was all that mattered. That we should be honest to ourselves, to other people, to each other. To *each other*, Mum! Or are you going to stand there and deny you ever said that? Are you going to lie to me *again*?'

'No, I . . . You're right, I did say that but –'

'*So how was this any different?*'

Susanna exhales. 'It wasn't,' she says at last. 'It shouldn't have been. But Emily, please . . .' She reaches for her daughter and Emily slides quickly away.

'You were saying?'

Susanna's outstretched hand floats in front of her. 'Just that . . . you were so young,' she says. 'I told myself I was protecting you. That I was keeping the truth from you because I didn't want to burden you. I wanted you to have a fresh start. I wanted us both to have a clean beginning.'

Susanna can see her daughter is about to interrupt. She holds up her hands.

'But that wasn't all. I see now, I admit: that wasn't all. By lying to you, by running away, really I was trying to protect myself. To lie to *myself*. I was so sad, Emily. Just . . . so sad. Your brother . . . I failed him. I loved him as dearly as I love you and it's my fault he died. You're right. It was. All of it . . . everything . . . with Adam, with you . . . it's all completely my fault.'

Susanna cannot stop herself weeping. It's been so hard. She was so happy – so mindlessly, complacently happy – and then it all fell apart. Even when Emily came along, when it seemed like she was finding her feet again, she always knew the floor would one day collapse from under her. That's why she has been stepping through this new life of hers so lightly: not making friends, not going out, doing her best, from a personal perspective, to avoid leaving even the faintest impression. But in the end the floor gave way anyway. The problem wasn't how lightly or not Susanna was stepping. It was the weight of the baggage she was carrying with her.

The tears flow so freely now it is as though she is bleeding, as though every wound she has ever borne has coalesced into one. But as Susanna cries she feels something touch her shoulder, and when she looks up she sees that her daughter, reaching out, is crying too.

'You should have told me, Mum. I thought we were

friends. I thought if you needed to you could tell me anything. I thought you *trusted* me.'

'Oh Emily. Oh my girl. My brave, beautiful girl. I do trust you. I *do*. And I'm sorry I betrayed your trust in me.'

Susanna attempts to draw her daughter close. When Emily this time allows her to, it is as though they have broken through a wall.

They walk side by side, their footsteps heavy on the gravel pathway. As they pass Jake's grave they pause to look.

'What was he like, Mum? How do I . . . I'm not sure how I'm supposed to feel about him. About *any* of it. That's why I've been coming here. To try to . . . to make sense of . . . of everything, I guess, but . . .' Emily ends by shaking her head.

'That's something I've been struggling with myself,' Susanna tells her. 'Some things, the things people do – they *don't* make sense, not when we're on the outside looking in.'

'But that's not *enough*. When something bad happens, you can't just shrug your shoulders and move on.'

For an instant Emily is the little girl Susanna walked with on Brighton pier. Young, yes, but precocious; already full of questions about the world. How was it that Susanna so misjudged her? How was it that all this time she failed to have *faith* in her?

'I'm not saying we shouldn't try to understand,' Susanna says. 'Just the opposite. What I'm saying is, it's not always possible, not to the extent we would like. And even when it is, we need to learn to look at things – at horrible things sometimes, *awful* things – from a different perspective. From the beginning. From the start. Not the way we usually do, which tends to be . . .' She pauses, searching for the words.

'Back to front,' Emily finishes.

Susanna smiles. 'Exactly.'

They move off, towards the cemetery gates, leaving Jake's grave behind them.

'I'm sorry, Mum,' says Emily, out of the blue. 'I was such an idiot. With Adam. If I hadn't trusted him . . . if I hadn't believed what he said . . . I even fell for him! And he's like . . . what? My *nephew*?'

She shudders, violently.

Susanna threads an arm around her daughter's shoulders. 'Hey,' she says. 'Hey.' She squeezes, gently. 'It's not your fault. Do you understand me? And I'm the one who's supposed to be apologizing to you. Remember?'

There is a smile in Emily's expression struggling to get out.

'Adam knew exactly what he was doing,' Susanna tells her. 'With you, with me. He manipulated us both. Although, at the same time, he was also being controlled in a way himself – compelled by events he played no part in.'

She feels Emily stiffen. 'You make it sound like you feel sorry for him. He tried to hurt you, Mum. He tried to hurt both of us.'

'He did,' Susanna says. 'You're right. But in a way I also hurt him. *Life* did.'

336

Emily has come to a stop. 'Are you saying . . . What are you saying, Mum? That you *forgive* him?'

'No. I don't know. I suppose all I'm saying is, try not to hate him, Emily. That's all. For your sake as much as his.' It is advice Susanna has repeatedly offered to herself. On occasion over these past two weeks, she has even found herself able to follow it.

They walk on. Emily isn't satisfied, Susanna can tell. For the moment, though, her daughter has lapsed into a brooding silence.

'Your friend,' Emily says, after a while. 'Ruth. Is she all right? What's going to happen to her?'

Susanna has been wondering the same thing herself. The threat of prosecution has gone away but that doesn't mean Ruth won't suffer. When a rational human being becomes responsible for another person's death, it isn't possible to escape without scars. Susanna is as much aware of this as anyone.

'Ruth will be OK,' Susanna says. 'I'll make sure she is. I'll try to, anyway. The same way she's always tried to take care of me.'

'I'd like to help,' Emily says. 'If I can. I mean, I don't know how exactly, but when we get home, if there's anything I can do . . .'

When we get home . . .

Susanna stops walking. They are at the gates now, on the threshold of returning to the world. And until this moment, Susanna didn't know which way they would turn. Which way Emily would, rather.

'Home,' Susanna says. 'Does that mean . . .'

337

'It means I love you, Mum. It means I've missed you. Dad, he's great. Quite . . . serious, I guess. And sort of quiet. Almost old before his time. Was he always like that?'

Susanna isn't sure whether to smile or cry. 'Not always,' she says. 'No.'

'He's been so kind to me,' Emily goes on. 'So . . . attentive, I guess is the word. And I'd like to visit, to get to know him better. But this isn't home. You know? Home's with you, Mum. Where you are.'

The tears come, then. Susanna cannot stop them.

'Oh Emily,' she says.

She pulls her daughter in tight, hugging her, holding her – wondering how she will ever let her go.

'What will survive of us is love.'

Philip Larkin

Acknowledgements

Within weeks of starting work on this novel, and following a freak impact injury to my neck, I suffered what turned out to be a series of strokes. I was incredibly lucky: not only was the underlying cause (a damaged vertebral artery) identified very quickly, all the major symptoms I experienced were gone within a few days. The recovery, though, took much longer – even longer than it took me to finish the book – and I am indebted to so many people for their incredible help and support during what proved to be a very challenging year. I cannot offer praise enough to the amazing staff at the Royal Sussex County Hospital here in Brighton. Thank you in particular to Dr Nicki Gainsborough, as well as to Dr Marius Venter at Charing Cross Hospital in London. Thanks as well to my amazing friends and wonderful family for their patience, love and support. There are too many of you to list here but hopefully you know who you are. Above all, love and thanks to my wife, Sarah, to whom this book is dedicated. It simply wouldn't have been written without her.

Caroline Wood has been my agent now for almost ten years, and I cannot think of anyone I would rather have in my corner. Thanks to her, and indeed to everyone at Felicity Bryan Associates. Thanks as well to Katy Loftus and Amanda Bergeron, my two incredible editors. And special mention to Jane McLoughlin and Caroline Pretty, as well as the fantastic teams supporting Katy and Amanda at Viking and Berkley. I am constantly amazed by the depth of your talents.

Also by Simon Lelic

THE HOUSE

**The perfect couple. The perfect house.
. . . the perfect crime.**

Londoners Jack and Syd moved into the house a year ago.
It seemed like their dream home: tons of space, the
perfect location, and a friendly owner who wanted a
young couple to have it.

So when they made a grisly discovery in the attic, Jack
and Syd chose to ignore it. That was a mistake.

Because someone has just been murdered outside
their back door.

AND NOW THE POLICE ARE WATCHING THEM.

'Hugely gripping and spooky as hell' Mark Billingham

'Lelic can plot like a demon' *Guardian*

'Read it' *Observer*

He just wanted a decent book to read ...

Not too much to ask, is it? It was in 1935 when Allen Lane, Managing Director of Bodley Head Publishers, stood on a platform at Exeter railway station looking for something good to read on his journey back to London. His choice was limited to popular magazines and poor-quality paperbacks – the same choice faced every day by the vast majority of readers, few of whom could afford hardbacks. Lane's disappointment and subsequent anger at the range of books generally available led him to found a company – and change the world.

'We believed in the existence in this country of a vast reading public for intelligent books at a low price, and staked everything on it'
Sir Allen Lane, 1902–1970, founder of Penguin Books

The quality paperback had arrived – and not just in bookshops. Lane was adamant that his Penguins should appear in chain stores and tobacconists, and should cost no more than a packet of cigarettes.

Reading habits (and cigarette prices) have changed since 1935, but Penguin still believes in publishing the best books for everybody to enjoy. We still believe that good design costs no more than bad design, and we still believe that quality books published passionately and responsibly make the world a better place.

So wherever you see the little bird – whether it's on a piece of prize-winning literary fiction or a celebrity autobiography, political tour de force or historical masterpiece, a serial-killer thriller, reference book, world classic or a piece of pure escapism – you can bet that it represents the very best that the genre has to offer.

Whatever you like to read – trust Penguin.

read more
www.penguin.co.uk